THE ALPS AND PYRENEES

THE ALPS AND PYRENEES

BY

VICTOR HUGO

TRANSLATED FROM THE FRENCH BY

JOHN MANSON

Fredonia Books
Amsterdam, The Netherlands

The Alps and Pyrenees

by
Victor Hugo

ISBN 1-58963-208-7

Reprinted from the 1898 edition

Fredonia Books
Amsterdam, The Netherlands
http://www.fredoniabooks.com

I AM greatly indebted to Mr. Swinburne for per-
mission to make use of the following extracts from
the review of " Alpes et Pyrénées " contained in his
" Studies in Prose and Poetry," as a preface to the
English translation of the work.

JOHN MANSON.

PREFACE.

I T is a fact not less singular than sig-
nificant that the volume containing
Victor Hugo's personal reminiscences
of men and events should have had more
than twice the sale of any other among his posthumous works. Full of interest, personal and historical, as is the many-coloured record of " Choses
Vues," its crowning interest consists in the fact that
the experiences recorded in that book are the experiences of the greatest writer born in the nine-
teenth century : the value of his other posthumous
works consists in the fact that, if no other legacy
had been bequeathed by him to time, they would
have sufficed to prove him the greatest poet of an
age which has been glorified by the advent of
Tennyson, Browning, and Leconte de Lisle. The
account of his excursions among the Alps at the
age of thirty-seven, which occupies less than a
quarter of the volume last issued, might perhaps
have been conjectured, by a careful and thoughtful
student of the man and his work, to belong to the
same date as the series of letters from the Rhine :

of which, as the prefatory note informs us, it is
simply the sequel.

Most readers will probably agree that the most
interesting and important episode in this epistolary
journal is the one which has been extracted from a
letter to the artist who had the honour of receiving
the previous letters from the Rhine. The six letters
addressed to the wife of the writer are full to over-
flowing of evidence to the wonderfully swift, keen,
and joyful observation of nature, the amazing quick-
ness of notice, and the astonishing vivacity of recollection, which make it hard for a duller eye and
a slower brain to follow the mere transcript of his
experiences and impressions. But the story of the
mountebanks at Berne, a truncated and incoherent
tragedy, could have been written as it is here
written by no other man that ever lived but the
author of "Notre Dame de Paris;" and it is impossible to imagine—though he has vouchsafed no
hint to that effect—that the creator of Esmeralda
was not reminded of his creation by the sorrowful
sight which he has registered for all time in that
letter. . . . The spectacle seen by the writer when
at breakfast—"reading while eating," and reading the leaf which accident laid before him of
the tragi-comic bible of life—is now as immortal,
though merely a record of actual fact, as though
it had been a creation of the spectator's fancy;
the glance, the touch, the sympathy of genius

have made reality for once as real as fiction at
its best. . . .

*   *   *

. . . I must avow that the second and larger
division of the book is to me yet more fascinating
than the first part. The style, if I may venture an
opinion, is terser, keener, more trenchant and more
vivid : the humour is riper and readier than before.
. . . At Bordeaux the writer of the famous pamphlet
headed "Guerre aux Démolisseurs" was moved to
utter a protest as eloquent and as earnest as anything in his two essays on the same subject which
were written respectively eighteen and eleven years
earlier. The whole of this letter from Bordeaux
should be studied and appreciated by all who feel
—and by all who need to learn—how close and
how inextricable must be the connection of all
serious and serviceable hope for the future with
sincere and earnest reverence for the past. . . .

The description of the ruined cloister could only
have been matched in verse by Shelley or in prose
by Ruskin ; and for English readers this can hardly
but suffice by way of comment or of commendation. In the next letter the journey from Bordeaux
to Bayonne is rendered into words of such living
simplicity and effect that we hear the sound and
smell the flowers of a summer day now dead these
forty-seven years since. The tender childish re-
collections evoked on entering Bayonne have all

the matchless and unfailing charm which which
Hugo could always touch and invest, by a natural
and sacred magic, the morning lights and shadows
of the unforgotten and thenceforward imperishable
past. But the charnel-house of St. Michael's at
Bordeaux will now be for ever remembered by all
students of his work as the subject of a realistic
and tragic poem in prose which may be ranked
among the greatest and most terrible triumphs of
his imaginative and descriptive genius.

*   *   *

We will not dwell on his shrinking anticipation
that Biarritz might some day possibly become
fashionable and be ruined ; but the story of his fly
could only have been told by Thackeray with such
quiet and serious humour. There is nothing funnier
in " The Irish Sketch Book ; " and there is nothing
so ingenious or so rascally recorded of an Irish
conductor in that kindly and delightful volume. A
penny to go, ten shillings to return, make up a
tariff worthy of commendation even by such a passenger as the one who found himself swindled on
this occasion ; and Sterne could not have registered
the experience with more delightful good-humour
and more kindly realism.   .   .   .

*   *   *

. . . From Bayonne to St. Sebastian the most
amusingly memorable record set down by Victor
Hugo is the anecdote of a porter, Oyarbide by

name. The letter from St. Sebastian leaves the
reader bewildered and compassionate at the thought
of so many fruitless revolutions, in which so much
noble devotion and courage and chivalry were
wasted ; but the shining instance of royal gratitude
on the part of Don Carlos and the noble incident
of loyal comradeship on the part of General Elio
serve excellently well to set off each other.

The letter describing the strange, enchanted, and
enchanting old town of Pasages is so delightfully
full of life and light and colour that no com-
mentary can convey or can suggest a sense of its
charm. The rival clamours of the boatwomen,
which startled the writer from meditation on an
insect and a flower ; the singularly flattering dis-
appointment of the girl whom Hugo paid for a
task on which he did not employ her ; the conversation with the admirer of the incomparable
rope-walk (Flaubert could not have recorded it
with more calm severity and precision of touch) ;
the dazzling and many-coloured prospect of a
" humble corner of earth and water which would
be admired if it were in Switzerland and famous if
it were in Italy, and is unknown because it is in
Guipuzcoa," compose an inimitable prologue to the
extraordinary scene which follows.   . . .

*   *   *

Pamplona, which the poet had so grandly celebrated fifteen years earlier, inspired on this occasion

the longest and one of the most interesting of his
letters. The noble, pathetic, and manly meditation
on the mysterious sufferings of misused animals
should remind us of a passage dealing with the
same sorrowful and shameful subject in a poem
(" Melancholia ") belonging to the third book of the
" Contemplations." The brilliant and grotesque description of the strange conveyance and its stranger
conductors which introduces this discourse on the
duty of pity is in its way as perfect as the sub-
limely characteristic and fantastic sketch of sunrise, touched and coloured by the dream or vision
of a suggested sense in awakening nature of pain
ineffable and pity inexpressible for the poor tormented and terrified and bewildered beasts of
burden or of draught—" those forsaken and miserable animals who are her children as we are, and
live nearer to her than we do."

*   *   *

The account of Gavarnie, " nature's Colosseum,"
may be matched against any of this great artist's
studies for terse and vigorous precision of imaginative outline.   The brief notice of Luz gives a
last touch of brightness to a book which then closes
in gloom as deep as death.   In the isle of Oléron,
a ghastly and hardly accessible wilderness of salt
marshes, with interludes of sterile meadow and un-
profitable vineyard, manured with seaweed and
yielding an oily and bitter wine ; with foul gray

fog rising in heavy reek from the marshlands, a
shore of mud, a desolate horizon, a lean and fever-
stricken population, a prison for some hundreds
of military convicts ; a heaviness like death, he tells
us, fell upon the visitor :

"Not a sound to seaward, not a sail, not a bird.
At the bottom of the sky, to westward, appeared a
huge round moon, which seemed in those livid mists
the reddened imprint of the moon with its gilding
rubbed off. . . . Perhaps on another day, at another
hour, I should have had another impression. But
for me that evening everything was funereal and
melancholy. It seemed to me that this island was
a great coffin lying in the sea, and this moon the
torch to light it."

Next day the writer of these words came by
chance on the tidings—in a newspaper taken up in
a coffee-house—that just five days earlier his eldest
daughter and her six-months' husband had been
drowned in a boating excursion on the Seine.

It was not till three years later that the first was
written of those matchless poems of mourning which
keep fresh for ever the record of his crowning
sorrow.

                         A. C. SWINBURNE.

PREFATORY NOTE.

HE Alpine Journey, with which this volume opens, was written, like the second Rhine Journey, of which it is a continuation, in 1839. With the exception of the incident of the Strolling Players, which is taken from a letter to Louis Boulanger, the Alpine Journey is composed of letters addressed to Madame Victor Hugo, dated from the various towns and stamped by the post.

The Pyrenean Journey (1843) was produced in a somewhat different manner. It was written in hurried fragments on the leaves of sketch-books in the actual places which it depicts. The two sketch-books containing it are full of pen-and-ink drawings made on the spot, and have as book-marks flowers and grasses gathered on mountain or in forest.

The Journey is continued in this way, without interruption or break, as far as Pampeluna. Thereafter, we have only isolated chapters. The traveller

made notes with the intention of completing his
narrative later ; but it was only those places and
things with which he was most struck that he described at once.   After the death of his daughter
Léopoldine, he had no heart to finish the Journey.

CONTENTS.

b

CONTENTS.

CONTENTS.

b

CONTENTS.

1839.

THE ALPS

THE ALPS.

I.

LUCERNE.—MOUNT PILATUS.

LUCERNE, 10*th September, midnight.*

REACHED Lucerne at night. I stayed at the Pension Lichman, an excellent hotel located in a fine old tower, and with machicoulis too! I supped, I asked for a room, I have opened my window, and I am probably going to spend the night in writing to you, my dear Adèle, for my mind is filled with visions and my heart with tenderness.

Whenever the landscape which fills my open window is worth the trouble, I make a sketch of it and send it to you. To-day, it is exquisite, notwithstanding the night; partly, perhaps, because of the night.

Beneath my eyes I have the Lake of Lucerne, the wonder of Switzerland. The water of the lake comes close up under my window, and beats softly against the old stones of the tower. I hear the faint sound of the fish leaping in it. The darkness is intense. On my right, however, I can distinguish a rotten wooden bridge, with sharp-pointed roofing, extending towards a bulky tower with a superb outline. Vague gleams of light run over the water. Facing me, some five hundred steps from my tower, several tall black poplars are reflected in the dark lake. A wide-stretching mist, spread by the night over the lake, hides the rest from me. It is not raised high enough, however, to prevent me from seeing the sinister growth of Mount Pilatus, planted before me in all its immensity.

Above the three teeth of its summit, Saturn, with the four beautiful stars of gold, amid which he is set, outlines a gigantic hour-glass in the sky. Behind Pilatus and on the shores of the lake a crowd of mountains—old, bald and deformed—jostle together confusedly : Titlis, Prosa, Crispalt, Badus, Galenstock, Frado, Furka, Mutthorn, Beckenviederberg, Urihorn, Hochstollen, Rathorn, Thierstock, and Brünig. I have a blurred impression of all these goitred, hunchbacked giants crouching in the shadow around me.

From time to time, through the darkness, the sound of distant bells is borne to me on the wind.

It is the cows and goats wandering in the aërial pastures of Pilatus and the Rigi shaking their little bells, and this soft music which reaches me here descends from a height of five or six thousand feet.

In this one day I have seen three lakes : the Lake of Zurich, which I left this morning ; the Lake of Zug, which vouchsafed me an excellent eel for lunch ; and the Lake of Lucerne, which has just provided me with a supper of its admirable salmon trout.

Seen as a bird flies, the Lake of Zurich has the form of a crescent, one of its horns resting at Zurich and the other at Utznach ; the Lake of Zug has the shape of a slipper, of which the road from Zug to Arth forms the sole ; the Lake of Lucerne resembles, up to a certain point, an eagle's crushed foot, the fractures of which form the two bays of Brunnen and Buochs, and of which the four claws bury themselves deep, one into Alpnach, another into Winkel, the third into Lucerne, and the last into Küssnacht, where Tell slew Gessler. The culminating point of the lake is Flüelen.

I became reconciled with the Lake of Zurich before leaving it. For it was indeed beautiful seen from the height of the flanks of the Albis. The white houses on the opposite road gleamed like pebbles in the grass, some boats with sails rippled

the glistening water, and the rising sun dispersed
from off the surface of the lake, one after another,
all the mists of the night, which the wind carried
away diligently to a huge pile of clouds heaped up
in the north.   The Lake of Zurich was magnificent
like this.

When I tell you that I have seen three lakes
during the day, I am over-cautious ; I saw four.
Between Albis and Zug, amid the most picturesque
sierras imaginable, in the depths of a ravine, wild,
and wooded, and solitary, one perceives a little
lake of sombre green called the Durlersee, of which
the plummet has never yet found the bottom.   It
appears that a waterside village sank into it and
was swallowed up.   The colour of this pool of
water is disquieting.   One would take it for a great
tubful of verdigris.—" A wicked lake ! " said an
old peasant to me as he passed.

The further one goes, the stranger become the
horizons.   At Albis, one seems to have four ridges
of mountains superimposed before one's eyes : the
first layer, the green Ardennes ; the second layer,
the dark Jura, with its abrupt outlines ; the third
ledge, the bare, precipitous Apennines ; behind, and
above all, the white Alps.   One might think them
the first four steps of the ancient stairway of the
Titans.

Then one goes down again into the valleys ; one plunges into the forests. The boughs weighted with leaves form over the road a reticulated vault, the meshes of which allow warmth and daylight to rain through. A few sparse cottages, genial and enticing, half hide their frontages of yellow wood, with their windows of round panes which one might think set in coarse tulle. A benevolent-looking peasant passes with his waggon drawn by oxen. The ravines make wide gaps in the trees, the eye escapes through the cuttings, and, if it is noon and the weather is fine, a magnificent interchange of lights and shadows takes place on every side between earth and sky. The wide curtains of mist overhanging the horizon are rent here and there, and, through the rents, the distant mountains suddenly appear in the depths of a cavern of light as in a magic mirror.

Zug, like Bruck and like Baden, is a charming feudal commune, still encircled with towers, its massive pointed gates blazoned and crenelated, and all battered by assaults and escalades. Zug has not the Aare, like Bruck ; Zug has not the Limmat, like Baden ; but Zug has its lake, its tiny lake, which is one of the loveliest in Switzerland. I seated myself upon a slight fence overshadowed by linden-trees, a few steps from my inn. Before me I had the Rigi and Pilatus, which formed four gigantic pyramids, two rising up into the sky, and two throwing themselves backwards into the water.

Stone fountains and carved and painted houses abound in Zug. The Hirsch Inn exhibits some traces of the Renaissance. At Zug the Italianate fresco already possesses itself of nearly all the walls. Wherever nature is highly ornate, man's dwelling and dress reflect it ; the dwelling decks itself, the dress puts on colour. It is a charming law. Our taverns of La Cunette and our suburban rustics dressed in tatters would be monstrosities here.

Over a door at Zug I saw a bas-relief representing a troglodyte with his club. Beneath is carved the date 1482. Over another door is inscribed this legend, more engaging than the troglodyte : "*Pax intrantibus, salus exeuntibus*, 1607." (Charlot will expound this Latin to his good mother.)

The church of Zug is enriched like a Flemish church. Altars with wreathed columns, and monumental tablets, varnished and gilded, are built into all the walls. A beadle showed me into the treasury of the church, which is magnificent, and overflows with silver plate and jewellery, some extremely rich, some extremely precious. For thirty sous I saw millions.

Fifteen years ago the road from Zug to Arth was

an impassable footpath, on which the best horse would have stumbled.   It is now an excellent high road, which does not even jolt the carrier's cart that plies along it loaded with passengers with packs on their backs.   At Zurich I had hired a little four-wheeled cabriolet, which bowled in the most delightful way imaginable along this pretty road, with its escarpments of trees and rocks on the left, and on the right the water of the lake scarcely ruffled by a breath of air.

The lake is graceful on leaving Zug ; it becomes magnificent as one approaches Arth.   For above Arth, a large village in the canton of Schwytz, is the Rossberg, which the country-folk call the " Sonnenberg " (the mountain in the sunlight), and the Rigi, which they call the " Schattenberg " (the mountain in the shadow).

The Rossberg is four thousand feet high,[1] the Rigi five thousand.[2]   They are the two highest brecciated mountains to be found in the world.   The Rossberg and the Rigi have no geological relationship with the Alps surrounding them.   The Alps are of granite ; the Rigi and the Rossberg are composed of flints embedded in mud which to-day is harder than cement, and gives the rocks that have

---

[1] In reality, 5,190 feet.—*Translator.*
[2] 5,906 feet.—*Translator.*

fallen by the roadside the appearance of fragments of a Roman wall. These enormous mountains are two diluvian mud-heaps.

And it sometimes happens that the mud dilutes and subsides. This occurred notably in 1806, after two months of rain. On the 2nd of September, at five in the evening, a piece of the summit of the Rossberg, a thousand feet broad, a hundred feet high, and a league in length, all at once broke loose, traversed a slope of three leagues in three minutes, and suddenly swallowed up a forest, a valley, three villages with their inhabitants, and half a lake. Goldau, which was crushed in this fashion, lies behind Arth.

At three o'clock I entered the shadow of the Rigi, leaving dazzling sunshine on the hills of Zug. As I approached Arth I thought of Goldau. I knew that that pretty, laughing town hid from the wayfarer the corpse of the crushed village. I gazed at that placid lake in which châlets and meadows were mirrored. It also conceals terrible things. Beneath the Rigi it is twelve hundred feet deep, and when it is swept by the two violent winds which the boatmen of Arth and Zug call the Arbis and the Wetterfœhn, this charming pool of water becomes more formidable and horrible than the ocean.

Before me, in the far distance, rose the Rigi, a

huge, dark, precipitous wall, up which the fir-trees clambered in confused and emulous haste, like battalions climbing to the assault.

Every landscape evokes a cloud of ideas, now sweet, now mournful. This one set free within me the triple thought of ruin, tempest, and war, and was causing me to dream, when a little barefooted maid, who was sitting by the roadside, came running towards me, threw three plums into my cabriolet as she passed, and fled with a smile. While I was feeling in my waistcoat pocket for some " batz," she had disappeared. A moment afterwards I turned round. She was again by the roadside, hiding herself in the bushes, and watching me through the willows with her bright eyes, like Galatea. All things are possible with the good God, when one meets with Virgilian eclogues in the shadow of the Rigi.

At five o'clock I emerged from this shadow of the Rigi. I had crossed the elbow which forms the lower end of the Lake of Zug, I had passed through Arth, and had just left the shore for a road with very steep banks, which ascends one of the low ridges of the Rigi at a tolerably steep incline. On either side of this road they were building some new houses in poor taste. It appears that the lovely wooden frontages are going out of fashion here. Parisian plaster is beginning to invade the façades.

It is a pity.   Switzerland needs to be warned that Paris herself is ashamed of her plaster to-day.

Suddenly the road grows lonely ; a dilapidated house emerges from a cluster of trees upon a little grass-plat.   My driver had stopped.   I was in the famous Hollow Way of Küssnacht.   On the 18th of November, 1307—five hundred and thirty-one years, nine months, and twenty-two days ago—at this very hour, and on this very spot, an arrow, firmly sped through this very forest, pierced a man to the heart.   The man was Austrian tyranny ; the arrow was Swiss liberty.

The sun sank, the road grew dark, the brambles above the bank quivered in the vivid western light. Two old beggars, the man and woman who keep the neighbouring ruin, held out their hands for my French sous.   A travelling showman, leading a muzzled bear by the nose, came down the road towards Küssnacht followed by the delighted cries of four urchins filled with wonder at the bear.   My driver applied the break to his carriage, and I heard the sound of iron made by the shoe-drag.   The parting of a couple of branches opened for me a window over the plain, and I saw some haymakers stacking their rick in the distance.   The birds sang in the trees, the cows lowed in the Rigi.   I had left the carriage and was gazing at the flint-stones in the Hollow Way, gazing upon nature, here serene as an untroubled conscience. Little by little the spectre of past things gained the mastery over present realities in my spirit, and obliterated them like some old handwriting which reappears on an ill-cleaned palimpsest in the midst of a new text ; I saw Gessler, the bailiff, lying bleeding in the Hollow Way, on those diluvian flints fallen from Mount Rigi, and I heard his dog howling through the trees at the gigantic shadow of William Tell standing erect in the coppice.

This old house, now a chapel, marks the very spot upon which the sublime ambush was accomplished. With the exception of the door, which is made of an old lancet panel-frame, the chapel has nothing remarkable about it. A dilapidated interior, wretched frescoes on the walls, a miserable altar decorated with Italianate frippery, coloured wooden vases and artificial flowers, two gibbering beggars who sell you William Tell souvenirs for a few sous —such is the monument of the Hollow Way of Küssnacht.

There is a Madonna over the altar. Before this Madonna is an open book in which passers-by may inscribe their names. The last traveller to enter the chapel had written in the book these two lines, which touched me more than all the declarations of

war upon tyrants with which it is filled : "I humbly
pray our holy Mother of God to deign, by her inter-
cession, to restore a little of my poor wife's sight."
I wrote nothing in the book, not even my name.
Beneath this sweet prayer the page was blank.   I
left it blank.

A corner of the Lake of Lucerne is seen from
the grass-plat before the chapel. On turning round
I perceived, on a rock-covered eminence at the foot
of the Rigi, the fragment of a tower which has the
appearance of a dismantled gable, and sticks up out
of the brambles like a tooth.   This ruin was the
fortress of Küssnacht, the keep in which Gessler
lived, and the dungeon designed for William Tell.
William Tell never entered it ; Gessler never re-
entered it.

A quarter of an hour afterwards, I was in Küssnacht.   The bear was dancing in the square, the
gossips were laughing by the fountains, three
English post-chaises were setting down passengers
in front of the ostentatious and comfortable hotel,
which breaks the harmony of the Gothic fronts of
the fifteenth-century cottages.   Two old women
were tending graves in the churchyard before the
church.   It was there that I stopped my carriage.
I visited the church, which is insignificant as an
edifice, but is very showy and ornate.

At Zurich the churches are bare. Here, as at Arth and at Zug, they are decked, and decked with excess, with violence, with passion. It is a reaction of the Roman churches against the Calvinistic churches. It is a war of flowers, volutes, fallals and chaplets, waged by the Catholic cantons against the Protestant cantons.

The churchyards especially are remarkable. On every grave there is a stone, and from the stone rises a cross of figured iron much varnished and gilded. The general effect of all these crosses is to give the churchyard the appearance of a great black thicket with yellow flowers.

The road from Kussnacht to Lucerne skirts the water like that from Zug to Arth. The Lake of Lucerne is even more beautiful than the Lake of Zug. Instead of the Rigi, I had now Mount Pilatus before me.

Mount Pilatus has kept me occupied during the whole day. I rarely lost sight of it on the journey from Zurich here. At this moment I can dimly distinguish it before my window.

Pilatus is a wonderful mountain. It is terrible in shape. In the middle ages it was called *Fracmont*, the broken mountain. There is nearly always a cloud over the summit of Mount Pilatus ; hence its name of *Mons pileatus*, the capped mountain. The

Lucerne peasants, who know the Gospel better than Latin, turn the word *pileatus* into *Pilatus*, and conclude from this that Pontius Pilate is buried beneath the mountain.

As for the cloud, it behaves, according to the old women, in a fantastic fashion : when present, it foretells fine weather ; when absent, it foretells a storm. Pilatus, like the eccentric giant that he is, puts on his cap when it is fine, and doffs it when it rains. So that this mountain-barometer dispenses four Swiss cantons from having at their windows those little hermits with movable hoods animated by means of catgut. The existence of the cloud is certain. I watched it all the morning. Within four hours it took twenty different shapes, but did not leave the mountain's brow. Sometimes it resembled a great white stork lying in the hollows of the summit as in a nest ; sometimes it split up into five or six little clouds, making an aureole of eagles hovering round the mountain.

You can understand how such a cloud over such a mountain was certain to give rise to many superstitions in the country below. The mountain is peaked, the slope is laborious; it is six thousand feet in height,[1] and its summit is surrounded by many

[1] The highest peak, the Tomlishorn, is 6,998 feet in height. —*Translator*.

terrors.   It therefore made the most daring chamois-
hunters hesitate long.—What could be the cause of
that strange cloud?—Two hundred years ago, a
freethinker who had the foot of a mountaineer,
risked his life and climbed Mount Pilatus.   Then
the cloud was explained.

On the mountain's very crest there is a lake, a
tiny lake, a bowl of water a hundred and sixty feet
long, eighty feet broad, and of unknown depth.
When it is fine the sun strikes upon this lake and
draws a cloud from it; when the weather breaks,
there is no more sun and no more cloud.

The superstitions did not disappear when the
phenomenon was explained.   On the contrary, they
only throve and became embellished.   For the
mountain after exploration was no less terrible than
the mountain while as yet untrodden.

Besides the lake, prodigious things were found
on Mount Pilatus.   First, a fir-tree unique in the
whole of Switzerland—a colossal fir-tree with nine
horizontal branches, and bearing on each of these
branches another great fir-tree, which must have
made it look like a gigantic seven-branched candlestick.   Then, in the Brundlisalp, which is the ridge
nearest the seven peaks of the summit, an echo,
which seems rather a voice than an echo, so perfect
is it and so clearly does it repeat words to their last

syllables and songs to their last notes.   And lastly,
in a fearful precipice in the middle of a perpendicular
wall of black rock more than six hundred feet in
height, the mouth of an inaccessible cavern, and, at
the entrance of this cavern, a supernatural statue of
white stone some thirty feet in height, sitting cross-
legged and leaning its elbows on a granite table, in
the redoubtable attitude of a spectre guarding the
threshold of the cavern.

It appears certain that the cave pierces the whole
mountain and comes out on the other side beneath
the Tomlisalp at an opening called the " Moon-
hole, " because, says Ebel, much "moon-milk "[1] is
found there.

Being unable to scale the wall six hundred feet in
height, they endeavoured to turn the statue and to
enter its retreat by the "moon-hole." This hole is
sixteen feet in diameter one way and nine in another.
It pours forth a torrent and an icy wind.   This in
itself was sufficiently dangerous.   They ventured it,
however.   They groped their way through vaulted
chambers ; they crawled on their faces, now beneath
fearful ceilings, now through running streams.   It
was labour lost.   No one was able to penetrate to

[1] " Lait de lune " ("moon-milk") is an earthy variety of
carbonate of lime found in the crevices of mountains.—
Translator.

the statue. It is still there, intact in the strict sense
of the word, contemplating the abyss, guarding the
cavern, serving its term of confinement, and dreaming of the mysterious workman who carved it. The
mountaineers call this figure Saint Dominic.

The middle ages and the sixteenth century concerned themselves with Pilatus as much as with
Mount Blanc. To-day no one thinks of it. The
Rigi is the fashion. The gloomy superstitions of
Mount Pilatus have fallen to the level of old
wives' tales, and there stagnate. The summit is no
longer dreaded except for the difficulty of climbing
it. General Pfyffer has made barometric observations upon it, and declares that the minster of Strasburg can be seen from it with a telescope.

A strange community of shepherds have taken up
their quarters and settled there. They are strong,
active, simple men, living to be centenarians, and
profoundly despising the human ants who inhabit
the plain.

Nevertheless, there are still at Lucerne ancient
laws prohibiting the throwing of stones into the
little lake at the summit of Pilatus, for the fantastic
reason that a flint causes a water-spout to rise out
of it, and that the lake repays every stone thrown
into it with a storm that covers the whole of
Switzerland.

Forbidding as it is, Mount Pilatus has been covered with pasture lands for the last hundred years. Thus it is not only a formidable mountain, but an enormous udder which suckles four thousand cows. These make an orchestra of four thousand small bells, to which I am listening at this moment.

Here is the history of these Alpine cows. A cow costs four hundred francs, is hired out at seventy to eighty francs a year, grazes six years in the mountains, and produces six calves ; then, lean, worn out and wasted, when she has given her whole substance in her milk, the cowherd gives her over to the butcher ; she crosses the St. Gothard, redescends the Alps by the southern slopes, and appears as beef in the dubious flesh-pots of the inns of Italy.

If this continues, however, the miraculous Mount Pilatus will become as prosaic as a whitewashed cathedral. A French company recently bought a forest of larch-trees half a league from the summit, and constructed a carriage road through it, so at present capitalism is shearing the giant.—A guide further declared to me at Küssnacht that, in 1814, a chamois-hunter named Ignatius Matt entered the cavern with ladders and ropes, and, of course at the risk of his life, boldly approached the gloomy sentinel of stone.

I must say that one of the old women of the churchyard, who heard the guide's story, protested energetically, declaring that Ignatius Matt was nothing but a rogue, that he had boasted of a stroke of luck which was impossible, and that the statue of the " Dominikloch" was still virgin.—In this matter, I believe the old women.

I covered the three leagues from Küssnacht to Lucerne in an hour and a half at full trot.   Nevertheless, it was quite dark when I reached Lucerne. But the drive along the shore of the Bay of Küssnacht in the twilight is superb.

In leaving Küssnacht, I had my eyes still fixed upon the Gessler ruin when they encountered another.   It is the donjon of Neu-Habsburg, another eagle's nest fallen half way up the hill among the heather.   From the road I saw a great fragment of wall which let the ends of its ivy steep in the water of the bay, like the drooping hair of a head that is thrown backwards.   Facing me, the green slopes of the Zinne, with their mingled network of trees and crops, were reflected in the already darkened mirror of the lake, giving it the appearance of herborized agate.   At the foot of the Rigi some unaccountable reflection shed a wan light upon the water.   A little craft, running in a pool of darkness beside it, was doubled in it by reflection

and cast the figure of a long sword, of which the
boat formed the handle, the boatman the guard,
and the glistening wake the fine, long, naked blade.

With the exception of the arsenal and the Rath-
haus, I have already seen everything in Lucerne.

The town is well built, set upon two confronting
hills, cut in two by the Reuss, which enters the lake
at Flüelen and rushes violently from it at Lucerne,
encircled with a fourteenth century wall, the towers
of which are all different, as at Bâle (a caprice
peculiar to Germanic military architecture), full of
fountains, nearly all curious, and of houses, voluted,
turreted, and gabled, for the most part well preserved. Overgrowths of vegetation encroach above
the battlements.

From the fronts of all the houses in the town,
which are arranged on tiers as in an amphitheatre,
the lake is seen buried magnificently among the
mountains.

There are three covered bridges of wood dating
from the fifteenth century, two over the lake and
one across the Reuss. The two bridges over the
lake are of inordinate length, and wind over the

water without any apparent purpose but that of
accosting some old towers in passing for the delight of the eye.   It is both curious and pretty.

The pointed roof of each bridge covers a picture
gallery.   The pictures are triangular boards set in
beneath the angle of the roof and painted on both
sides.   There is a picture to every joist.   The
three bridges form three series of pictures, which
have each a distinct purpose, a subject from which
they do not depart, the well-defined intention of
acting through the eye upon the mind of those who
come and go.   The series of the chief bridge, which
is fourteen hundred feet long, is devoted to sacred
history. That of the Kapellbrücke, which is over the
outlet of the lake and is a thousand feet in length,
contains two hundred pictures, ornamented with
coats-of-arms, illustrating the history of Switzerland.
The series of the bridge over the Reuss, which is
the shortest of the three, is a Dance of Death.

Thus the three great sides of human thought are
there : religion, patriotism, philosophy.   Each of
these bridges is a book.   The passer-by lifts up his
eyes and reads.   He came out upon business, and
he goes back with an idea.

Nearly all these paintings date from the sixteenth
and seventeenth centuries.   Several of them are of
a very fine character.   Others have been spoiled

during last century by clumsy and gluey restoration. The Dance of Death of the Reussbrücke is of capital execution throughout, and full of spirit and meaning.   Each of the panels represents Death mixing in all human affairs.   She is attired as a notary and is registering the new-born child upon which the mother is smiling ; she is a coachman in lace livery, dashingly driving the emblazoned carriage of a pretty woman ; a Don Juan is having a debauch—she turns up her sleeve and pours him out to drink ; a doctor is bleeding his patient—she wears the assistant's apron and supports the sufferer's arm ; a soldier is wielding a two-handed sword— she is his opponent ; a fugitive is spurring for life —she bestrides his horse's crupper.   The most terrible of these pictures is Paradise.   In it all the animals are mixed up together, lambs and lions, tigers and sheep—good, gentle, harmless.   The serpent is there too ; one can see him, but through a skeleton ; he crawls about dragging Death along with him.   Mylinger, who painted this bridge at the beginning of the seventeenth century, was a great painter and a great intellect.

On the Kapellbrücke is a charming, almost a bird's-eye view of Lucerne as it was two hundred years ago.   Happily for itself, the town has changed but little.

So far I have seen only the outside of the Rath-
haus.

Its bastard style notwithstanding, it is a tolerably
fine edifice, with a belfry surmounted by a helmet-
shaped roof which gives it a comic air.   Between
Bâle and Baden the spires are pointed with coloured
tiles ; between Baden and Zurich they are daubed
with crude red ; between Zug and Lucerne they
resemble helmets, crested and visored, plated and
gilded.

The canonical church, which is outside the town
and is called the Cathedral, has two slate obelisks
of fine proportions ; but, except for a Louis
XIII. portal and an exterior bas-relief of the
fifteenth century representing Jesus on the Mount
of Olives, crowned with lilies and rejecting the
chalice, the church itself is not worth seeking out.

On the quay is the Church of the Jesuits, in loud
and aggressive rococo, and, in a little square behind
the Jesuits, another church which, although it hides
itself, possesses more of interest than all the others.
The nave is decorated with painted flags.   The
pulpit, of seventeenth-century workmanship, is a
fine piece of joiner-work ; so, too, are the choir
stalls.   I observed also, in a rock-work chapel, a
magnificent grille of the fifteenth century.

There is something of everything in Lucerne,

things great and small, things dismal and charming. In the middle of the quay a flock of water-fowl, at once both wild and tame, are playing with the water of the lake in the shadow of Mount Pilatus. The town has taken these poor lively fowls under its protection.   A penalty is inflicted for the killing of them.   One might take them for a flock of little black swans with white beaks.   Nothing could be more delightful than to see them plunging and fluttering in the sun.   They come when one whistles. I throw them bread crumbs from my window.

In all these small towns the women are inquisitive, shrinking, and bored.   Of this inquisitiveness and boredom is born a longing to see into the street. The timidity gives birth to a fear of being seen. Hence, on all the housefronts, there is a spying apparatus, more or less discreet, more or less elaborate.   In Bâle, as in Flanders, it is a simple little mirror hung outside the window ; in Zurich, as in Alsace, it is a little turret, occasionally pretty, receiving light from all sides and half sunk into the front of the house.

At Lucerne, the spying machine is simply a kind of little cupboard pierced with holes and placed outside the window on the sill like a meat-safe.

The women of Lucerne make a great mistake in hiding themselves, for nearly all of them are pretty.

By the way, I have seen the Lion of the 10th of August; it is declamatory.

15th September.

I am at Lucerne still, my Adèle. But I have just made two delightful excursions, the tour of the lake and the ascent of the Rigi.

I left for the Rigi on the morning of the 12th, after undergoing a preliminary shave by a fearful hairdresser called Fraunezer, who cut my chin in three places and mulcted me in sixteen French sous for this surgical operation.

I will tell you all about it. The Rigi is superb.

Here is a little sketch for Didine. The kind of saucer which is over the tower is a stork's nest, you will explain to her.

And then kiss Dédé, and Toto, and Charles. I hope they are industrious. A hand-clasp to Vacquerie.

Good-bye, my Adèle; I will write to you soon. In another month I shall see you again, and will kiss you all, my well-beloved.

Your own Victor who loves you.

II.

BERNE.—THE RIGI.

HEREVER I go, my dear Adèle, my very first care is to write to you. I am no sooner settled down than I have a table and inkstand brought to me, and I begin to talk to you once more—to you all, my well-beloved children. Take, each of you, your own share of my thought, as you have your share of my heart.

I reached Berne, like Lucerne and Zurich, at night. I do not at all dislike this plan of arriving at a place. There is a medley of light-rays and shadows in a town which one approaches by night, lights that reveal things and shadows that hide them, producing a strangely distorted and fantastic effect which has a charm of its own. It is a combination of the known and the unknown in which the imagination makes what dreams it will. Many objects which are but prose by day assume in the gloom a certain poetry. At night the outlines of things are dilated; by day they shrink.

It was eight in the evening; I had left Thun at five. The sun had set two hours before, and the moon, which is in its first quarter, had risen behind me among the lofty, rugged crests of the Stockhorn. My four-wheeled cabriolet rolled along an excellent road.—I have still my cabriolet; it has merely changed its driver, by what arrangement I know not.

My present driver is not a little picturesque. He is a big black-whiskered Piedmontese with a wide glazed hat, buried in an immense hackney coachman's overcoat of buff leather lined with black sheepskin and embellished on the outside with pieces of skin, red, blue, and green, laid over the yellow ground and forming fantastic flowers upon it. When it opens slightly, the overcoat discloses a waistcoat of olive velvet, leather breeches and gaiters, the whole being set off by a gewgaw made of a forty-sous piece bearing the effigy of the Emperor, into the edge of which a watch-key has been screwed.

Well, before me I had the white sky of the twilight, and behind me the gray sky of the moonlight. Seen under this double light the landscape was entrancing. At intervals I perceived, on my left, the Aare making silvery windings at the bottom of

a black ravine. On either side of the road the
houses, which are little wooden structures of the
most elaborate description, and are frequently
châlet-shaped, showed their points feebly animated
by the moonlight, and their big roofs pulled down
over their ruddy windows.

I note, in passing, that the cottage roofs are immense in this country of torrents and floods. The
roof develops under rain: in Switzerland, it in-
vades almost the whole house; in Italy, it effaces
itself; in the East, it disappears.

I resume.—I was observing the proportions of
the trees, which always interest me, and had just
been admiring the enormous spread of a walnut-
tree in a meadow a hundred paces from the road,
when the driver got down to put on the break. It
is a good sign when the break is applied. It is the
scene-shifter's whistle. The scenery is about to
change.

The road, in fact, sank like a crupper, and, on
my left, through the row of trees bordering it, in
the rays of the moon, in the depths of a valley of
which I caught a confused glimpse, a town, an apparition, a dazzling picture, surged suddenly into
view.

It was Berne and its valley.

I should rather have taken it for a Chinese town

on the night of the Feast of Lanterns. Not that
the roofs had their ridges much and fantastically
carved. But there were so many lights lit in this
living chaos of houses—so many candles, so many
lanterns, so many lamps, so many stars at all the
windows ; a sort of great white street traced such a
strange milky way among these constellations
scattered over the ground ; two towers, one square
and stunted, the other slender and tapering, marked
so whimsically the two extremities of the town, one
on the hill, the other in the hollow ; the Aare, bent
like a horseshoe at the foot of the walls, severed
from the earth this heap of shadowy edifices pricked
with luminous holes—so strangely, like a sickle
that cuts beneath a lump of stone ; the crescent
moon just facing me, poised low in the heavens
like a torch lighting the scene, threw over the whole
a light so sweet, so pale, so harmonious, so ineffable,
that it was no longer a town that I beheld,—it was a
shadow, a phantom city, an impossible isle of the
air riding at anchor in a valley of the earth and
illuminated by spirits.

In descending, the beautiful silhouettes of the
town were decomposed and recomposed several
times, and the vision was half dissipated.

My carriage then crossed a bridge and stopped
under an ogive gateway. An old fellow between

two soldiers in green uniform came and demanded
my passport.   By the light of the street lamp I
discerned a rope-dancer's poster embellished with a
picture and pasted on the wall, and I fell from the
height of my Chinese dream into Berne, the capital
of the largest of twenty-two cantons, the chief town
of three hundred and ninety-nine thousand inhabitants, the residence of ambassadors, a city
situated in latitude 46° 57′ 14″ north and longitude
25° 7′ 6″ east,[1] and seventeen hundred and eight
feet above the level of the sea.

After recovering a little from this fall I continued
my journey, and here I am now in the Hôtel des
Gentilshommes !   And this is another fall, for the
Hôtel des Gentilshommes seems to me but a dilapidated inn ; the rooms smell fusty, the white curtains
are yellow with age, the brasses of the chests of
drawers are covered with verdigris, and the ink is
black mud.   In short, the Hôtel des Gentilshommes
has an originality of its own.   Nothing could have
been more unforeseen than this oasis of Breton filth
in the midst of Swiss cleanliness.

I must now tell you about my excursion to the
Rigi.

It was not the Rigi that I wished for while stay-

---

[1] Reckoning from Paris.—*Translator.*

ing at Lucerne ; it was Pilatus. Pilatus is a steep,
wild mountain, stamped with the wonderful, difficult of approach, and forsaken by tourists. It
tempted me greatly. The Rigi is lower than Pilatus
by fourteen hundred feet[1] ; it can be climbed on
horseback ; it has only such declivities as the bourgeois soul requires, and is covered every day with a
swarm of visitors. The Rigi is the boast of everybody. It therefore excited my taste but little. The
weather, however, persisted in remaining unfavour-
able for the ascent of Pilatus. Odry, a flat-nosed
guide, thus surnamed by some French tourists,
refused to take me ; so I have had to content myself
with the Rigi. After all, I do not complain of the
Rigi, but I should have liked Pilatus.

After having been shaved by that fearful flayer,
Fraunezer, I left Lucerne for the Rigi on the 12th
at eight in the morning. At nine, the steamer
" Ville de Lucerne " landed me at Weggis, a pretty
little village on the shore of the lake, where I break-
fasted tolerably well. At ten, I left the inn at
Weggis and began to climb the mountain. I had
a guide for formality's sake, and my stick for my
entire baggage.

On the way I met two or three caravans with
horses, mules, donkeys, bags of provisions, alpen-

---

[1] Pilatus is the higher by only 1,092 feet.— *Translator.*

D

stocks, guides for leading the animals, guides for explaining the prospect, etc.   There are travellers who treat the Rigi like Mont Blanc, Don Quixotes of the mountains, who are determined to "make an ascent," and who scale a hillock with all the appliances of Cachat-le-Géant.   Now the Rigi is very fine, but you can go up and down it with your stick in your hand.   You remember, my Adèle, our excursion to the Montenvers?   The Rigi is only double that height : the Montenvers is about two thousand five hundred feet high,[1] the Rigi about five thousand.

The ascent of the Rigi from Weggis takes three hours, and may be divided into four zones.

It takes about an hour to climb each of the first two zones ; the last two take half an hour each.

First, there is a road running through woods, where the branches catch on to the lace of English lady tourists, and pretty little barefooted girls offer you pears and peaches.   These woods are interspersed with orchards.   From time to time the blue of the lake pierces the green of the trees, and between a couple of plums one sees a boat.   Then there is a pathway, very difficult in places, which ascends the steep slope that nearly all mountains

[1] The Montenvers is actually 6,303 feet, the Rigi 5,906 feet, in height.— *Translator*.

have between their base and their summit ; next, a
grassy slope, over which the path grows comfortably
wider, and which separates the house called the
Kaltbad from that called the Turnpike ; and, from
the Turnpike up to the summit (*Kulm*) a path, very
rough here and there, from which Lucerne is seen
again, and which runs along the edge of a precipice with Küssnacht at its foot.

The first zone is merely a pleasant walk ; the
second is rather trying.   The day was very fine,
the sun beating perpendicularly upon the white
mountain walls along which the path climbed,
supported at different points by scaffolding and
masonry.   The old diluvian wall has crumbled
away beneath the rains and torrents.   Polished
pebbles cover the road, and I advanced somewhat
slowly over the heads of brecciated nails.   From
time to time I encountered a rude painting representing one of the stations of the Cross hanging on
the wall of rock.

Half-way up there is a chapel, decorated by a
beggar, and, a couple of hundred yards higher, a
great rock detached from the mountain called the
Felsenthor,[1] under which the road passes.   A good

[1] The author's allusion is to the "pierre-tour" (stone
tower), but it is, apparently, the Felsenthor (rock gate) that is
meant.—*Translator*.

deal of cool shade and a little cold water fall from
this vault upon the wayfarer bathed in perspiration.
Beneath it they have placed a treacherous bench
on which pleuritics are sitting.

The Felsenthor, moreover, is strange to see.   It
is surmounted by an inaccessible platform upon
which some tall fir-trees have peacefully shot up.
A few yards off, over the precipice, falls a lovely
cascade which roars in April and by summer-time
is reduced to a few silvery threads.

I was out of breath on reaching the top of the
slope, and sat down for a few moments on the
grass.   Dense dark clouds had hidden the sun,
every human habitation had disappeared, and the
gloom which fell from heaven gave that vast, solitary
landscape an aspect inexpressibly sinister.   Beneath
my feet lay the lake with its mountains and head-
lands, of which I could clearly distinguish the
haunches, the ribs, and the long necks, and I
seemed to see an immense herd of hairy monsters
gathered round that blue drinking-trough, lying on
their bellies drinking, their muzzles stretched out
into the lake.

Having rested a little, I began to climb again. . . .

I had surmounted the first two zones, and entered
the third.   I observed at a certain height, half-

way up, on a sloping grass-plat, the wooden
house called the Kaltbad.   In five minutes I had
reached it.

The house is in no way remarkable.   It is
covered with little bits of wood cut into scales,
imitating the bark of the fir-tree.   Note, here, that
nature gives scales to everything that has to contend
against water, to the fir-tree in the torrent as to the
fish among the surge.   There were some English-
women sitting in front of the house.

I turned aside from the road and found, among
some big, fallen rocks, the clear sparkling spring
which has there caused to blossom, two thousand
feet[1] above the plain, first a chapel and then a health
retreat.   This is the usual sequence of things in
this country made religious by its mountains : first,
the soul ; afterwards, the body.   The spring falls
from the rock in long crystal threads.   I took the
pilgrims' old iron drinking-bowl from its rusty nail
and drank the delicious water.   I then entered the
chapel which is close to the spring.

A somewhat dilapidated altar encumbered with
Catholic   profusion,   a   Madonna,   innumerable
withered flowers, innumerable vases with the
gilding worn off, a collection of votive offerings

---

[1] The height of the Kaltbad peak is 4,728 feet.—*Translator.*

in which there is something of everything : wax legs, tin hands, painted signboards representing shipwrecks on the lake, images of children granted or saved, the iron collars of convicts with their chains, and even hernial bandages—such is the interior of the chapel.

I had no need to hurry. I took a walk in the vicinity of the spring while my guide rested and drank some kirsch in the house.

The sun had reappeared. A faint sound of bells led me on. In this way I reached the edge of a very steep ravine. Some goats were browsing on the slope, hanging on by the bramble bushes. I went down, like them, very much on all fours.

There everything was delightfully small. The grass was fine and fragrant, beautiful blue flowers with long bodies leaned out of their windows among the briers, and seemed to be admiring a pretty yellow and black spider executing somer-saults like an acrobat on an invisible tight-rope stretched from one bramble to another.

The ravine appeared to be closed in like a room. After having watched the spider, as the flowers were doing (which, be it said in passing, seemed to flatter it, for its audacity and agility were wonderful so long as it saw that I was present), I discovered a narrow passage at the extremity of the ravine, and

as soon as I had made my way through it the scene
suddenly changed.

I was on a narrow platform of rock and grass
hanging like a balcony to the immense wall of the
Rigi. Before me I had in their entire development
the Bürgen, the Buochser Horn, and Pilatus ;
beneath me, at a stupendous depth, the Lake of
Lucerne, parcelled out into creeks and bays, in
which these giant faces were reflected as in a
broken mirror. Above Pilatus, on the edge of the
horizon, glistened a score of snowy summits. The
powerful muscles of the hills were covered over by
the shadows and the vegetation, while the colossal
skeleton of the Alps was made to stand out by the
sun. The wrinkled granite heights were knit in the
distance like careworn foreheads. The rays showered
down from the clouds gave an air of enchantment
to those valleys which, at certain hours, are filled
with the terrible noises of the mountain. Two or
three microscopic craft sped over the lake, trailing
behind them a great track opening like a silver
tail. I saw the roofs of the villages with their
smoke ascending, and the rocks with their cascades
looking like smoke descending.

It was a marvellous assemblage of harmonious
and magnificent things filled with divine grandeur.
I turned round, asking myself for what superior

chosen being nature had served that wonderful feast of mountains, clouds and sunshine, and seeking some sublime witness of that sublime landscape.

There was indeed a witness—one only, for the platform, moreover, was wild, rugged and solitary. I shall never forget it all my life. In a hollow of the rock, his legs dangling over a big stone, sat a goitred idiot, with a lank body and an enormous head, laughing a stupid laugh, and staring vacantly before him, his face full in the sun.   O abyss ! The Alps were the spectacle, the spectator was a cretin.

I became lost in this terrible antithesis : man in opposition to nature; nature in her most magnificent attitude, man in his most abject posture.   What could be the meaning of this mysterious contrast ? To what end this irony in a solitude ?   Must I believe that the scene was destined for him, a cretin, and the irony for me, a passer-by ?

The cretin, moreover, took no notice of me.   In his hand he held a big hunch of black bread, out of which he took a bite from time to time.   He is a cretin whom they feed at the Hospice of the Capuchins, situated on the other side of the Rigi. The poor idiot had come there in search of the noonday sun.

A quarter of an hour afterwards I had returned

to the path. The Kaltbad and the chapel, the
ravine and the cretin, had disappeared behind me in
one of the swellings made by the southern slope of
the Rigi.

After having passed the Turnpike, at which they
demand six " batz " (eighteen sous) for each horse, I
sat down at the edge of the precipice and, like the
cretin, let my feet dangle over a ruined castle, buried
in the briers seven hundred fathoms beneath.

A few steps behind me three small English
children, exceedingly pretty and elaborately tricked
out, laughed and chattered as they rolled on the
grass, playing with their white-aproned nursemaid
as if at the Luxembourg, and wished me good
morning in French.

Here the Rigi is very wild, and the proximity of
the summit makes itself felt. A few châlets grouped
together like a village are buried in a deep ravine
which gashes the summit of the mountain, and, on
the Küssnacht side, down in the abyss, I saw
clambering up towards me in a host those tall fir-
trees which will one day be the masts of ships, and
which will have had but two destinies—on mountain
and on ocean.

From the spot where I was the summit can be
seen. It seems quite near. One fancies one might
reach it in three strides, but it is half a league away.

At two o'clock, after a four hours' climb much broken by halts and " caprices," in the etymological sense of the word, I stood upon the Rigi-Kulm.

There are only three things at the top of the Rigi : an inn, an observatory constructed of a few planks raised over some rafters, and a cross. That is all that is necessary. The stomach, the eye, and the soul have a threefold need. The need is satisfied.

The inn is called the Rigi-Kulm Hotel, and appeared to me pretentious. The cross is pretentious also. It is of wood, and bears the date 1838.

The summit of the Rigi is a great grass-covered ridge. On arriving there I was alone upon the mountain. While thinking of you, dear love, and of you, my Didine, I plucked a lovely little flower at the edge of a precipice four thousand feet deep. I am sending it to you.

The Rigi is nine times [1] the height of Strasburg steeple ; Mont Blanc is only thrice the height of the Rigi.

On heights like the Rigi-Kulm, one must look, but must not describe. Is it beautiful, or is it terrible? Truly I do not know. It is at once terrible and beautiful. It is no longer scenery, it is unnatural aspects that one sees. The horizon

---

[1] Actually over twelve and a half times.—*Translator*.

is unreal, the perspective is impossible ; it is a chaos of absurd exaggeration and terrible belittlement.

Mountains eight hundred feet high are wretched warts ; forests of fir-trees are tufts of furze ; the Lake of Zug is a washhand-basin full of water ; the Goldau valley, that waste of six square leagues, is a spadeful of mud ; the Bergfall, the wall seven hundred feet high along which glided the enormous landslip that engulfed Goldau, is the groove of a sleigh-slide ; the roads, on which three stage-coaches can pass each other, are spiders' threads ; the towns of Küssnacht and Arth with their illuminated steeples are toy villages to be put in a box and given to children as New Year's gifts ; men, oxen, and horses are no longer even grubs ; they have vanished.

At this height the convexity of the globe enters, to a certain extent, into all the lines and disturbs them. The mountains assume extraordinary postures. The point of the Rothhorn floats upon the Lake of Sarnen ; the Lake of Constance mounts upon the summit of the Rossberg. The landscape has gone mad.

In the presence of this ineffable spectacle one understands Switzerland and Savoy swarming with cretins. The Alps make many idiots. It is not given to every intelligence to keep house with such wonders, and to cast from morning until evening a terrestrial visual ray fifty leagues in length round a circumference of three hundred, without being dazzled and stupified.

After an hour spent on the Rigi-Kulm one becomes a statue ; one is rooted to one point or another of the summit.   One's emotion is intense. For the memory is no less occupied than the eye, the mind is no less occupied than the memory.   It is not only a segment of the globe that one has beneath one's eyes, it is a segment of history also. The tourist comes there in quest of a " prospect. " The thinker finds an immense book, in which every rock is a letter, every lake a sentence, every village an accent, and from which ascend, mingled together like a cloud of smoke, two thousand years of memories.   There the geologist may examine the formation of a chain of mountains ; there the philosopher may study the formation of one of those chains of men, races, or ideas which are called nations—a study still more profound, perhaps, than the other.

From the spot where I stood I saw eleven lakes (clever people see fourteen), and these eleven lakes were the whole history of Switzerland.   It was Sarnen that saw the fall of Landerberg, as the Lake of Lucerne saw the fall of Gessler ; Lungern, where Swiss beauty dwells among the peoples of the

Hasli; Sempach, where Winkelried embraced the pikes, and the Avoyer of Gundoldingen had himself slain on the banner of his town; Heideck, which reflects a fragment of the Castle of Waldeck torn from its rock in 1386 by the people of Lucerne; Hallwyl, laid waste by the civil wars of Berne and the Catholic cantons, and the lamentable battles of Wilmorgen; Egeri, resplendent with the memory of Morgarten, and dominated by the gigantic forms of her fifty peasants crushing an army by hurling down stones; Constance, with her Council, her two chairs in which the Pope and the Emperor sat, her promontory still called the Romanshorn (*Cornu romanorum*), her defile of Bregenz, blood-stained by the vengeance of the Swabian knights upon the knights of Appenzell; Zurich, which beheld Nicholas of Flac fight at the battle of Winterthur, and Ulpien Zwingli at the battle of Kappel.

Away down beneath my feet was Lowerz, where Goldau was crushed; Zug, which possesses the shade of Peter Collin and the relics of the battle of Bellinzona, and on the shore of which I saw, as I passed on the previous evening, a tombstone, already hidden by the brambles, bearing the inscription: KARL-MARIA WEBER, appear suddenly between two trees; and, finally, that wonderful lake of which the shores are formed by the four cantons constituting the very heart of Switzerland—by Schwytz, the patriarchal canton ; Unterwald, the pastoral canton; Lucerne, the feudal canton ; Uri, the heroic canton.

Looking towards the north, I had Swabia on my right in the extreme distance ; on my left, the Black Forest ; on the west, the Jura as far as the Chasseral; and, with a glass, I should, perhaps, have distinguished Bienne (the Petenissa of Antoninus), its forest of beeches and oak-trees, its lake, its deep spring, which started and was troubled on the day of the earthquake of Lisbon, and its delightful island from which Jean-Jacques was expelled by Berne in 1765.

Nearer to me I had an immense girdle of cantons : Appenzell, in which are the calcareous Alps, and which is divided by two religions into two peoples —Catholicism makes the shepherds, Calvinism the merchants ; St. Gallen, which replaced its abbé by a landamman and was the scene of the battle of Ragatz ; Thurgau, which witnessed the battle of Diessenhofen, and from which Conradin set out, the last of the Hohenstaufens, to die at Naples, as the Duke of Enghien died in our own day at Vincennes ; the Grisons, which are ancient Rhætia, and have sixty valleys, a hundred and eighty castles, the three sources of the Rhine, Mont Julier with the Julian columns, and that lovely valley of the Enga-

dine where the earth quakes and the water is solid
(the lakes were still frozen on the 4th of May, 1799,
the day on which the French artillery crossed them) ;
Schaffhausen, which has the Falls of the Rhine, as
Bellegarde has the Perte du Rhône, with the gloomy
memories of Heinz and Stern, and the defeat of
Paradies in 992 ; Aargau, which in 1415 saw the
fall of the Austrian fortress of Aarburg, and where
the peasants still vote like the old Romans in their
comitia, in the open air, with uplifted hand, and in
separate bands ; Soleure, called by the Italians
Soletta, which possesses some paintings by Dominico
Corvi, and whose regiment would do no discredit to
the Spanish infantry of the seventeenth century of
which Bossuet spoke.

Neuchâtel and the battlefields of Grandson and
Morat were hidden from me by Mount Pilatus ; but
the two shades of Nicolas of Scharnachthal and
Charles the Bold rose up in my spirit above the
height of Mount Pilatus, and completed that horizon
of great mountains and great events.

I had still beneath my eyes Frutigen, from which
the bailiff of Tellenburg was driven ; the Entlebuch,
where one may pluck the Alpine rhododendron,
where the peasants have Greek games and sing
every year their secret Chronique Scandaleuse of
Hirschmontag ; on the east, Berne, which witnessed

the first battle of the oppressed Swiss, Donnerbües, in 1291 ; on the north, Bâle, which saw the last victory of free Switzerland, Dornach, in 1499.

Stretching from east to north I saw the whole of the calcareous Alps from the Sentis to the Jungfrau, while the great granitic Alps surged together in fearful confusion in the south.

I was alone, dreaming—who would not have dreamed ?—and the four giants of European history came of themselves before the eye of my thought and placed themselves as if standing erect at the four cardinal points of that colossal landscape : Hannibal, in the Allobrogean Alps ; Charlemagne, in the Lombardic Alps ; Cæsar, in the Engadine ; Napoleon, in the St. Bernard.

Beneath me in the valley, at the foot of the precipice, I had Küssnacht and William Tell.

I seemed to see Rome and Carthage, Germany and France, represented by their four greatest figures, contemplating Switzerland personified in her great man—they leaders and despots, he a shepherd and a liberator.

It is a solemn hour, and one filled with meditations, in which one has Switzerland beneath one's eyes, that sturdy knot of strong men and tall mountains inextricably knit into the heart of Europe, which notched the battle-axe of Austria and broke the formidable sword of Charles the Bold.   Providence made her mountains—William Tell made her men.

How did I spend the whole day at the top of the Rigi ?   I cannot tell.   I wandered, gazed, dreamed. I lay down on my face at the edge of the precipice, and stretched out my head to peer into the abyss ; I made a bird's-eye visit to Goldau ; I threw stones into the hole which they call the Kessisbodenloch, but must say that I did not see them come out again at the mountain's foot ; I purchased a castle of carved wood from a mountaineer ; I climbed the observatory and thence sketched the Mythen, a prodigious granite cone with a reddish stone at its summit, which makes the Mythen look as if it had been mended with Roman cement like the pyramid of Luxor.   Seen from the Rigi, the Mythen has the exaçt form of the pyramids of Egypt.   But Cheops would disappear in its shadow—as the Bedouin's tent disappears in the shadow of Cheops, as Ramses disappears in the shadow of Jehovah.

The Rigi-Kulm had become peopled while I was sketching.   The first visitors climbed the mountain by the Arth road, which is steeper but more shady than the Weggis road, over which I had had to struggle against the sun and the sirocco.

They were young German students with knap-

E

sacks on their backs, painted faïence pipes in their mouths, and sticks in their hands. With an air at once thoughtful and naïve they came and sat beside me. Then a pretty, fair Englishwoman climbed the observatory. She had come from Lombardy and had travelled to Lucerne by the St. Gothard. The students, who had come down into Switzerland by way of Zurich and Schwytz, talked of Rapperswyl, Herrliberg, and Affoltern ; the Englishwoman went into ecstasies in a small, melodious voice over Giamaglio, Bucioletto, Rima, and Rimella.

For all this is Switzerland. The vowels and consonants share Switzerland between them like the flowers and rocks. Towards the north, where the shadow is, and the cold wind, and the ice, the consonants crystallize and bristle confusedly in the names of all the towns and mountains. The sun-rays cause the vowels to blossom ; wherever they fall vowels sprout and bloom in crowds, so they cover the whole southern slope of the Alps. They scatter themselves gaily over all those lovely golden declivities. The same summit—the same rock— has on its dark side consonants, on its sunlit side vowels. The formation of languages is laid bare in the Alps, thanks to the central position of the chain. There is but one mountain, the St. Gothard, between the Teufelsbrücke and Airolo.

Towards half-past five visitors came crowding from all quarters almost with one accord, on foot, on horseback, on donkeys, on mules, and in sedan-chairs; Englishmen buried in overcoats, Parisiennes in velvet shawls, invalids who spend the summer in the Kaltbad; a senator driven from Zurich by the little revolution of a week ago; a French com-mercial traveller who said he had visited Chillon and the prison "*in which Bolivar died*," and so forth. At two o'clock I had arrived alone; at six, we numbered sixty.

The size of the miserable little inn contrasted with this great throng exercised the mind of one of the young Germans, and he solemnly informed me that we should all die of starvation.

Just then the valley became magnificent. The sun was setting behind the jagged crest of Pilatus. It now illumined only the topmost peaks of all the mountains, and its horizontal rays rested upon those monster pyramids like golden architraves. The great valleys of the Alps were all filled with mists. It was the hour when the eagles and bearded vultures return to their nests.

I had advanced to the edge of the precipice surmounted by the cross and looking towards Goldau. The crowd remained on the observatory, and I was there alone with my back turned towards

the west.   I do not know what the others saw, but
my own view was sublime.

The immense cone of darkness projected by the
Rigi, with its sharply-defined edges and without
visible penumbra because of its distance, slowly
climbed the precipitous flank of the Rossberg, fir by
fir, and rock by rock.   The mountain of shadow was
devouring the mountain of light.   That vast, dark
triangle, with its base lost beneath the Rigi and its
apex every instant more and more approaching the
summit of the Rossberg, already covered Arth,
Goldau, ten valleys, ten villages, half of the Lake of
Zug, and the whole of the Lake of Lowerz.   Red
copper clouds floated into it, and there became
transformed into tin.   At the bottom of the gulf
Arth swam in a twilight glow, star-studded here
and there with lighted windows.   Already poor
women were spinning there beside their lamps.
Arth lives in the night ; there the sun sets at two
o'clock.

A moment afterwards the sun had disappeared ;
the wind was cold, the mountains were gray, and
the visitors had re-entered the inn.   Not a cloud
was in the sky.   The Rigi had again become
solitary, with a vast blue sky above it.

In one of my first letters to you, dear love, I
wrote : " Those billows of granite called the Alps."

I did not know I was speaking so truly. The image which then came to my mind appeared to me in all its reality on the summit of the Rigi after the sun had gone down. These mountains are indeed billows, but giant billows. They have all the forms of the sea. There are dark, green swells, which are the fir-covered mounds ; light and earth-coloured sheets, which are the granite slopes gilded by the lichens ; and, on the highest undulations, the snow is rent and falls in tatters, as does the foam. One seems to behold an immense ocean frozen in the midst of a tempest by the breath of Jehovah.

The thought of what would happen to the horizon and to the mind of man, were those mighty waves to be suddenly set in motion again, is a fearful dream.

III.

THE STROLLING PLAYERS.

HE dining-room of the new hotel in which I am staying is on the ground floor. In accordance with my custom, I installed my table near the window, and, while doing justice to an excellent lunch with an excellent appetite, I looked into the square.

As you know, I call this "reading at meals." To dreamers everything seen has a meaning. The eyes see, but it is the mind that pierces beneath, comments, and interprets. A public square is a book. You spell out the buildings, and in them you find history; you decipher the passers-by, and in them you find life.

After a few moments my attention became fixed upon a strange-looking little group bivouacked, so to speak, a few steps from the window from which I was looking.

The group, which was scattered over the ground

in a somewhat picturesque fashion, shaded by a
big banner not very firmly planted in the ground,
was composed of four personages : a man, two
women, and an animal.   One of the women was
asleep, the man was asleep, the animal was asleep.

I could distinguish nothing of the sleeping
woman, who was hidden by a wide head-dress
turned down over her face.

The man's face, which was turned towards the
roadway, was also hidden from me.   I saw only
his black hands, his frayed nails, his coarse, dirty,
bristling hair, the holed and worn-out sole of his
boots, gray with dust, and, through the sole, one
of the toes of his left foot.

He was fantastically accoutred in heavy-cavalry
breeches   and   a   French-fashioned   coat.   The
breeches, which were composed more of leather
than of cloth, appeared tolerably new, although
soiled with ashes and mud.   The coat was falling
in tatters.   It was an old threadbare coat of black
velvet strewn over with gold spangles, and had at
one time been exceedingly dashing and showy.   In
ageing, the velvet had assumed a hue of reddish
smoke, and the spangles had nearly all become
extinct ; and so it came about that the coat had
the appearance, as Trivelin says, of an illumination
at three in the morning.

During his sleep the man grasped in his right
hand a very thick cane with a carved silver knob,
which had probably paraded the Boulevard de
Gand as the coat had graced the Œil-de-Bœuf.
Two epochs of French elegance were mingled in
the wretched man's rags. The cane, which remained
rich and brilliant at the top, was burnt and
blackened at its lower extremity.   One felt that it
had more than once stirred and poked noɛturnal
fires.   Towards the middle it was flattened and
crushed.   One would have said that it had been used
in carrying weights, and that it had been its fate
to lift up doors.

An old round hat, which had now become poly-
hedral in form, lay partly on the pavement and
partly on the sleeper's head.   A tin dish thrown in
front of his feet seemed to await the coppers of the
passers-by.

As for the animal, without doubt the visible
breadwinner of these people, it lay, half-buried in
sand, behind the bars of a sort of cage, in which I
could with difficulty distinguish it.   In sleeping,
however, parts of it moved, and I saw enough of it
to recognize something horrible, one of those monsters that are not for human eyes to see, that prove
the imagination of nature—one of those creatures
that are nightmares, a sort of living thistle, a prickly

lizard, a hideous thing like the *Moloch horridus* of New Holland.

Five or six pretty children were examining this monster and eyeing it with delight. Among them I admired two charming little French boys, who doubtless belonged to some Parisian family which was staying at the inn.

The cage rested on a square box, on the outside panel of which some strange chance had inlaid a tolerably fine bas-relief of St. Francis of Sales with his hand resting on a death's head. The little French children gazed at this panel. After a few moments' inspection the elder said to the younger, " Oh, that is the good God with His apple ! "

The other woman—the one who was not asleep —was sitting beside the man on a piece of old carpet. I wish I could tell you that she was ugly, for nothing is more trite and stale in literature than the beauty of beggars and open-air actresses. To my regret, however, I am forced to confess that this creature, although tanned by the sun and " speckled with bran," as the popular metaphors say, was really a charming and delicate creature.

Her forehead was intelligent. Her mouth, which was ornamented with perfect teeth, was graceful and shapely. Her eyes, which were not very large, were deep and clear. Rich, light-coloured veins glistened through the thick locks of her chestnut hair, which was very coquettishly, but above all very becomingly arranged. In the litheness of her figure, the fullness of her hips, the perfect harmony of her forehead, nose, and chin, the smallness of her feet and hands, the transparency of her nails, the delicacy of her ankles, and the height of her instep, there was breeding. Her whole person—her whole attire—was as neat and seductive as her head-dress. One felt that she probably took advantage of every brook she came to, first to wash, then to admire herself.

Her belt, which was set off with all manner of trinkets, told of her travels. She wore blue stockings with clocks ornamented with white arabesques, like those worn by the Swabian girls; a full petticoat of brown cloth with innumerable plaits, like the mountain women of the Black Forest; and a tight silk vest like the peasant women of Brescia. This vest, the cut of which was naïve and a little unbecoming, was almost hidden, and, as it were, redeemed by a wide Flemish frill, on which were embroidered several enamelled cathedral catharine-wheels knit into one another. Her trinkets, which were all Italian, and had probably been purchased each in the particular place where it was made, finished and completed the tale of her wanderings.

By her filigrane earrings one divined that she had
been in Genoa ; by her gold bracelet, enamelled
and ornamented with miniatures, that she had
stayed in Venice ; by her mosaic bracelet, that she
had been to Florence ; by her cameo bracelet, that
she had passed through Rome ; by her necklet of
coral and shells, that she had seen Naples.

Altogether, the girl was delightful and magnificent—the jewels of an idol and the air of a goddess.

It was clear that the finery of this woman
covered with trinkets was the chief concern of the
man covered with rags.

Nor was she ungrateful.   She appeared to adore
him, and that surprised me greatly.   I well knew
that women often take pleasure in feeling that they
form half of an antithesis ; I was not unaware that
the most beautiful, young, and charming women
willingly lend themselves — through what inexplicable sentiment I know not—to play their part
in that figure of living rhetoric, idolizing their old
husband because of his age, and their hunchbacked
lover because of his hump.   But that cleanliness in
the form of a woman should have had any liking
for dirtiness in the form of a man, I never should
have believed.   Between the human species that
washes and the human species that does not
wash there is a great gulf fixed, and I did not

imagine that that gulf could be bridged. From
this day forth nothing of the kind could surprise
me any longer. In this public square, I saw a girl
of sixteen, bright and pretty as a wet pebble, kissing every other minute with a sort of passionate
admiration the greasy hair and black hands of a
horrible sleeping man who was not even conscious
of those sweet caresses. I saw her with her rosy
fingers dust the showman's coat, from which her
graceful fillips brought out little clouds of dust. I
saw her drive off the flies that importuned the dirty
sleeper, bend over him, listen to the sound of his
breathing, and tenderly contemplate his down-at-
heel boots. And now, I am quite prepared to
applaud any writer who may care to produce a
novel entitled, "The Melancholy History of the
Loves of a Turtle-Dove and a Swine."

Verily, nature contains every combination, and
woman contains every caprice. With woman, as
with God, all things are possible.

While with her eyes she brooded over her companion lying beside her, she mended and polished
with a serge rag a kind of spinet, antique in shape
and inlaid with little ivory wheels, like the viola
d'amore of the great Girgiganto.

The banner by which the couple were shaded
was certainly the most unintelligible of charlatans'

placards that I have ever met with. That, however, is not injurious to success.

Imagine a big sheet painted in blue, peeled by the sun and furrowed by the rain, and, in the middle of it, nothing whatever but this hieroglyph painted in black :

If I am not mistaken in the little I know of the late M. Champollion's elucidations, this phrase, which is perfectly Egyptian, signifies, " *To-day, as for ever, throughout eternity.*" But what meaning did that mountebank attach to it? That I cannot so easily understand, unless, indeed, it may have been a passionate declaration made by the swine to the turtle-dove in the mystic language of Horus, Epiphanes, and Ammon Ra.

To contemplate a woman who is contemplating a man, even when the woman is very pretty and the man very ugly, is after all but a poor pleasure; so, as soon as I had made these various observations, I resumed breakfast. Suddenly, however, a French word uttered beneath my window in the clearest and sharpest fashion recalled my attention to the square. You will excuse me from repeating it. It was one of those words that are an outrage, one of

those words that are hard to pronounce from the
scanty decency of their syllables, and that have
exceedingly evil communications within them.

I raised my eyes.

The sleeping woman had awakened. She was
sitting up, and her hat, which was now thrown back,
disclosed the face of an old woman with the ugliness
of an ogress.

It was she who had just thrown the word I had
heard at the young girl, and her look full of anger
seemed to be casting it at her still.

The girl made no answer; her pretty mouth
assumed an expression of ineffable scorn, and she
bent over the man and kissed him.   The old
woman, exasperated by this caress, repeated the
insult.

I shall never forget with what a proud, fiery
glance the young girl, without uttering a word,
answered her.

From this little scene I drew two conclusions :
first, that the old woman had probably awakened
while the young one was bestowing some caress
upon the sleeping player ; second, that this man—
the swine—was loved by the two women.

A story which, after all, is more or less that of
everybody.   Alas !   Who has not found himself
caught in life between the young and the old,

between the present and the past, between to-day and yesterday, between the turtle-dove and the hawk.

The haughty tranquillity of the beauty exasperated the other. And then, without a gesture or exclamation, for fear of gathering a crowd, speaking in an undertone, but in a terrible and determined fashion, she uttered, for more than a quarter of an hour, and always in French, all that that wretched slave, the despised mistress, could say to the favourite sultana, the happy queen.

She told, with that abundance of passion which repeats the same thing a score of times in a different accent, the story of both, and the man's story, and the story of all men and women, seasoning the whole, I am obliged to say, with the most degrading, the most frightful, and the most obscene abuse.

After all, this occurs among others than street buffoons. Even among those classes who think themselves educated and polished, there are those who steep their anger in foul language as a waggoner soaks his whip in a brook to make the lash more cutting.

The young girl suffered visibly beneath this overflow of hate. She was pale and her lips trembled, but she made no answer.

She had merely placed her right hand on the

shoulder of the heavily-sleeping man, and had been cautiously pushing it with a slow, gentle, regular movement while the old woman was speaking. Nothing could have been stranger than this sort of silent tocsin, full at once of respect, alarm, anguish, and love.

At length the beauty succeeded, and the man awoke. He turned round with a yawn and said in Spanish : " Que demonio de ruido haceis, mugeres ? "

Then, raising himself up and turning to the old woman, he said : " Calla te, vieja." The old woman was silent.

The player then got upon his feet, and leaned upon his cane, listening with an absent air of superiority to the young girl, who, without replying to his question, was addressing him with all manner of affectionate and incoherent expressions.

While this was going on, I examined him at my leisure. He might have been forty-five years of age. His face was browned like a sailor's. One saw by the almost painful manner in which his eye-brows were knit together that he had wandered much in the south beneath the glaring sun. It was the deep and pronounced features of one of those rude and vigorous beggars' faces that obliged Callot to employ for his etchings the hard varnish used by lute-makers.

After making my examination I did not discover so much degradation in the face of the man as in his costume.   It was still animated by something strong and generous.   Like the two women, he evidently belonged to that underground society which undermines the visible and lawful society and lives in the saps.   All things considered, however, I should still prefer the savage physiognomy of that revolted Titan, that escaped gladiator, that lion-faced thief clothed in a marquis's coat and a soldier's breeches, to the polished and treacherous mien of some pamphleteer, some popular declaimer or public calumniator, some literary spy who stealthily warms himself at the genial fire of a secret pension.

Nothing could express the tender accents in which the girl spoke to the player.   She spoke in French ; he answered in Spanish.   This bi-lingual dialogue, of which the Bernese passers-by understood nothing, did not seem to incommode either of them.

There was, moreover, something fantastically mingled with the words of the beautiful street-player which expressed to me her indecipherable origin. Her voice, which was pleasant and sympathetic, was at intervals hollow and tremulous.   (You could not believe with what pain I write this particular, which, I fear, points to rum and brandy.   But what

F

would you have? Truth is inexorable, and I desire
only to be truthful.)

Her language, which was now coarse, now affected,
was composed of words picked up in the streets and
words culled in the salons. Imagine to yourself a
précieuse gliding at times into a fishwife, the Hôtel
de Rambouillet modified by the stall, the guard-
room, and the tavern.

This produced the strangest style imaginable. It
was at once argot and gibberish. She said "un
esbrouf" like the gipsies of the Fair of St. Germain,
and "un farimara" like the duchesses of the Petit-
Marly.

Towards her rival she was quite a great lady.
She did not do her the honour of concerning herself
about her, and in what she said to the man there
was not a word about the old woman, either of
complaint or of reproach.

But the one personage who never loses anything,
the Devil, had an interest there as elsewhere. It
was clear that the fair favourite's soul was filled with
anger. From time to time she cast a side-glance at
the other, and the look that came from those charming eyes was almost savage.

Here, my friend, is an observation which I have
made, and which I permit you to apply to all the
lions and turtle-doves of humankind. Nothing

looks so harmless as a lion in repose, and nothing
so wicked as a turtle-dove in a passion.

I beg of you here not to give the word "lion" that
ridiculous sense with which they have endowed it
in Paris during the past few years, a lamentable
and foolish fashion, like most English fashions,
disfiguring one of the finest words in the language,
and degrading one of the noblest beings in creation.

However, beneath the man's "Be quiet, old
woman!" the other had remained crushed and
stupid, motionless, her eyes fixed on the pavement,
seeming neither to listen nor even to hear.

At a certain moment, however, as one of the inn
waiters was passing in front of the door a few steps
from her, she made him a sign to come to her.   To
this detail the amorous and happy couple paid not
the slightest heed.

The waiter came and bent down near the gipsy,
who said a few words in his ear.

The waiter answered with a sign of intelligence
and re-entered the inn.

With an air of profound indifference the old
woman began, with the point of her finger, to make
and unmake plaits in her petticoat, which, it may be
said in passing, was similar to that of the favourite.
Only the young girl had a new petticoat and the
old woman had an old one.

A clatter of dishes and plate was heard in the inn.

The man made a sign to the young girl to rise :

" Vámos. Ahora es menester entrar en la posada."

" Yes," she answered, " it is time. It is the hour of table d'hôte."

And she raised herself as lightly as a bird.

" Que cantarás ? "

" That song of the valley of Luz ; you know ? "

" Muy bien."

She picked up the tin dish. He took the spinet, passing the shoulder-strap round his neck, and then half-turned towards the other woman, saying :

" Vas á quedar aquí, vieja ! "

They then entered the inn together.

The old woman's eyes had again fallen on the pavement, and mine upon my plate. I was quietly finishing my lunch when the sound of singing arose in the next room, a long hall in which the guests at the table d'hôte were noisily dining.

The voice, which was sweet, low, but slightly hoarse, and was accompanied by a spinet hoarser still, was probably that of the young girl.

Although the door was ajar I could not hear the words, thanks to the Pantagruelic accompaniment of spoons and forks which drowned them.

Here I must say that I have never seen without a sort of anguish those poor itinerant singers, those

pariahs of the tavern and the wine-shop, slink
trembling and abashed into those pandemoniums
of voracious and dreadful creatures engaged in
carousing, to submit their wretched baritone or thin
contralto to the mercy of the fearful orchestra of
glasses, knives, dishes, and bottles, which has for its
maestro that huge, big-bellied devil, with the starting eyes, stopped ears, and terrible teeth, called
Appetite.

I was, then, a prey to somewhat melancholy reflections, when the festive din of the table d'hôte
was suddenly transformed into an extraordinary
tumult.

The singing subsided, the clatter of the glasses
and dishes suddenly ceased, and an indescribable
hubbub succeeded.

Imagine to yourself a medley of cries, an uproar
of voices, footsteps, blows given and received, chairs
overturned, swaying tables, dishes broken—a surging
crowd, clamouring men-servants, a house upside
down, a tempest ; in short, what the Milanese so
well call in their picturesque dialect, " barataclar
per ca."

Above the tumult rose the cry, " Ein Dieb ! ein
Dieb ! "

I rose in surprise and made my way towards the
room from which the uproar came.

At this moment my eyes, which had been wandering mechanically over the square, alighted on the old woman.

I confess that I went no further.

The woman was transfigured.   She had risen and was standing listening eagerly to the noise, fixing on the inn flashing, terrible, almost beautiful eyes, full of anger, full of hate, and full of joy.

The flame in her eyes then went suddenly out. The expression of her face, which, like that of all old people, was by no means plain to read, became sullen and icy again.

A throng of people were coming out of the house, and had just appeared at the door of the inn.   I leaned over to see.

It was a crowd of all sorts of people, men-servants, women-servants, travellers with their dinner-napkins in their hands, surrounding, with a tornado of gestures and cries, a struggling man and woman.

The man was the player ; the woman was the beautiful girl.

The man, who was held by the collar by seven or eight vigorous hands, was driving back the crowd, but with the calmest, boldest, and most unconcerned demeanour possible.   He went on, but resisted as he went.

As for the poor girl, pale, with dishevelled hair,

brutally handled and buffeted by five or six grooms, with her trinkets torn off and her silk-lace all rent, she was weeping and crying in supplicating tones, and I must say that she defended herself with all the solicitude of innocence.

Some men in uniform, like sergents de ville, had already sprung from somewhere or other and mingled in the scuffle, for the police have the peculiar faculty of suddenly rising up from beneath the pavement. A clumsy thief has but to strike his heel against the ground and a gendarme will jump up out of it.

I observed that the waiter who held the young girl's arm was the same person to whom the old woman had spoken in an undertone.

As for the old woman, she did not stir. She silently watched her two companions being led away. She had become a statue.

In passing in front of her the man called out to her: "Vete, muger!"

A moment afterwards, the whole of the stormy crowd, the two prisoners, the inn servants, the police and the passers-by, had disappeared round the corner of the house.

"Where are they going?" I inquired of a waiter who came near me.

"To prison," he replied.

The particulars given me by the same waiter were these :

While the beautiful girl was standing singing at the end of the table d'hôte, with her eyes raised to heaven, one of the hotel servants—the same, the waiter informed me, who had held her by the arm as she was taken out—had noticed a quantity of pepper and salt scattered on the ground behind her, in the shadow of a sideboard on which the waiters were placing the dessert. The man who was accompanying the singing on the spinet leaned his back against this sideboard from time to time as if fatigued. The servant spoke to the landlord about the pepper and salt, and the silver plate was examined.

A large silver salt-cellar had disappeared.

The servant hereupon rushed towards the beautiful songstress shouting : " Search this woman !"

In spite of her resistance and that of the man, they had searched her, and found the salt-cellar in a pocket concealed beneath the ample folds of her petticoat.

Hence the tumult, the cries of " Ein Dieb !" the appearance of the police, and the prison as dénouement.

You may laugh at me, my friend, but this adventure wrung my heart.

I alone knew the secret of it.

To everyone—to the two prisoners themselves—it was merely a punished theft. To me it was a drama. It was for love that the girl had stolen ; it was through jealousy that she was punished. To me it was plain that the old woman had informed against her rival in advance to the same servant of the inn who, a few moments later, had noticed the spilt salt, searched the singer, and led her off to prison.

A wretched story, trivial in appearance, poetic in reality ; burlesque, if you like, in the baseness of the characters ; tragic, to my thinking, in the grandeur of the passions.

Be that as it may. In spite of the warning cry of " Vete, muger ! " charitably uttered by the man, her unconscious victim, the old woman had remained where she was.

Her look of triumph had gone, and her glassy eye had become horrible and sad. The after-taste of revenge is bitter.

She was still in the same place, when a little troop of soldiers, led by a police officer, and augmented by a swarm of street urchins, appeared and suddenly surrounded her. The soldiers seized the cage, pulled up the banner, and ordered the old woman to march along with them.

Her head fell on her breast, and she obeyed without uttering a syllable.

The urchins, however, leaping about her with glee, deafened her with their jeering and hooting, and one, the biggest of them, who knew several taunts in French, persecuted her with the inexplicable relentlessness of childhood, which is so sweet when it is sweet, so cruel when it is cruel.

At first the Egyptian bore this abuse with an air of disdain ; but suddenly, escaping from among the stupified soldiers, and taking three strides through the group of children, she stretched out her arm at the biggest, crying with her hawk-like voice : " See your gibbet ! "

In this attitude she remained for several instants.

Hitherto I had not remarked the tall figure of the woman. Dressed as she was in black, pale, gaunt, and standing erect with extended arm among the children, she was the very image of a living gibbet.

The soldiers seized her again, the children redoubled their laughter and shouts, and, a minute afterwards, she had disappeared, like the two others, round the corner of the house.

IV.

ON THE ROAD TO AIX-LES-BAINS.

24th September, seven in the morning.

WAY on the green, rugged ridges of the Jura the yellow beds of the dried-up torrents drew Y's in every direction.

Have you observed how picturesque the letter Y is, and how numberless are its significations?—A tree is a Y ; the parting of two roads is a Y ; the confluence of two rivers is a Y ; an ass's or an ox's head is a Y ; a glass standing on its foot is a Y ; an iris upon its stem is a Y ; a supplicant lifting his arms to heaven is a Y.

This observation, moreover, may be extended to everything that primarily constitutes human writing. Everything that is in the demotic language has been derived from the hieratic language. The hieroglyph is the necessary cause of the character. All letters were first of all signs, and all signs were first of all images.

Human society, the world, the whole man is contained in the alphabet. In it masonry, astronomy, philosophy—all the sciences, have their point of departure, imperceptible but real. And this must be so. The alphabet is a fountain-head.

A is a roof, a gable with its traverse, an arch, *arx;* or it is the embrace of two friends kissing one another and clasping each other's hands ; D is the back ; B is a D above a D, a back upon a back, a hump ; C is a crescent, the moon ; E is a basement, an upright, a console and stem, an architrave —the whole architecture of ceilings in a single letter ; F is a gibbet, the gallows, *furca;* G is a horn ; H is the front of an edifice with its two towers ; I is an engine of war hurling its projectile ; J is a ploughshare and a horn of plenty; K is the angle of reflection equal to the angle of incidence, one of the keys of geometry ; L is a leg and foot ; M is a mountain, or a camp with its tents joined together ; N is a closed door with its diagonal bar ; O is the sun ; P is a porter standing with his load on his back ; Q is a horse's crupper with the tail ; R is repose, the porter leaning on his staff ; S is a serpent ; T is a hammer ; U is an urn ; V is a vase (hence they are often confounded) ; I have just said what Y is ; X is crossed swords, a combat ; who will be the victor ?—no one knows ; thus the Hermetics chose X as the sign of destiny, the algebraists as the sign of the unknown ; Z is the lightning—God.

First, then, man's house and its architecture ; then man's body, its structure and deformities ; then justice, music, the church ; war, agriculture, geometry ; mountains ; nomadic life, the life of the cloister ; astronomy ; labour and rest ; the horse and the serpent ; the hammer and urn, which, if overturned and joined together, form a bell ; the trees, rivers, and roads ; and, finally, destiny and God—that is what the alphabet contains.

Hence, to some of those mysterious constructors of the languages which go to make the foundations of human memory, and which the human memory forgets, A, E, F, H, I, K, L, M, N, T, V, Y, X, and Z, may have been none other than the various timbers forming the framework of the temple.

V.

GENEVA.

AM at Aix-les-Bains, turning rapidly towards the south. The weather in Switzerland is terrible. Several of the roads to the north are blocked.

I passed through Lausanne the day before yesterday, my Adèle, and my thoughts were full of you. We had only a glimpse of Lausanne, you remember, one lovely moonlit night in 1825. The church, although fine, is inferior to the idea that I had retained of it. In the evening, by a strange coincidence, precisely the same moonlight recurred, and I again saw the church as beautiful as in 1825. The moon is the folly-veil of architects. The cathedral of Lausanne rather needs its moon.

Geneva has lost much, and imagines, alas! that she has gained much. The Rue des Dômes has been demolished. The old row of worm-eaten houses, which gave the town such a picturesque

frontage on the lake, has disappeared. It is replaced
by a white quay, embellished with a string of big,
white barracks which these good Genevese take for
palaces. During the last fifteen years Geneva has
been cleaned and scraped, levelled, twisted and hoed
in such a fashion that, with the exception of the
Butte Saint-Pierre and the bridges over the Rhône,
there is no longer an old edifice remaining.—At
present Geneva is a platitude surrounded by
excrescences.

But they may do what they please. They may
prettify their city as much as they like, but as they
will never be able to scrape out Mont Salève, to
touch up Mont Blanc, or to bleach the lake, my
mind is quite at ease.

Nothing could be more dismal than these little
would-be Parises which one encounters nowadays
in the provinces of France, and outside of France.
One expects an old town with its towers, its carved
fronts, its historic streets, its Gothic or Renaissance
spires, and one finds a sham Rue de Rivoli, a sham
Madeleine resembling the façade of the Théâtre de
Bobino, a sham Colonne Vendôme looking like an
advertisement post.

The provincial would have the Parisian admire
this. The Parisian shrugs his shoulders, and the
provincial loses his temper. That is how I have

already fallen out with the whole of Brittany ; that is how I shall fall out with Geneva.

None the less, Geneva is an admirably situated town, with many pretty women in it, some fine intellects, and any number of delightful children at play beneath the trees on the shores of the lake.   With these, one can forgive her her ridiculously inept and meddling little government, her pitiful and grotesque inquisition of passports, her shops for the sale of imitations, her new quays, her Island of Jean-Jacques shod with its stone horse-shoe, her Rue de Rivoli with its yellow and its white, its plaster and its chalk.

Only a little more, and Geneva would become a wearisome town.

Yesterday there was a fête, an "ensuissement," as they call it, and they fired off guns.   Everybody talked Genevese.   I had lost the key of my watch, and it was impossible for me to find a watchmaker working.   Geneva no longer knew herself.   People went on the water in spite of the seyches ; urchins gambolled in the bergues, and holiday-makers trampled down the grassy banks.

I laughed, and yet I did not laugh.   I wandered alone in the town where I walked with you fourteen years ago.   I was sad, and full of sweet and tender thoughts, to have known of which, my Adèle, would, perhaps, have made you glad.

From Bâle to beyond Lausanne I travelled with an estimable and delightful Swiss family—six of them. The father, a distinguished-looking old man, literary, amiable, and full of useful information, reminded me of your father. The eldest daughter was an attractive young widow (something like Madame François). She wanted to see Chillon. I offered her my arm, which she accepted. The eldest brother, a good-hearted, irrepressible student, joined the party, and we all three made the expedition to the castle. At Coppet the Swiss family left me, and I missed them greatly.

But what I miss is you, and all of you, my dear ones. I shall see you all again within a month. My journey is a task ; but for this I would shorten it. I am longing so much to embrace you all, for all of you are dear to me.

And, of course, I am not excepting my dear Vacquerie.

G

1843.

—

THE PYRENEES

THE PYRENEES.

I.

THE LOIRE.—BORDEAUX.

OU, who never travel otherwise than in the spirit, passing from book to book, from thought to thought, and never from country to country; you, who spend all your summers in the shadow of the same trees, and all your winters at the corner of the same fireside— you want me, the wanderer, whenever I leave Paris, to tell you, the recluse, everything I have done and everything I have seen. Well, I obey.

What have I done since the 18th of July, the day before yesterday? A hundred and five leagues in thirty-six hours. What have I seen? I have seen Étampes, Orleans, Blois, Tours, Poitiers, and Angoulême.

Will you have more? Must you have descriptions? Do you wish to know what manner of towns these are, and under what aspects they appeared to me ; what historical, artistic and poetic booty I have gathered on my way—in a word, all that I have seen ? So be it. Again I obey.

Étampes is a big town seen dimly in the twilight over the roofs of a long street on the right, where one hears postillions saying : " Another accident on the railway ! Two coaches smashed, and the passengers killed ! The engine broke down with the train between Étampes and Étrechy. At any rate, we never break down."

Orleans is a candle standing on a round table in a low room, in which a pale-faced girl serves you a thin soup.

Blois is a bridge on the left, with a Pompadour obelisk. The traveller surmises that there may be houses towards the right, perhaps a town.

Tours also is a bridge, a big wide street, and the face of a clock indicating nine in the morning.

Poitiers is a meat soup, a duck with turnips, an eel stew, a roast chicken, a fried sole, beans, a salad, and strawberries.

Angoulême is a gas lamp, with a wall bearing the inscription : CAFÉ DE LA MARINE ; and, on the left, another wall adorned with a blue poster on which one reads : LA RUE DE LA LUNE, VAUDEVILLE.

Such is France as we see her from the mail-
coach.   What will it be when we see her from the
railway train ?

———————

I have some recollection of having already said
so elsewhere : the Loire and Touraine have been
far too much praised.   It is time to do and render
justice.   The Seine is much more beautiful than
the Loire ; Normandy is a much more charming
" garden " than Touraine.

A broad, yellow strip of water, flat banks, and
poplars everywhere—that is the Loire.   The poplar
is the only tree that is stupid.   It masks all the
horizons of the Loire.   Along the river and on the
islands, on the edge of the dyke and far away in the
distance, one sees only poplars.   In my mind there
is a strangely intimate relationship, a strangely in-
definable resemblance, between a landscape made
up of poplars and a tragedy written in Alexan-
drines.   The poplar, like the Alexandrine, is one of
the classic forms of boredom.

It rained ; I had passed a sleepless night.   I do
not know whether that put me out of temper, but
everything on the Loire seemed to me cold, dull,
methodical, monotonous, formal, and lugubrious.

From time to time one meets convoys of five or

six small craft ascending or descending the river.
Each vessel has but one mast with a square sail.
The one that has the biggest sail precedes the
others and tows them.   The convoy is arranged in
such a fashion that the sails grow smaller in size
from one boat to the other, from the first to the
last, with a sort of symmetric decrease unbroken by
any unevenness, undisturbed by any vagary.   One
involuntarily recalls the caricature of the English
family ; one might imagine one saw a chromatic
scale sweeping along under full sail.   I have seen
this only on the Loire ; and I confess that I prefer
the Norman sloops and luggers, of all shapes and
sizes, flying like birds of prey, and mingling their
yellow and red sails with the squall, the rain, and
the sun, between Quillebœuf and Tancarville.

The Spaniards call the Manzanares " the viscount
of waterways ; " I suggest that the Loire be called
" the dowager of rivers."

The Loire has not, like the Seine and the Rhine,
a host of pretty towns and lovely villages built on
the very edge of the river and mirroring their gables,
church-spires, and house-fronts in the water.   The
Loire flows through a great alluvion caused by the
floods and called La Sologne.   It carries back from
it the sand which its waters bear down and which
often encumber and obstruct its bed.   Hence the

frequent risings and inundations in these low plains which thrust back the villages. On the right bank they hide themselves behind the dyke. But there they are almost lost to sight. The wayfarer does not see them.

Nevertheless, the Loire has its beauties. Madame de Stael, banished by Napoleon to fifty leagues' distance from Paris, learned that on the banks of the Loire, exactly fifty leagues from Paris, there was a château called, I believe, Chaumont. It was thither that she repaired, not wishing to aggravate her exile by a quarter of a league. I do not commiserate her. Chaumont is a dignified and lordly dwelling. The château, which must date from the sixteenth century, is fine in style ; the towers are massive. The village at the foot of the wooded hill presents an aspect perhaps unique on the Loire, the precise aspect of a Rhine village—of a long frontage stretching along the edge of the water.

Amboise is a pleasant, pretty town, half a league from Tours, crowned with a magnificent edifice, facing those three precious arches of the ancient bridge, which will disappear one of these days in some scheme of municipal improvement.

The ruin of the Abbey of Marmoutiers is both great and beautiful. In particular there is, a few

paces from the road, a structure of the fifteenth
century—the most original I have seen : by its
dimensions a house, by its machicoulis a fortress,
by its belfry an hôtel de ville, by its pointed doorway a church.   This structure sums up, and, as it
were, renders visible to the eye, the species of hybrid
and complex authority which in feudal times ap-
pertained to abbeys in general, and, in particular,
to the Abbey of Marmoutiers.

But the most picturesque and imposing feature
of the Loire is an immense calcareous wall, mixed
with sandstone, millstone, and potter's clay, which
skirts and banks up its right shore, and stretches
itself out before the eye from Blois to Tours with
inexpressible variety and charm, now wild rock,
now an English garden, covered with trees and
flowers, crowned with ripening vines and smoking
chimneys, perforated like a sponge, as full of life as
an ant-hill.

There there are deep caves which long ago hid
the coiners who counterfeited the E of the Tours
mint, and flooded the province with spurious sous
of Tours.   To-day the rude embrasures of these
dens are filled with pretty window-frames coquettishly fitted into the rock, and from time to time
one perceives through the glass the fantastic head-
dress of some young girl occupied in packing

aniseed, angelica, and coriander in boxes. The confectioners have replaced the coiners.

And since I am on the subject of the charms of the Loire, I thank chance for having led me naturally to tell you about the fair maidens who work and sing in the midst of that fair landscape.

> " La terra molle, e lieta, e dilettosa,
> Simili a se gli habitatori produce."

Unlike the Loire, Bordeaux has not been extolled enough, or, at least, it has been extolled injudiciously.

People praise Bordeaux as they praise the Rue de Rivoli—for its regularity and symmetry, its great white frontages all like one another, and so forth ; which, to a man of sense, mean insipid architecture—a town wearisome to the eye. Now, with regard to Bordeaux, nothing can be less correct.

Bordeaux is a quaint, original, perhaps a unique town. Take Versailles and intermix Antwerp with it, and you have Bordeaux.

I withdraw from the mixture, however—for one must be just—the two greatest beauties of Versailles and Antwerp, the palace of the one and the cathedral of the other.

There are two Bordeaux's. the new and the old.

Everything in modern Bordeaux breathes of grandeur as at Versailles; everything in old Bordeaux relates history as at Antwerp.

The fountains, the rostral columns, the vast well-planted avenues, the Place Royale, which is simply half of the Place Vendôme placed by the water's edge, the bridge with a length of three furlongs, the superb quay, the wide streets, the enormous and monumental theatre—these are things effaced by none of the splendours of Versailles, and which, even in Versailles, would worthily surround the great palace which lodged the Grand Siècle.

The inextricable cross-roads; the labyrinths of passages and buildings; the Rue des Loups, recalling the time when the wolves came and devoured children in the interior of the town; the fortress-houses, haunted of old by demons in such inconvenient fashion that, in 1596, a decree of Parliament declared it enough that a habitation should be frequented by the devil for its lease to be legally cancelled; the mushroom-coloured façades carved by the fine chisel of the Renaissance; the doorways and staircases ornamented with balustrades and wreathed pillars painted in blue in the Flemish manner; the charming and delicate Porte de Caillou built to commemorate the battle of Fornova; the other fine gate of the Hôtel de Ville which discloses the belfry so proudly suspended beneath an open arch ; the shapeless stumps of the gloomy fort of Hâ; the old churches—St. André with its two spires, St. Seurin, whose greedy canons sold the town of Langon for twelve lampreys a year, Ste. Croix, which was burnt by the Normans, St. Michel, which was burnt by the lightning—that whole pile of old porches, old gables, and old roofs, those memories that are monuments, those edifices that are dates, are indeed worthy of being mirrored in the Scheldt as they are mirrored in the Gironde, and of being grouped among the most fantastic of timeworn Flemish buildings round the Cathedral of Antwerp.

Add to this, my friend, the magnificent Gironde crowded with vessels, a soft horizon of green hills, a lovely sky, a warm sun, and you will love Bordeaux —even you, who drink nothing but water and never look at pretty girls.

Here they are charming with their orange or red madrases, like those of Marseilles with their yellow stockings.

It is an instinct with women in every country to add coquetry to nature. Nature gives them their tresses, but that does not suffice them, and they add a head-dress. Nature gives them a white, supple neck ; that is but a little thing, and they encircle it by a necklet. Nature gives them a dainty, supple

foot ; that is not at all enough—they must heighten
its charms by foot-gear.   God made them beautiful ;
that does not suffice them—they make themselves
pretty.

And at the bottom of coquetry there is a thought,
a sentiment, if you like, that goes back to our
mother Eve. Allow me to utter a paradox, a
blasphemy, which, I greatly fear, contains a truth :
It is God who makes woman beautiful ; it is the
devil who makes her pretty.

What matter, friend ?   Let us love woman even
with what the devil hath added unto her.

But it really seems to me that I have been
preaching, and that scarcely suits me.   Let us return,
if you please, to Bordeaux.

The double physiognomy of Bordeaux is curious.
It is time and chance that have made it, and it
ought not to be spoiled by man.   Now it is impossible to pretend not to see that the mania for
" clean-cut streets," as they say, and structures in
" fine taste," is gaining ground every day, and is
gradually effacing the old historic city from off the
earth.   In other words, Bordeaux-Versailles tends
to devour Bordeaux-Antwerp.

Let the Bordelese see to it !   In art, history, and
the past, Antwerp, taking it altogether, is more

interesting than Versailles. Versailles represents
only a man and a reign; Antwerp represents a
whole people and several centuries.   Maintain,
then, the balance between the two cities ; put an
end to the contest between Antwerp and Versailles.
Beautify the new town ; preserve the old town.
You have had a history, you have been a nation.
Remember it, be proud of it.

There is nothing more desolating and humiliating
than great demolitions.   The demolisher of his
house is the demolisher of his family ; the destroyer
of his city is the destroyer of his country ; the
destroyer of his dwelling is the destroyer of his
name.   These old stones are the repository of
ancient honour.

All these despised old buildings are illustrious ;
they have a voice, they speak, they bear witness to
the deeds of our fathers.

The amphitheatre of Gallienus says : " I saw
Tetricus, governor of the Gauls, proclaimed Emperor ;
I saw the birth of Ausonius, poet and Roman
consul ; I saw St. Martin preside over the first
Council ; I saw the passage of Abd-al-Rahman, the
passage of the Black Prince."   Ste. Croix says : " I
saw Louis Le Jeune wed Eleanor of Guyenne,
Gaston de Foix wed Madeleine of France, Louis
XIII. wed Anne of Austria."   The Peyberland

says : " I have seen Charles VII. and Catherine de'
Medici." The belfry says : " Beneath my vault sat
Michel de Montaigne, who was mayor, and Montes-
quieu, who was president." The old wall says :
"It was through my breach that the Constable Mont-
morency entered."

Is not all this worth a street made straight as a
stretched cord ? All this is the past ; the past—a
thing great, venerable, and prolific.

As I have said elsewhere, let us respect buildings
and books. In them alone does the past live ; everywhere else it is dead. And the past is a part of ourselves, the most essential, perhaps. The whole flood
that bears us along, the whole of the sap that vivifies
us, comes to us from the past. What is a river without its source ? What is a people without its past ?

Has M. de Tourny, the intendant in 1743, who
began the demolition of old Bordeaux and the construction of the new quarters, been beneficial or
harmful to the town ? That is a question into which
I do not enter. They have raised a statue to him ;
there is the Rue Tourny, the Quai Tourny, the Cours
Tourny—which is all very well. But, admitting that
he rendered the city such great services, is that any
reason why Bordeaux should present herself to the
world as never having possessed anybody else but
M. de Tourny?

What! Augustus built you the Temple de
Tutelle; you have thrown it down.   Gallienus
erected the amphitheatre; you have dismantled it.
Clovis gave you the Palais de l'Ombrière; you
have made ruins of it.   The kings of England constructed a great wall from the Fossé des Tanneurs
to the Fossé des Salinières; you have levelled it with
the ground.   Charles VII. built you the Château-
Trompette; you have demolished it.   One after
another you tear up all the pages of your ancient
book, to keep only the last; you drive from your
town and efface from your history Charles VII.,
the kings of England, the dukes of Guyenne, Clovis,
Gallienus, and Augustus, and you raise a statue to
M. de Tourny!   Herein you overthrow a thing of
exceeding greatness to raise up something that is
exceedingly small.

21st July.

The bridge of Bordeaux is the plaything of the
town.   There are always four men on the bridge,
engaged in patching the roadway and furbishing
the pavement.   By way of contrast, the churches
are very sadly dilapidated.

But is it not true that everything in a church,
even to the stones, is worthy of reverence?   This is

H

readily forgotten by the priests, who are themselves the first demolishers.

The two principal churches in Bordeaux, St. André and St. Michel, have, instead of spires, campanili isolated from the main edifice, as at Venice and Pisa.

The campanile of St. André, the Cathedral, is a rather fine tower, the form of which recalls the Tour de Beurre of Rouen, and which is called the Peyberland, from the name of Archbishop Pierre Berland, who lived in 1430. The Cathedral has, besides, the two bold, pierced spires of which I have already told you. The building of the church, begun in the eleventh century, as the Romanesque pillars of the nave attest, was abandoned for three centuries, to be resumed under Charles VII., and was completed under Charles VIII. The delightful epoch of Louis XII. gave it the finishing touches, and constructed, at the extremity opposite the apsis, the exquisite porch which supports the organs. The two great bas-reliefs in the wall beneath this porch are pictures in stone, most beautiful in style, and, one might almost say—so powerful is the modelling—most magnificent in colour. In the picture on the left the eagle and the lion are adoring Christ with a profound and intelligent expression, as it is fitting that genii should adore

God. The portal, although only lateral, is of great
beauty.

But I make haste to tell you about an old
ruined cloister which flanks the Cathedral on the
south, and which I entered by chance.

Nothing could be more dismal and more charming, more imposing and more abject. Picture it to
yourself. Gloomy galleries pierced with flamboyant
ogive fenestration; over these ogive windows, a
trellis of wood; the cloister transformed into
a shed, all the flagstones torn up, dust and
spiders' webs everywhere; latrines in an adjacent
court; sconces of rusty copper, black crosses, silver
hour-glasses, all the discarded trappings of hearses
and funeral mutes lying in the dark corners; and,
beneath these sham cenotaphs of wood and printed
calico, real tombs of which one catches a glimpse with
their stern statues, resting too securely to be able
to rise, sleeping too soundly to be able to wake. Is
it not scandalous? Is not the priest to be charged
with the degradation of the church and the profana-
tion of the tombs? For myself, had I to lay down
to priests their duty, I should do it in two words:
" Pity for the living, pity for the dead ! "

In the middle, enclosed by the four corridors of
the cloister, the débris and rubbish fill a little
corner, formerly a cemetery, in which the long

grass, the wild jasmine, the briers and the brambles, grow and intermingle with, one might almost say, unspeakable joy. It is vegetation that is over-coming the building; it is the work of God prevailing over the work of man.

But this joy contains nothing that is wicked or bitter. It is the innocent and royal exuberance of nature, nothing more. Amid ruins and grasses, a thousand flowers bloom. Sweet and lovely flowers! I felt their perfumes float towards me, I saw them nodding their pretty heads, white, yellow, and blue, and it seemed to me that they were all trying to outdo one another in comforting the poor, abandoned stones.

And then, it is destiny. The monks go their way before the priests, and the cloisters crumble away before the churches.

From St. André I went to St. Michel. . . .— But I am called ; the Bayonne coach is about to leave. I will tell you in my next what happened to me on this visit to St. Michel.

II.

FROM BORDEAUX TO BAYONNE.

BAYONNE, 23rd July.

ONE must be a tough and hardened traveller to feel comfortable on the top of the Dotézac diligence which runs from Bordeaux to Bayonne. Never in my life have I met with a seat so ferociously stuffed. This divan, moreover, may render a service to literature by furnishing those in need of it with a new metaphor. We may renounce those ancient classical comparisons which for three thousand years have expressed the resisting powers of things; we may allow steel, bronze, and the tyrant's heart to rest. Instead of saying,

> " La Caucase en courroux,
> Cruel, t'a fait le cœur plus dur que les cailloux ! "

poets will say : " Harder than the seat of the Dotézac coach."

One does not, moreover, scale that lofty and rude

position without some difficulty.   Needless to say,
one must first of all pay one's fourteen francs ; and
then one must give one's name to the conductor.
I therefore gave mine.

When I am asked regarding my name in the
coach offices, I am fain to remove its first syllable,
and answer, " Monsieur Go," leaving the ortho-
graphy to the fancy of the inquirer.   When I am
asked how the thing is written, I answer, " I don't
know."   With this the clerk of the register is
usually satisfied.   He lays hold of the syllable I have
given him, and embroiders the simple theme with
more or less imagination, according as he may or
may not be a man of taste.   This mode of pro-
cedure has procured me, in my various excursions,
the satisfaction of seeing my name written in the
diverse manners here set out : " M. Go.—M. Got.—
M. Gaut.—M. Gault.—M. Gaud.—M. Gauld.—M.
Gaulx.—M. Gaux.—M. Gau."

None of these scribes has as yet conceived the
idea of writing " M. Goth."   Up to the present, I
have observed this gradation only in the satires
of M. Viennet and in the feuilletons of the
" Constitutionnel."

The scribe of the Dotézacs' office first wrote
" M. Gau."   He then hesitated for a moment,
scrutinized the word he had just traced, and, doubt-

less thinking it a little nude, affixed an " x." It was, then, under the name of Gaux that I mounted to the redoubtable penitent's bench upon which Messrs. Dotézac Brothers transport their victims a distance of fifty-five leagues.

I have already observed that hunchbacks love the outside of coaches. I do not wish to fathom the affinities ; but the fact is that on the top of the Meaux diligence I met one, and, on the top of the Bayonne diligence, two. They were travelling together, and what made the conjunction curious was that one had his hump behind and the other in front ! The first appeared to exercise a strange ascendency over the second, whose waistcoat was partly open and disordered, and just as I arrived he said to him with an authoritative air : " My dear fellow, button up your deformity."

The conductor of the coach examined the two deformed men with an expression of humiliation. This worthy man bore a perfect resemblance to M. de Rambuteau. As I contemplated him I said to myself that it would no doubt be only necessary to shave him in order to transform him into a prefect of the Seine; and that, too, it would only be necessary for M. de Rambuteau never to shave again in order to make an excellent diligence conductor.

Moreover, in the process of assimilation, as they say in the language of politics nowadays, there is nothing either irksome or offensive. A diligence is much more than a prefecture ; it is a perfect representation of a nation with its constitution and government. The diligence, like the State, has three compartments. The aristocracy is in the coupé, the bourgeoisie in the inside, and the people in the rotunda. Outside, above all, are the dreamers, the artists, the nondescripts. The conductor is the Law, which people are prone to call a tyrant ; the postillion is the Ministry, changed at each relay. When the coach is too heavily loaded with luggage, that is to say, when society places material interests above everything, it runs the risk of being over-turned.

Since we are in the way of rejuvenating the ancient metaphors, I would counsel those worthy men of letters whose style so frequently buries in the mud " the chariot of State," to say henceforth " the diligence of State." It will be less dignified, but more correct.

The road, however, was very fine, and we went along in great style. This comes of a contest at present going on between the Dotézac diligence and another coach which the Dotézac postillions contemptuously refer to as " the opposition," with-

out otherwise designating it. This coach appeared
to me to be a good one. It is new, showy, and pretty.
From time to time it *passed us*, and then it would
bowl along twenty yards in front of us for an hour
or two until we did as much for it. It was very
unpleasant. In the ancient classic combats one
made one's enemy bite the dust ; in these, one is
content to make him swallow it.

Between Bazas and Mont-de-Marsan the Landes
are nothing but an interminable pine forest, sprinkled
here and there with big oaks, and cut into by
immense glades covered as far as the eye can reach
by the green moors, the yellow furze, and the purple
heather. In the most solitary parts of the forest
man's presence is revealed by long strips of bark
torn from the trunks of the pine-trees for the running
off of the resin.

There are no villages, but at intervals are seen
two or three houses with big roofs, covered with
hollow tiles in the Spanish fashion, and sheltered
beneath clusters of oak-trees and chestnuts. At
times the landscape becomes bleaker, the pines
vanish on the horizon, and all is heath and sand.
A few low thatched cottages, buried under a sort of
fur of dry ferns spread over the walls, appear here
and there, and are then lost to sight, and one no
longer meets with anything on the roadside but the

mud cottage of a road-mender, or, at times, a great circle of burnt turf and black ashes, indicating the place of some nocturnal fire.

All kinds of herds are grazing on the heath : herds of geese and pigs driven by children, herds of black or red sheep driven by women, herds of big-horned oxen driven by men on horseback. As the herd, so is the herdsman.

Without perceiving it, and thinking only to depict a desert, I have just penned a maxim of State.

And, by the way, would you believe that, just as I was crossing the Landes, everybody was talking politics ? This is scarcely fitting in such a country, is it? A breath of revolution seemed to agitate those old pines.

It was the very moment of Espartero's downfall in Spain. As yet nothing was known, and one had a foreboding of everything. The postillions, as they climbed into their seats, said to the conductor : " He is at Cadiz.—No, he has embarked.—Yes, for England.—No, for France.—He will have none either of France or England.—He is going to a Spanish colony.—Pshaw !"

The two hunchbacks mingled their politics with the postillion's politics, and the one with the hump in front observed gracefully : " Espartero has taken prisoner Lafuite and Caillard."

As we approached Mont-de-Marsan the roads were covered with Spaniards, on foot, on horseback, and in coaches, travelling separately or in bands. On a cart loaded with men in rags I noticed a young and gracefully-dressed peasant-girl with the most exquisite hat one could imagine on her head, at once pretty, sweet, and stately. It was something black trimmed with something red. It was charming. What manner of politics, then, must they be, the blasts of which are capable of driving from her country a poor, pretty girl so nicely bonneted?

While fresh refugees are arriving, the old refugees are going off. In two post-berlins which were driving in opposite directions and must have passed each other, I met Madame the Duchess of Gor, who was leaving for Madrid, and Madame the Duchess of San Fernando, who was leaving for Paris. Two diligences full of Spaniards crossed each other half-way between Captieux and Traverses, and, in accordance with a custom of the postillions in such circumstances, exchanged teams. The same horses that had just brought back to their country the outlaws of yesterday, carried away into exile the outlaws of to-day.

But whatever the fresh revolution might be which was being accomplished so near to us, it troubled that severe and tranquil scene only on the surface.

The wind which displaces powers and moves thrones did not make the pine-apple, trembling at the end of its branch, fall sooner from the tree.   The waggons with their teams of oxen passed along among those flying post-chaises and scared diligences with all their old heaviness.

Nothing could be more quaint, I may say in passing, than these teams of oxen.   The waggon is of wood and has four wheels of the same size, which indicates that it never turns round but always goes straight forward.   The oxen are completely covered with a white cloth which trails on the ground.   Between their horns they have a sort of wig made of a sheep-skin, and over their muzzles a white net with a fringe, which is a wonderful caricature of a beard. Some oak branches twined round their heads complete the accoutrement.   Thus decked out, the oxen have the look of high priests of tragedy ; they resemble, to the point of deception, the figurants of the Théâtre Français made up as flamens and druids.

At Bazas, just as we alighted, one of these oxen passed close to me with such a majestic and pontifical gait that I was tempted to say to it :

" Les prêtres ne sont pas ce qu'un vain peuple pense."

I think I really did say it.   To be accurate, I ought to add that it did not bellow me any reply.

Beyond Roquefort, the landes are enlivened by the tile-kilns which one meets with from time to time, some abandoned and very old, going back to the time of Louis XIII., as the master-keystone of their archivaults attests, others at work and in full production, and smoking all over like a faggot of green wood on a big fire.

I travelled through this district thirty years ago, when quite a child. I remember that the coaches used to go at a walking pace, the wheels having sand up to the nave. There was no made road. From time to time one found a road-end formed of the stems of pines placed side by side and lashed together like the flooring of rustic bridges. To-day the sands are crossed from Bordeaux to Bayonne by a wide road lined with poplars which has almost the beauty of a Roman causeway.

Within a given time this road, the product of industry and perseverance, will sink to the level of the sands, and will then disappear. The soil tends to sink beneath it and swallow it up, as it swallowed up the military road made by Brutus, which went from Cape Breton (*Caput Bruti*) to Boïos, now Buch, and that other road, the work of Cæsar, which traversed Gamarde, Saint-Géours and Saint-Michel de Jouarare.

I note by the way that those two words, *Jovis ara*,

ara Jovis, have given birth to many names of towns
which, although having the same origin, resemble
one another but little to-day, from Jouarre in
Champagne and Jouarare in the Landes, to Aranjuez
in Spain.

Between Roquefort and Tartas the pines give
place to a host of other trees. A rich and varied
vegetation takes possession of the plains and hills,
and the road runs through a delightful garden.
Every moment one passes charming rivers, seen in
crossing old bridges with pointed arches. First the
Douze, then the Midou ; then the Midouze, formed,
as the name indicates, by the Douze and the Midou,
and then the Adour. The syllable " dour " or
" dou " which is met with in all these names,
evidently comes from the Celtic word *our*, signifying
a stream of water.

All these rivers are steeply banked, limpid, green,
and pleasant. The young girls beat their linen at
the water's edge ; the goldfinches sing in the thickets ;
the sweet scene breathes of happy life.

At times, however, between a couple of branches
playfully parted by the wind, one perceives far
away on the horizon the heath and the piñadas
suffused with the red glow of sunset, and one remembers that one is in the Landes. One reflects
that, beyond this laughing garden strewn with all

these pretty towns, Roquefort, Mont-de-Marsan, and Tartas, traversed by all these cool rivers, the Adour, the Douze, and the Midou, there is, a few leagues distant, the forest ; and, beyond the forest, the heath, the lande, the desert—that gloomy solitude in which the grasshopper chirps, where the birds are silent, where every human habitation disappears, and which at long intervals is silently crossed by caravans of great oxen clad in white shrouds. One reminds oneself that beyond these solitudes of sand there are the marshes, solitudes of water—Sanguinet, Parentis, Mimizan, Léon, and Biscarosse, with their wild population of wolves and polecats, wild boars and squirrels, their tangled vegetation of cork-oak, cherry-bay, locust-trees, sage-leafed rock-rose, enormous holly, gigantic hawthorn, and thorn-broom twenty feet high, and their virgin forests, into which one cannot venture without a hatchet and a compass. One pictures to oneself, in the heart of these immense woods, the great Cassou, that mysterious oak whose boughs used to spread superstition and terror over the whole country. One thinks that beyond these marshes there are the dunes, mountains of sand that move, that drive the marshes before them, that engulf piñadas, villages, and church-spires — mountains whose shape is changed before the tempest. And one tells oneself

that beyond the dunes there is the ocean. The
dunes devour the marshes ; the ocean devours the
dunes.

The landes, the marshes, the dunes, the sea—
these, then, are the four zones traversed by one's
thought. One pictures them to oneself one after
another, each more terrible than the other. One
sees vultures flying over the landes, cranes over the
lagoons, and sea-gulls over the sea. One watches
turtles and serpents crawling over the dunes. The
spectre of a sullen landscape appears before you.
The reverie fills one's spirit. Unknown and fantastic
scenes tremble and glitter before your eyes. Men
propped up by long sticks and mounted upon
stilts pass like big spiders over the crest of the hills
in the mists of the horizon. One imagines one sees
the enigmatic pyramids of Mimizan rise up in the
undulations of the dunes, one turns one's ear as if
one heard the wild, sweet song of the peasant
women of Parentis, and one gazes far away as if one
saw the lovely girls of Biscarosse, crowned with sea
immortelles, walking with their bare feet in the
waves.

For thought has its mirages. The journeys
which the Dotézac diligence does not make, are
made by the imagination.

We reach Tartas, however, a pretty town on the

Midouze, and the ancient capital of the Tarusates. In the Middle Ages it was the seat of one of the four seneschals' courts of the Duchy of Albret. The three others were Nérac, Castel-Moron and Castel-Jaloux. In passing, I saluted, on the left side of the road, a remnant, still upright, of the venerable wall which in 1440 resisted the redoubtable Captal of Buch and gave Charles VII. time to arrive. The people of Tartas make inns and taverns of this wall, which made a country for them.

As we left Tartas an enormous hare came out of a neighbouring thicket and crossed the road. It then stood still in a meadow within pistol-shot, and boldly gazed at the diligence. The temerity of the hares in this country is doubtless due to their knowledge that it was they who gave their name to the House of Albret.[1] Pride has taken hold of them, and they comport themselves, when occasion offers, like gentlemen hares.

But night was falling. Evening, which furnished Virgil with so many fine lines, all similar in idea, all different in form, shed darkness over the landscape and sleep upon the travellers' eyelids. As the darkness grew denser and blurred the shapeless

[1] Formerly Lebret, possibly a corruption of the Latin word "leporetum."—*Translator*.

I

silhouettes on the horizon, it seemed to me—was it an illusion of the night?—that the country became wilder and more rugged, that the piñadas and the glades reappeared, and that we were making in reality, amid the profound darkness, that journey through the Landes which I had made in imagination a few hours before. The sky was star-lit, the earth seemed to the eye but a sort of dark plain in which strange ruddy lights flickered here and there, as if herdsmen's fires were lit upon the heath. Without seeing or distinguishing anything, one heard the clear, shrill clang of the small bells resembling an harmonious tingling; then all entered into silence and night, and the coach seemed to roll blindly along through a gloomy solitude, in which only broad pools of light, appearing at long stretches amid the black trees, revealed the presence of the marshes.

But I felt happy. I had several times traversed the smell of the bindweed which brings back my childhood. I thought of all who love me, I forgot all who hate me, and I looked into the darkness with rapt gaze, as it were, allowing the vague shapes of night which passed confusedly before my eyes to mingle with my reverie.

The two hunchbacks had left me at Mont-de-Marsan. I was alone on my seat, and it was growing cold. I wrapped myself in my cloak, and in a little while I fell asleep.

The sleep vouchsafed by a coach carrying you along at a gallop is a lucid sleep through which you feel and hear. At one particular moment the conductor alighted and the diligence stopped. The conductor's voice said, " Messieurs les voyageurs, we are at the Pont de Dax." Then the doors were opened and shut again, as if the passengers were getting out, and the coach gave a lurch and went on again. A few seconds afterwards the horses' hoofs sounded as if they were going over wood. The diligence, leaning sharply to the front, gave a violent jolt. I opened one eye. The postillion, leaning low over his horses, seemed to be peering ahead of him with uneasy precaution. I opened both eyes.

The unwieldy, heavily-laden coach, drawn by five horses fastened with chains, was going at walk- ing pace over a wooden bridge in a sort of narrow pathway, bounded on the left by a very low parapet and on the right by a pile of beams and timber. Beneath the bridge a fairly broad river flowed at a considerable depth, which was still further increased by the uncertainty of the darkness. At certain moments the diligence leaned over ; in certain places the parapet was missing. I sat up. I was on the top; the conductor had not resumed his place; the coach was still moving. The postillion, still bending over his team, and scarcely visible by the light of the coupé lantern, was muttering all manner of energetic exclamations. At length the horses climbed a little slope; the coach was shaken by a fresh jolt; then it stopped. We were on the road.

The passengers who had crossed the bridge on foot before the coach now re-entered the three compartments, and, as he was opening and closing the doors, I heard the conductor saying:

"A devil of a bridge!—always being repaired! When will it ever be sound? The police are not worth much at Dax; the carpenters leave their tools right in the way of the coach to upset it. At one time I thought the diligence was in the river. You can't imagine how dangerous it is. You will see there will be an accident one of these days. Did I not do well, Messieurs les voyageurs, to make you get down?"

Having said this, he climbed to his place again. "Why, Monsieur!" he exclaimed, upon perceiving me, "I had forgotten you!"

III.

BAYONNE.

THE CHARNEL-HOUSE OF BORDEAUX.

26th July.

 WAS unable to enter Bayonne without emotion. To me Bayonne is a memory of childhood. I was quite little when I came to Bayonne in my seventh or eighth year at the time of the great wars, about 1811 or 1812. My father was following his calling as a soldier of the Emperor in Spain, holding in respect two provinces which had been incited to rise by El Empecinado—Avila, Guadalajara, and the whole valley of the Tagus.

My mother, in going to join him, had stopped at Bayonne to await an escort; for, to perform the journey from Bayonne to Madrid in those days, one had to be accompanied by three thousand men and preceded by four pieces of cannon. Some day I will write that journey, which has a certain interest, were it only for the preparation of historical

memoirs.   My mother had taken with her my two
brothers Abel and Eugène, and myself, the youngest
of the three.

On the day after our arrival in Bayonne, I
remember, a kind of corpulent signor, decorated
with gaudy ornaments and gibbering Italian,
presented himself at my mother's.   To us children,
who saw him enter through a glass door, this man
had all the appearance of a street mountebank.   He
was the director of the Bayonne theatre.

He came to beg my mother to take a box at his
theatre.   My mother hired one for a month, which
was about the time we were to remain in Bayonne.

The taking of this box made us leap with joy.
For us children to go to the play every evening for
a whole month !—we who had hitherto entered a
theatre only once a year, and who had in our minds
no dramatic memory other than " The Countess of
Escarbagnas ! "

That very evening we plagued my mother, who
yielded, as mothers always do, and took us to the
theatre.   The check-taker installed us in a magnificent front box decorated with red calico hangings
with saffron catharine-wheels.   They played " The
Ruins of Babylon," a famous melodrama which at
that time was having an immense success throughout the whole of France.

It was magnificent—in Bayonne, at least. Apricot-coloured knights, arrayed from head to foot in chain armour, rushed on every moment and annihilated each other to the accompaniment of fearful prose, in the midst of pasteboard ruins full of caltrops and wolf-traps. There were the Caliph Haroun and Giafar the eunuch. We were in ecstasies.

Next day, when evening came, we again tormented our mother, and again she obeyed us. There we were again in our box with the catharine-wheels. What were they going to play? We were anxious to know. The curtain rose, and Giafar appeared. They were playing "The Ruins of Babylon." That did not trouble us. We were glad to see that fine production again, and were once more exceedingly interested by it.

On the third day my mother, as usual, was most indulgent, and we again went to the theatre. They gave "The Ruins of Babylon." We saw the piece with pleasure. We should, however, have preferred some other ruins. On the fourth day the play was to be changed without fail. We went to see it, my mother letting us have our own way and accompanying us with a smile. They gave "The Ruins of Babylon!" This time we slept.

On the fifth day we sent Bertrand, my mother's

footman, to look at the poster early in the morning.
They were to give " The Ruins of Babylon."   We
begged our mother not to take us.   On the sixth
day " The Ruins of Babylon " was given again.
This lasted the whole month.   One fine day the
bill was changed.   That day we left.

It is this recollection which has made me speak
somewhere of "that vexing chance which sports
with childhood."

Save for " The Ruins of Babylon," however, I
recall that month spent in Bayonne with pleasure.

Beneath the trees by the water's edge there
was a lovely promenade where we used to walk
every evening.   As we passed, we made faces at
the theatre in which we no longer set foot, and
which inspired us with a sort of boredom mingled
with horror.   There we would sit on a seat, and watch
the ships, and listen to our mother talking to us—
that good and noble woman who to-day is but an
image in my memory, but an image which will shine
within my soul and upon my life until the day I die.

The house in which we lived was delightful.   I
remember my window with its beautiful hanging
clusters of ripe maize.   During the whole of that
long month we had not a moment's weariness—
I except always " The Ruins of Babylon."

One day we went to see a ship of the line

anchored at the mouth of the Adour. An English squadron had given chase to her. After a fight of several hours she had taken refuge there, and the English held her blockaded. I can still see the splendid vessel as if she were before my eyes. She lay a quarter of a league off the coast, lit by a lovely gleam of sunlight, with all her sails clewed up, resting proudly on the waves, and seemed to me to have an attitude of inexpressible menace, for she had just issued from the fire of grape-shot, and was, perhaps, about to re-enter it.

The back of our house was against the fortifications. It was there, on the slopes of green turf, among the guns turned with their touch-holes to the grass, and the mortars reversed with their mouths to the earth, that we used to go to play from morning onwards.

In the evenings we—Abel, poor Eugène, and myself—used to gather round our mother, and besmear the dishes of a paint-box in our efforts to surpass each other in colouring in the most barbarous fashion the engravings in an old copy of "The Thousand and One Nights." This copy had been given me by General Lahorie, my godfather, who died on the field of Grenelle a few months after the time of which I am speaking.

Eugène and I used to purchase from the little

boys of the town all the goldfinches and green-
finches that they brought us. We put these poor
birds in wicker cages. When one cage was full we
would buy another. In this way we came to have
five cages full. When the time came for us to leave,
we set all these pretty birds free. To us this was
at once a pleasure and a grief.

It was a lady of the town—a widow, I believe—
who let the house to my mother. This widow
herself occupied a pavilion beside our house. She
had a daughter of fourteen or fifteen. My memory,
after the lapse of thirty years, has not lost a single
detail of that angelic form.

I see her still. She was fair and slender, and to
me seemed tall. She had a sweet, far-away look.
Her features were Virgilian, such as one dreams of
in Amaryllis or Galatea taking refuge beneath the
willows. Her neck was admirably poised, and
exquisite in its purity ; her hand small, her arm
white with a little redness at the elbow, which was
accounted for by her years, a circumstance of which
mine were then ignorant. She had usually on her
head a tea-coloured madras with a green border,
tightly drawn from the crown of the head to the
nape of the neck, so as to leave her forehead
uncovered and hide only half her hair. I do not
remember the dress she wore.

This beautiful child used to come and play with us. Sometimes my elder brothers Abel and Eugène, who were bigger and more serious than I—" acting the man " as my mother used to say—went to see the firing practice on the ramparts, or went up to their room to study Sobrino and finger the leaves of Cormon. At such times I was alone and would begin to feel wearied. What was I to do? Then she would call me and say : " Come, and I will read you something."

In the courtyard there was a door raised above the ground by a few steps, and closed by a big, rusty bolt which I can see still—a round bolt with a handle like a pig's tail, such as one sometimes finds in old cellars. It was on these steps that she used to go and sit. I used to stand behind her, my back leaning against the door.

She would read to me from some book—I no longer remember what—lying open on her knees. We had over our heads a brilliant sky and a lovely sun, which penetrated the limes with light, and transformed the green leaves into golden leaves. A warm wind came through the chinks of the old door and caressed our faces. She was bending over her book, reading aloud.

While she read, I did not listen to the meaning of the words ; I listened only to the sound of her voice.

At intervals I lowered my eyes. My glance fell on her neckerchief half-open beneath me, and I saw with agitation, mingled with a strange fascination, her round, white throat gently rising and falling in the shadow, vaguely gilded by a warm ray of sunshine.

At such a moment it sometimes happened that she suddenly raised her big, blue eyes, and said to me : " Why, Victor !   Are you not listening ? "

I would be quite disconcerted. I would blush and tremble, and pretend to be playing with the big bolt.   I never kissed her of my own accord.   It was she who used to call me and say : " Come, then ; kiss me."

On the day on which we left I had two great sorrows—parting with her and setting free my birds.

What was this, my friend ?   What was it I felt— I, so small—by the side of that tall, beautiful, innocent girl ?   I did not know then.   I have often thought of it since.

Bayonne has remained in my thoughts as a rosy, smiling place.   The earliest memory of my heart is there.   A time of innocence, yet sweetly troubled already !   It was there that I saw break forth, in the innermost recesses of my being, that first ineffable gleam—the divine dawn of the soul.

Do you not think, friend, that a memory like this is a bond, and a bond that nothing can destroy?

The strange thing is that two beings can be united by this chain for life, and yet not feel the need of one another or seek each other out, but be strangers the one to the other and not even know each other! The bond which binds me to that sweet child has not been severed, but some of the threads have snapped.

I had hardly arrived in Bayonne before I made a tour of the town by the ramparts, looking for the house—looking for the bolt. I found nothing, or, at least, recognized nothing.

Where is she? What is she doing? Is she dead? If she is alive, she is doubtless married and has children. Perhaps she is a widow and is ageing in her turn. How comes it that beauty goes and the woman remains? Is the woman of to-day indeed the same being as the young girl of other days?

Perhaps I passed her only just now. Perhaps she is the woman of whom I chanced just now to ask my way, and who saw me disappear like a stranger.

What a bitter sadness there is in all this! We are, then, but shadows. We pass close to one another, and efface one another like clouds of smoke in the deep, blue sky of eternity. Men are in space what the hours are in time. When they have struck,

they vanish away. Whither goes our youth?—
whither our childhood? Alas!

Where is the fair damsel of the year 1812?
Where is the child I was then? In those days we
used to touch one another; and now, perhaps, we
touch each other still—and there is a gulf between
us. Memory, that bridge from the past, is broken
between her and me. She would not know my face,
and I should not recognize the sound of her voice.
She no longer knows my name, and I do not know
hers.

27th July.

I have little to tell you about Bayonne. The
town is as prettily situated as could be imagined,
among green hills, at the confluence of the Nive and
the Adour, which there forms a little Gironde. But
of this pretty town and this lovely spot they must
needs make a fortress.

Woe to those landscapes which it is thought fit to
fortify! I have said it once already, and cannot
refrain from saying it again : what a sad ravine is a
zigzagged trench! What a hideous hill is a scarp
with its counterscarp! This is one of Vauban's
masterpieces. That may be, but it is certain that
the masterpieces of Vauban disturb the masterpieces
of the good God.

The cathedral of Bayonne is rather a fine church of the fourteenth century, mushroom-coloured and gnawed all over by the sea wind. Nowhere have I seen richer and more capricious fenestration than that traced by the framework within the pointed arches. In it there is all the strength of the four-teenth century mingled with all the fantasy of the fifteenth, but without chilling it. Here and there some fine stained glass remains, nearly all of the six-teenth century. On the right of what was the chief doorway I admired a little bay, the design of which is composed of flowers and leaves intertwined in wonderful fashion into catharine-wheels. The doors are magnificent in character—great black moons studded with big nails and set off with knockers of gilded iron. Only one of these knockers remains ; it is of fine Byzantine workmanship.

The church is flanked on the south by a vast cloister, of the same period, which they are at present restoring with tolerable intelligence. It formerly communicated with the choir by a magni-ficent doorway, now walled up and whitewashed, the ornamentation and statuary of which recall, by their impressive style, Amiens, Reims, and Chartres.

In the church and cloister there used to be a great number of tombs, which have now been taken away. Several mutilated sarcophagi still adhere to the wall.   These are empty.   I cannot tell what dust, hideous to behold, now replaces the human dust they once contained.   The spider spins her web in those gloomy abodes of death.

I stopped in a chapel where there is nothing now left of one of these tombs but its site, which is still to be recognized by the fragments that have been torn from the wall.   Yet the dead man had taken his precautions to preserve his tomb.   " This tomb is his property," as an inscription in black marble set into the stone still declares to-day. " On April 22, 1664," if we are to believe the same inscription, which I quote textually, " C. Reboul, notary-royal, and Messieurs of the chapter " gave " Pierre de Baraduc, burgess, and man-at-arms in the old castle of the town, the title and possession of this tomb, *in order that he and his may have the enjoyment thereof.*"

By the way, my visit to St. Michel of Bordeaux, of which I promised to tell you, comes back to my mind.

I had just come out of the church, which dates from the thirteenth century and is very remarkable, especially for its portals, and which contains an

exquisite Chapel of the Virgin carved, I ought rather
to say worked, by the admirable plaster-casters of
the time of Louis XII. I examined the campanile
which is at the side of the church and is surmounted
by a telegraph. It was formerly a superb spire
three hundred feet in height; it is now a tower of
the strangest and most original appearance.

To anyone who is unaware that the spire was
struck by lightning in 1768, and was destroyed by a
fire which devoured the timber-work of the church
at the same time, there is quite a problem contained
in this enormous tower, which seems at once military
and ecclesiastic, rude as a donjon, and enriched like
a belfry. There is no longer any penthouse on the
upper bays; there are no bells, or chimes, or clock-
hammers. Although still surmounted by a block
with eight sides and eight gables, the tower is worn
away and mutilated at its summit. One feels that
it is decapitated and dead. The wind and the
light sweep through its long ogives, windowless and
frameless, as through a great skeleton. It is no
longer a belfry, but the skeleton of a belfry.

I was alone, then, in the courtyard, planted with
a few trees, in which this isolated campanile stands.
This courtyard is the old churchyard.

Although a little troubled by the sun, I contemplated this sullen, magnificent wreck of an edifice,

K

and endeavoured to read its history in its architecture
and its misfortunes in its wounds.   You know that
a building interests me almost as much as a man:
To me it is, in some sort, a person whose adventures
I am trying to learn.

I was there, deep in reverie, when I suddenly
heard, a few paces from me, the words : " Monsieur !
monsieur ! " I looked—I listened.   There was no
one to be seen.   The courtyard was deserted.
Some sparrows were chattering in the old trees of
the cemetery.   But a voice had called me—a feeble,
sweet, broken voice, which sounded in my ear
still.

I took a few steps and again heard the voice :
" Monsieur ! " This time I turned round sharply,
and perceived, at the angle of the court near the
gate, the face of an old woman projecting from a
dormer window.   This window, which was terribly
dilapidated, allowed one to catch a glimpse of the
interior of a wretched room.   Beside the woman
there was an old man.

Never in my life have I seen anything more
decrepit than that hovel, unless it were that old
couple.   The interior of the den was whitened with
that whitewash which reminds one of a shroud, and
I saw in it no furniture other than two stools on
which were seated, watching me with their small

gray eyes, those two figures, tanned, wrinkled and
worn, looking as if they were coated all over with
bistre and bitumen, and enveloped, rather than
clothed, in old mended winding-sheets.

I am not like Salvator Rosa, who said :

" Me figuro il sepolcro in ogni loco."

Even in broad daylight, however, under that warm,
quickening noonday sun, the apparition startled me
for a moment, and I seemed to hear myself called
from the depths of some antediluvian crypt by a
couple of spectres four thousand years old.

After a few moments' reflection I gave them
fifteen sous. They were simply the keeper of the
churchyard and his wife—Philemon and Baucis.

Philemon, dazzled by the fifteen-sous piece, made
a hideous grimace of astonishment and joy, and put
the coin into a sort of old leather pouch nailed to
the wall—" autre injure des ans," as La Fontaine
says ; while Baucis, with an amiable smile, asked :
" Would you like to see the charnel-house ? "

The word " charnel-house " awakened in my spirit
an undefinable, vague memory of something which
I really believed I knew, and I answered : " With
pleasure, Madame."—" I thought you would," replied the old woman. " Wait," she added ; " here
is the bell-ringer. He will show it to you. It is very

fine to see."—As she spoke she amicably laid her red, transparent, trembling hand—cold and hairy like the wing of a bat—upon mine.

The bell-ringer, the new personage who had just made his appearance, and who had no doubt scented the fifteen-sous piece, was standing a few paces distant on the outside staircase of the tower, of which he had half-opened the door.

He was a fellow of about six-and-thirty, strong and thick-set, fat, fresh and rosy, with all the appearance of a good liver, as becomes one who lives at the expense of the dead. My two spectres were completed by a vampire.

The old woman introduced me to the bell-ringer with a certain degree of ceremony: "This is an English gentleman who wishes to see the charnel-house."

Without uttering a word, the vampire remounted the few steps he had come down, pushed open the door of the tower, and beckoned to me to follow him. I entered. Still silent, he closed the door behind me.

We found ourselves in profound darkness. There was, however, a night-light in the corner of a step behind a big paving-stone. By the glimmer of this light I saw the bell-ringer bend down and pick up a lamp. The lamp lighted, he proceeded to descend the steps of a narrow cork-screw staircase. I followed his example.

After going down about ten steps, I think I stooped to pass through a low doorway, and then mounted two or three steps, still conducted by the bell-ringer. I cannot now remember these details. I was plunged in a sort of reverie which made me walk as if in sleep. On reaching a certain point the bell-ringer held out his big, bony hand to me, and I heard our footsteps sound upon a wooden floor. The place we were in was very dark—a sort of gloomy vault.

I shall never forget what I then saw.

The bell-ringer, silent and motionless, stood erect in the middle of the vault, leaning against a post buried in the floor, the lamp in his left hand raised above his head. I looked round about us. A hazy, diffused light dimly lit the vault, and I distinguished its pointed arch.

All at once, as I turned my eyes upon the wall, I saw that we were not alone.

Strange shapes, standing upright against the wall, surrounded us on every side. I had a confused glimpse of them by the light of the lamp through the haze that fills such dark, underground places.

Imagine a circle of terrifying faces with myself

in the centre. Their black, naked bodies were
buried and lost in the darkness ; but I distinctly
saw, standing out from the gloom and bending
forward, as it were, towards me, a crowd of sinister,
fearful heads, which seemed to be calling to me with
mouths that were all gaping wide, but voiceless,
and to be gazing at me with orbits that were
eyeless.

What were these shapes ?   Statues, doubtless.   I
took the lamp from the bell-ringer's hands and approached them.   They were corpses.

In 1793, while the burying-ground of kings was
being violated at St. Denis, the burying-ground of
the people was being violated at Bordeaux.   The
monarchy and the people are alike sovereignties.
The populace insulted both at the same time.
Which proves — those who are ignorant of this
grammar may here be told—that " people " and
" populace " are not at all synonymous.

The churchyard of St. Michel at Bordeaux was
despoiled like the rest.   They tore the coffins from
the earth, and scattered all their dust to the winds.
When the pickaxe approached the foundations of
the tower, they were surprised to encounter neither
rotten coffins nor broken vertebræ any longer, but
entire bodies, desiccated and preserved by the clay
which had covered them for so many years.   This

suggested the creation of a charnel-house museum.
The idea fitted the times.

The little children of the Rue Montfaucon and
the Chemin des Bègles used to play knuckle-bones
with the scattered remains of the churchyard.
These were taken from them, everything that could
be recovered was gathered together, and the bones
were placed in the lower vault of the campanile of
St. Michel. They made a pile seventeen feet in
height, and over them a floor with a balustrade
was constructed.

The whole was surmounted by the corpses, so
curiously preserved, which had just been dis-
interred. There were seventy of them. They were
set upright against the wall in the circular space
reserved between it and the balustrade. It was this
floor that had echoed beneath my feet ; it was over
those bones that I was treading ; it was those corpses
that were gazing at me.

When the bell-ringer had produced his effect—
for this artist stage-managed the thing like a melodrama—he came nearer to me and condescended
to speak. He explained his dead to me. The
vampire transformed himself into a cicerone. He
might have been a museum catalogue chattering.
At times he had the eloquence of a bear-showman.

" Look, Monsieur," said he, " at this one : he is

number one. He has all his teeth. See how well
number two is preserved ; yet he is nearly four
hundred years old. As for number three, you
might think he breathed and heard us. It isn't
surprising ; it is scarcely sixty years since he died.
He is one of our youngest. I know people in the
town who knew him."

Thus he pursued his round, gracefully passing
from one spectre to another, repeating his lesson
with an imperturbable memory. When I interrupted him with a question in the middle of a sentence, he answered me in his natural voice, and
then resumed his sentence at the precise place
where I had broken in. He tapped the corpses
from time to time with a small stick which he
carried in his hand, producing a leathery thud like
the sound of an empty travelling-bag. What, indeed, is man's body after thought has gone out of
it but an empty travelling-bag ?

A more fearful review I cannot conceive. Dante
and Orcagna never dreamt of anything more grue-
some. The Dances of Death of the Bridge of
Lucerne and the Campo Santo at Pisa are merely
the shadow of this reality.

There was a negress suspended from a nail by a
cord passed under her armpits, who laughed at me
with a hideous laugh. In one corner were grouped

a whole family who died, they say, from being poisoned by mushrooms. There were four of them. The mother, with her head bent down, seemed still to be trying to calm her youngest child who was agonizing at her knees; the elder son, whose profile seemed to have retained a youthful expression, leaned his forehead against his father's shoulder. A woman who had died of a cancer in the breast bent back her arm curiously, as if to show her wound enlarged by the horrible travail of death. Beside her stood a gigantic porter who had one day made a wager that he would carry two thousand pounds from the Porte de Caillou to the Chartrons. He did carry them, won his wager, and died. The man killed by a wager was elbowed by a man killed in a duel. The sword-hole by which death had entered was still visible to the right on that fleshless breast.

A poor child of fifteen who, they say, was buried alive, was writhing a few paces off. This is the height of horror. The spectre suffers. After six hundred years it still struggles against its vanished coffin. It raises the lid with its skull and its knee; it presses against the oaken plank with its heel and its elbow; it tears its nails in despair against the sides; its breast dilates; the muscles of its neck swell in a manner terrible to see : it cries out.

One no longer hears the cry, but one sees it.   It is horrible.

The last of the seventy is the oldest.   It dates from eight hundred years ago.   With some playfulness the bell-ringer drew my attention to its teeth and hair.   Beside it is a little child.

As I retraced my steps I observed one of these phantoms seated on the ground near the door.   Its neck was strained, its head thrown back, its mouth most piteous, its hand open.   It had a piece of cloth round the middle of its body; one leg and foot were bare, and from its other thigh projected a fleshless tibia, resting on a stone like a wooden leg.   It seemed to be asking me for alms.   Nothing could be more strange and mysterious than such a beggar at such a door.

What could one give?   What alms could one bestow?   What coins are wanted by the dead?   I remained a long time motionless before this apparition, and my reverie gradually became a prayer.

When one remembers that all these spectres, to-day imprisoned in that icy silence, in those heart-rending attitudes, have lived and throbbed, suffered and loved ; when one remembers that they have seen the spectacle of nature, the trees, the country, the flowers, the sun, and, instead of this leaden vault, the azure vault of heaven : when one remembers that they, like us, have given vent at merry-makings to long bursts of laughter filled with lightness and forgetfulness ; when one remembers that they have been what we are, and that what they are we shall be ; when one finds oneself thus, alas ! face to face with one's hereafter, a feeling of melancholy steals over the heart, one seeks vainly to cling to the human things one possesses, which all crumble away, one after another, in one's hands like sand, and one feels oneself falling into an abyss.

To one who regards these human remains with the eye of the flesh, nothing could be more hideous. They are hardly hidden by their tattered shrouds ; the naked ribs appear through rent diaphragms ; the teeth are yellow, the nails black, the hair scanty and frizzled ; the skin is a fawny tan which secretes a grayish dust ; the muscles, which have lost their prominence, the viscera, and the intestines, have been dissolved into a sort of reddish tow, from which horrible threads hang down, silently unwound in the darkness by the invisible distaff of death. Behind the open belly one perceives the spinal column.

" How well preserved they are, Monsieur ! " said the man to me.

To one who regards them with the eye of the spirit, nothing could be more dreadful.

The bell-ringer, seeing me prolong my reverie, had silently gone out, leaving me alone. The lamp had been left on the ground. Now that the man was no longer there, it seemed to me as if something oppressing me had gone. I felt myself, as it were, in direct and intimate communication with the dismal inhabitants of the vault.

I beheld with a sort of dizziness this circle, at once motionless and convulsive, by which I was surrounded. Some dropped their arms, others contorted them ; some clasped their hands. Certain it is that all those faces that had seen the inside of the sepulchre bore an expression of terror and of anguish. In whatever fashion the tomb may treat them, the bodies of the dead are terrible.

To me, as you have already been able to perceive, they were not mummies ; they were phantoms. I saw all those heads turned one towards another, all those ears which appeared to listen leaning towards all those mouths which appeared to whisper, and it seemed to me that those dead, torn from the earth and doomed for ever, lived in that darkness a life fearful and eternal, that they spoke to one another through the dense mist of their dungeon, that they related to each other the gloomy adventures of the soul within the tomb, and that they told each other below their breath unutterable things.

What grim dialogues! What could they be telling each other? O gulf, in which thought is lost! They know that which is behind life. They know the secret of the journey. They have doubled the promontory. For them the great cloud has been rent. As for us, we are still in the land of conjectures, of hopes, of ambitions, of passions, of all the follies which we call wisdom, of all the chimeras which we call truth. But they—they have entered the region of the infinite, of the immutable, of the real. They know the things that are, and the only things that are. All those questions which engage us night and day—us dreamers, philosophers —all the subjects of our endless meditations : the purpose of life, the object of creation, the persistence of self, the future state of the soul—of these things they know all. They know the key to all our enigmas, they know the end of all our beginnings. Why do they wear that terrible look? Whence have they that despairing, that formidable aspect?

If our ears were not too dull to hear their speech, if God had not placed that insurmountable wall of flesh and life between them and us, what would they tell us? What revelations would they make? What counsels would they give us? Should we come from their hands wiser or mad? What do they bring back from the tomb?

If the appearance of these spectres is to be relied upon, it must be terror. But that is merely an appearance, and it would be madness to rely upon it. Whatever we may do, we dreamers only pierce the surface of things to a certain depth. The sphere of the infinite is no more to be fathomed by thought than the terrestrial globe is to be fathomed by the plummet.

The various philosophies are nothing but artesian wells. From the same soil they all jet forth the same water, the same truth mingled with human mud and warmed with the breath of God. But no well, no philosophy, reaches to the centre of things. Genius itself, which is of all plummets the most powerful, cannot touch that kernel of flame, Being— that geometric, mystic point, the ineffable centre of truth. We shall never draw anything from the rock but here a drop of water, there a spark of fire.

But let us think. Let us strike the rock, let us dig into the earth. That is the fulfilment of law. Some must think, as others must work.

And then, let us resign ourselves. The secret which philosophy would wrest is guarded by nature. And who shall ever vanquish thee, O nature?

We see but one side of things. God sees the other.

The human shell terrifies us when we contemplate it. Yet it is only a shell—something empty, and vain, and uninhabited. To us it appears that this ruin reveals horrible things. No. It frightens us, and nothing more. Do we see the mind ? Do we see the soul ? Do we see the spirit ? Do we know what the spirit of the dead would tell us, were it given us to meet it in its glorious resplendence ? Let us not, then, believe the body, which disintegrates in horror and is revolting in its dissolution ; let us not believe the corpse, or the skeleton, or the mummy, but let us remember that if there be darkness in the tomb there is a light also. In this light the soul walked while the body was enveloped in night. And this light the soul contemplates. What matter if the body be contorted, if the soul smiles ?

I was immersed in this chaos of thought. Those dead who were communing with one another no longer inspired me with dread. I felt almost at ease among them. Suddenly, I remembered—I know not how—that at that very moment, on the summit of that tower of St. Michel, two hundred feet above my head, above those spectres exchanging all manner of mysterious communications through the gloom, the telegraph, a poor wooden machine worked by a cord, was gesticulating in the clouds, sending through space, one after another, in that mysterious language which it too possesses, all those invisible things which to-morrow will constitute the newspaper.

Never have I felt the vanity of all that agitates us more deeply than at that moment. What a poem is this tower of St. Michel! What a contrast, and what a lesson! On its summit, in the light and warmth of the sun, in the midst of the azure sky, within sight of the busy crowd swarming in the streets, a telegraph, gesticulating and straining like Pasquin on his trestles, is telling and minutely detailing all the trifles of the history of the day and the politics of the moment—the fall of Espartero, the rise of Narvaez, the expulsion of Mendizabal by Lopez; all the great microscopic events—infusoria who become dictators, volvoces who become tribunes, vibrios who become tyrants; all the littlenesses that compose the passing man and the fleeting moment,—and all this time, at its base, within the massive building upon which the tower rests, in a crypt penetrated by neither a ray of light nor a sound, a council of spectres, seated in a circle amid the darkness, are discoursing in low tones of the tomb and of eternity.

IV.

BIARRITZ.

OU know, my friend, the three spots on the coast of Normandy which delight me most: the village of Aŭlt, Le Tréport, and Étretat—Étretat with its immense arches cut in the cliff by the waves; Le Tréport with its old church, its old stone cross, and its old harbour swarming with fishing boats; Aŭlt with its big Gothic street debouching suddenly on the open sea. Well, place Biarritz henceforth with Le Tréport, Étretat, and Aŭlt, among those spots which I should choose for "the pleasure of my eyes," of which Fénélon speaks.

I know no spot more charming and magnificent than Biarritz. There are no trees, say those people who criticise everything—even the good God in his finest works. But one must be prepared to choose —either the ocean or the forest. It is the sea wind that shaves off the trees.

L

Biarritz is a white village with red roofs and green outside shutters, resting upon mounds of grass and heather, the undulations of which it follows. One leaves the village, descends the dune, the sand crumbles beneath one's heels, and suddenly one finds oneself on a gentle, smooth, sandy shore in the midst of an inextricable labyrinth of rocks, chambers, arcades, grottos, and caverns—a strange architecture, flung in confusion among the surge, which the sky fills with sunbeams and azure, with lights and shadows, the sea with foam, the wind with sound.

Nowhere have I seen old Neptune devastate old Cybele with greater violence, exultation, and majesty. This whole coast is filled with tumult. The Gascon sea gnaws it and tears it, and prolongs among the reefs its boundless murmurings. Yet whatever the hour might be, I have never wandered over this desert shore without feeling a great peace rise to my heart. The tumults of nature do not trouble solitude.

You could not imagine all that lives, palpitates, and vegetates amid the apparent confusion of a crumbling coast. A crust of living shell-fish covers the rocks. Zoophytes and molluscs float and swim, themselves transparent in the transparency of the waves. The water filters drop by drop, weeping in long pearls, from the vault of the grottos. Crabs and slugs crawl about among the drift and seaweed, which describe on the wet sand the form of the waves that bore them in. Above the caves grows a whole flora, curious and almost unknown : the milk-vetch of Bayonne, the Gallic carnation, the sea-flax, the pimpernel-leafed rose-tree, the thyme-leafed snap-dragon.

There are little narrow creeks where the poor fishermen, crouching round some old sloop, are cutting up and gutting the fish they have caught during the night, to the accompaniment of the deafening roar of the tide rising or falling among the rocks. Young barefooted girls go and wash the skins of the dogfish in the waves ; and each time that the sea, white with foam, suddenly springs towards them, like a lion turning upon its tormentors, they pull up their skirts and run backwards with loud bursts of laughter.

The bathing at Biarritz is the same as at Dieppe and at Havre, except that there is a certain freedom provoked by the lovely sky and tolerated by the mild climate. Women wearing the latest Parisian millinery on their heads, with lace veils over their faces, enveloped from head to foot in great shawls, enter with lowered eyes one of the canvas tents with which the shore is covered. A moment after-

wards they come out, with bare legs, dressed in a
mere tunic of brown wool which often scarcely falls
below the knee, and skip laughingly down to the
sea.   This freedom, mingled with the delight of
man and the glory of the sky, has a charm of its
own.

Both the village girls and the pretty grisettes of
Bayonne bathe in serge chemises, often full of holes,
without troubling themselves overmuch about what
the holes may show or what the chemises may
conceal.

On the second day upon which I went to Biarritz,
as I was walking at low tide among the grottos,
looking for shell-fish and frightening the crabs, which
fled obliquely from me and buried themselves in the
sand, I heard a voice which came from behind a
rock singing the following stanza with some mixture of patois, but not enough to prevent me from
distinguishing the words :

> " Gastibelza, l'homme à la carabine,
> > Chantait ainsi :
> Quelqu'un a-t-il connu doña Sabine,
> > Quelqu'un d'ici ?
> Dansez, chantez, villageois, la nuit gagne
> > Le mont Falou.
> Le vent qui vient à travers la montagne
> > Me rendra fou."

It was a woman's voice.   I turned the corner of

the rock. The songstress was a bather. She was a young and beautiful girl, clad in a white chemise and a short petticoat, swimming in a little creek shut in by two rocks at the entrance of a grotto. Her peasant's clothes lay on the sand at the back of the grotto. On perceiving me, she came half-way out of the water and began to sing her second verse. Seeing that I was standing motionless on the rock listening to her, she said to me with a smile, in a jargon composed of French and Spanish :

"Señor estrangero, conoce Usted cette chanson ? "

"I think I do," said I to her. "A little."

Then I withdrew ; but she did not send me away.

Do you not see in this some resemblance to Ulysses listening to the syren ? Nature, while ever rejuvenating them, is constantly casting up and giving us again those innumerable themes and motives upon which the human imagination has constructed all the old poetry and all the old mythologies.

To sum up, Biarritz, with its kindly people, its pretty white houses, its broad dunes, its fine sand, its enormous grottos, and its magnificent sea, is a delightful spot.

I have but one fear, and that is that it may become fashionable. Already people come from Madrid ; soon they will be coming from Paris.

Then Biarritz, this village, so rustic, so rude, and, as yet, so honest, will be seized with the evil appetite for money—*sacra fames*. Biarritz will place poplars on her hills, hand-rails along her dunes, stairways over her precipices, kiosks upon her rocks, seats in her grottos, bathing-drawers on her naïads. Biarritz will become modest and rapacious.   Prudishness, which, as Molière says, "has nothing chaste in its whole body but its ears," will replace the free and innocent familiarity of those young women sporting with the sea.   They will read the newspapers at Biarritz ; they will play melodrama and tragedy at Biarritz.   O Zaïre, what hast thou to do with me ? In the evening people will go to the concert—for there will be a concert every evening—and some singer with a name ending in " i," some nightingale weighted with some fifty years, will sing soprano airs a few steps distant from that old ocean which sings the eternal music of the tides, the hurricane, and the tempest.

Then Biarritz will be Biarritz no longer.   She will be something colourless and bastard like Dieppe and Ostend.

There is nothing greater than a hamlet of fisher-men, full of the old, simple customs, lying by the ocean's edge.   There is nothing greater than a city which seems to have the august function of thinking

for the whole human species, and of suggesting to
the world those innovations, often difficult and formidable, demanded by civilization. There is nothing
more mean, pitiful, and ridiculous than an imitation
Paris.

Towns that are bathed by the sea should sacredly
preserve the physiognomy which their situation has
given them. The ocean has every grace, every
beauty, every grandeur. When one has the ocean,
where is the use of copying Paris?

Already several symptoms seem to announce this
approaching transformation of Biarritz. Ten years
ago people came there from Bayonne in cacolets;
two years ago they came in coucous; at present
they come by omnibus. A hundred years—twenty
years ago, one bathed at the old port, a little bay
overlooked by two old dismantled towers. To-day,
one bathes at the new port. Ten years ago, there
was hardly an inn in Biarritz. To-day, there are
three or four " hôtels."

It is not that I have any fault to find with the
omnibus, or with the new port, where the waves
break more freely than at the old, and where one's
bath is more efficacious in consequence, or with the
" hôtels," which have no defect other than that of
having no windows overlooking the sea ; but I am
fearful of the other possible improvements, and I

would have Biarritz remain Biarritz. So far, all is well; but do not let us go further.

Moreover, the omnibus from Bayonne to Biarritz was not established without opposition. The coucou is struggling against the omnibus, as the cacoet doubtless contended against the coucou ten years ago. All the coach-hirers in the town are in revolt against two saddlers, Castex and Anatole, who conceived the idea of omnibuses. There is league, competition, coalition. It is an Iliad of hackney-coachmen, who subject the traveller's purse to fantastically fluctuating demands.

On the day after my arrival in Bayonne I wished to go to Biarritz. Not knowing the road, I addressed myself to a passer-by, a Navarrese peasant who was arrayed in a grand costume: wide breeches of olive velvet, a red sash, a shirt with a broad turned-down collar and fastened with a silver ring, a waistcoat of rough chocolate-coloured cloth embroidered all over with brown silk, and a little Henri II. hat, trimmed with velvet and decked with a black, curled ostrich feather. It was of this magnificent wayfarer that I asked the way to Biarritz.

"Take the Rue du Pont-Magour," said he, "and follow it as far as the Porte d'Espagne."

"Is it easy," I further inquired, "to get a coach for Biarritz?"

The Navarrese looked at me, smiled a grave smile, and with the accent of his country said these memorable words, the profundity of which I did not appreciate until afterwards :

" Monsieur, it is easy to get there, but it is difficult to get back."

I took the Rue du Pont-Magour.

In ascending it I encountered several posters of different colours on which the coach-hirers offered to the public carriages for Biarritz at various reasonable prices. I observed, but somewhat negligently, that these announcements ended with this invariable formula : " The prices will remain unaltered until eight o'clock in the evening."

I reached the Porte d'Espagne. There a crowd of conveyances of all sorts—chars-à-bancs, cabriolets, coucous, gondolas, calashes, coupés, omnibuses— were drawn up and huddled together in confusion. Scarcely had I cast my eye over this throng of vehicles than I found myself suddenly surrounded by another throng. These were the drivers. In a moment I was deafened. I was assailed by all the voices, all the accents, all the patois, all the oaths, and all the offers at once.

One took hold of my right arm : " Monsieur, I am M. Castex's driver ; get into the coupé—a seat for fifteen sous." Another seized my left arm :

" Monsieur, I am Ruspit ; I have a coupé too—a seat for twelve sous." A third blocked my way : " I am Anatole. Here is my calash ; I will drive you for ten sous."

" Monsieur," said a fourth in my ear, " come with Momus ; I am Momus. Full speed to Biarritz for six sous ! "

" Five sous ! " exclaimed others round about me.

" See, Monsieur, the pretty coach—' The Sultan of Biarritz ' ; a seat for five sous ! "

The first to speak to me, who was holding me by the right arm, at last dominated the whole tumult.

" Monsieur," said he, " it was I who spoke to you first. I should have the preference."

" He asks fifteen sous ! " cried the other drivers.

" Monsieur," answered the man coolly, " I ask three sous."

There was a great silence.

" I spoke to Monsieur first," said the man.

Then, profiting by the amazement of the other combatants, he hastily opened the door of his coupé, pushed me inside before I had time to collect myself, closed the door again, mounted his box, and went off at a gallop. His omnibus was full. Apparently he had only been waiting for me.

The coach was quite new and a very good one; the horses were excellent. In less than half an hour we were in Biarritz.

On arriving there, being unwilling to take advantage of my position, I took fifteen sous from my purse and gave them to the driver. I was about to go off, but he held me by the arm.

"Monsieur," said he, "it is only three sous."

"Pshaw!" I answered; "you told me fifteen sous at first. It shall be fifteen sous."

"Not at all, Monsieur; I said I would take you for three sous, and it is three sous."

And he returned me the surplus, almost forcing me to take it.

"Pardieu!" said I, as I went off, "there is an honest man!"

Like myself, the other passengers had paid only three sous.

After walking all day about the beach, evening came, and I thought of returning to Bayonne. I was tired, and it was not without a certain pleasure that I thought of the excellent coach and the virtuous driver who had brought me there. It was striking eight on the distant clocks on the plain as I climbed the slope from the old port. I paid no attention to the crowd of pedestrians, who were coming from all quarters and seemed to be hurrying towards the entrance of the village where the coaches stopped.

The evening was magnificent; a few stars were beginning to pierce the clear sky of twilight; the sea, which was scarcely ruffled, had the dull, opaque lustre of an immense sheet of oil.

A lighthouse with a revolving light had just been lit on my right. It flashed, then went out, then suddenly revived, and threw out all at once a brilliant ray as if seeking to match itself with eternal Sirius, who shone effulgently through the haze at the other extremity of the horizon. I paused and contemplated for a time this melancholy spectacle, which to me was like the representation of human endeavour in the presence of the divine power.

But the darkness grew denser, and at a certain moment the thought of Bayonne and my inn suddenly traversed my contemplations. I resumed my walk, and reached the place from which the coaches started. There was only one remaining. I saw it by the light of a large lantern placed on the ground. It was a calash seated for four. Three of the seats were already occupied.

" Hollo, Monsieur! " cried a voice as I approached. " Make haste; it is the last seat, and we are the last coach."

I recognized the voice of my driver of the morning.

I had found that human curiosity again. Chance seemed providential to me, and I thanked heaven. A moment later, and I should have been obliged to do the journey on foot—a good league of country.

"Pardieu! my fine fellow," said I, "I am glad to see you again."

"Get in quickly, Monsieur," answered the man.

I hastily installed myself in the calash.

When I was seated, the driver, with his hand on the handle of the door, said to me:

"Monsieur knows that it is past the hour?"

"What hour?" said I.

"Eight o'clock."

"True. I heard something like that strike."

"Monsieur is aware," rejoined the man, "that after eight o'clock in the evening the fare is altered. We come and fetch the passengers to oblige them. It is customary to pay before starting."

"Most certainly," I answered, pulling out my purse. "How much is it?"

"Monsieur," replied the man sweetly, "it is twelve francs."

I understood the operation instantly. In the morning they announce that they will drive sight-seers to Biarritz at three sous a head, and there is a crowd. In the evening they take this crowd back again to Bayonne at twelve francs a head.

Only that morning I had experienced my driver's stoical inflexibility. I answered not a word, and paid.

As we drove back to Bayonne at a gallop, the excellent maxim of the Navarrese peasant came back to my mind, and for the instruction of the passengers I made this translation of it into the vulgar tongue: "COACHES FOR BIARRITZ. Fare, per person, going: *Three sous*; returning: *Twelve francs*." —Don't you think this fluctuation delightful?

Some distance from Bayonne one of my travelling companions pointed out to me in the shadow of a hill the Château de Marrac, or, at least, what remains of it to-day.

The Château de Marrac is celebrated for having been the residence of the Emperor in 1808, at the time of the Bayonne interview. On this occasion Napoleon had a great idea, but Providence did not favour it; and although Joseph I. governed the Castiles like a good and wise prince, the project of giving a new dynasty to Spain, however beneficial it might have been to Europe, to France, to Spain, and to civilization, was fatal to Napoleon as it had been fatal to Louis XIV.

Josephine, who was a Creole and superstitious,

accompanied the Emperor to Bayonne. She appeared to have all manner of presentiments, and, like Nuñez Saledo in the Spanish romance, she frequently repeated, " Evil will come of this."

To-day, when we see the other side of those events, already buried in history at a depth of thirty years, we perceive all their sinister elements even in the smallest details, and it seems as if all their threads were held by destiny.

Here is one incident which is quite unchronicled, but is worthy of being preserved :

During his stay at Bayonne, the Emperor desired to inspect the works which he was having executed at Boucaut. Those Bayonnese who were then grown up remember that one morning the Emperor crossed the Allées Marines on foot, with the object of walking to the brigantine moored in the port, by which he was to be conveyed to the mouth of the Adour.

He gave Josephine his arm. As everywhere, he was there attended by his suite of kings, and on this occasion it was the princes of the south and the Bourbons of Spain who composed his retinue : old King Charles IV. and his wife ; the Prince of the Asturias, who was afterwards king and was called Ferdinand VII. ; and Don Carlos, now pretender under the name of Charles VI.

The whole population of Bayonne was in the Allées Marines and surrounded the Emperor, who walked without any guard. The crowd soon became so numerous and so importunate in its meridional curiosity that Napoleon hastened his steps. The poor panting Bourbons followed him with much difficulty.

The Emperor reached the brigantine's boat with such precipitation that Josephine, in trying to catch hold of the hand held out to her by the captain of the ship as she entered, fell into the water up to her knees. In any other circumstance such a thing would merely have made her laugh. "It would have been," said Madame the Duchess of C——, in relating the incident to me, "an opportunity for her to exhibit her leg, which was charming." This time, it was remarked that she shook her head sadly. The omen was bad.

Everything that had a part in this adventure came to a melancholy end. Napoleon died in exile ; Josephine died divorced ; Charles IV. and his wife died dethroned. As for those who were then young princes, one, Ferdinand VII., is dead ; the other, Don Carlos, is a prisoner. The brigantine boarded by the Emperor was lost, vessel and crew, two years afterwards, beneath Cape Ferret, in the Bassin d'Arcachon ; her captain, who had held out his hand to the Empress, and whose name was Lafon, was condemned to death in consequence of the occurrence, and shot. And finally, the Château de Marrac, in which Napoleon lodged, after being transformed successively into a barrack-room and a seminary, disappeared in a fire. One stormy night in 1820, a hand which has never been discovered set fire to it at its four corners.

M

V.

THE OX-CART.

I T was on the 27th of July, 1843, at half-past ten in the morning, between Bidart and St. Jean-de-Luz, just as I was about to enter Spain, that I once more saw an old Spanish ox-cart at the door of a humble inn. By this I mean the little Biscayan cart with two oxen, and two broad wheels which turn round with the axle-tree, making a fearful noise that can be heard a league away among the mountains.

Do not smile, my friend, at the tender care with which I record this memory so minutely. If you knew how that sound, so horrible to everybody else, is delightful to me! It brings back to me years of bliss.

I was quite little when I crossed these mountains and heard it for the first time. Merely on hearing it yesterday, as soon as ever it struck my ear, I felt myself suddenly rejuvenated, and it seemed to me that my whole childhood was renewed again within me.

I cannot tell you by what strange, supernatural process my memory became fresh as an April dawn, and all came back to me at once. The slightest details of that happy time appeared to me, clear, bright, and illuminated as by the rising sun. As the ox-cart approached with its savage music, I distinctly saw that delightful past again, and it seemed to me that between that past and to-day there was nothing. It was but yesterday.

Oh, blissful days! Oh, sweet and smiling years! I was a child, I was little, I was loved. I had not experience, but I had my mother.

The travellers round about me stopped their ears, but I had ecstasy within my heart. No chorus of Weber, no symphony of Beethoven, no melody of Mozart, ever called forth within a soul all the divine, unutterable things awakened within me by the furious grating of those two ill-greased wheels upon that ill-paved road.

The cart disappeared in the distance. Little by little the sound became fainter, and, as fast as it was extinguished among the hills, the dazzling vision of my childhood was extinguished within my mind. Then all was colourless, and, when the last note of that song—to me alone melodious—had died away in the distance, I felt myself falling rudely into reality, into the present, into life, into night.

Blessings on the poor unknown teamster who had the mysterious power to illuminate my mind, and who, without knowing it, wrought that magic evocation in my soul! May heaven be with the wayfarer who can rejoice the gloomy spirit of the dreamer with such unexpected light.

This, my friend, has filled my heart. I will write you nothing more to-day.

VI.

FROM BAYONNE TO SAN SEBASTIAN.

29th July.

I LEFT Bayonne at sunrise. The road
is charming; it runs along a lofty
plateau, with Biarritz on the right and
the sea on the horizon. Nearer, there is
a mountain; nearer still, a great green pool at which
a perfectly naked child is watering a cow. The
landscape is magnificent—a blue sky, a blue sea, a
dazzling sun. From the top of a hill an ass is
surveying the whole:

> " Dans le mol abandon
> D'un mandarin lettré qui mange du chardon."

Here there is a pretty Louis XIII. château, the
last in the south of France on this side.

At Bidart the horses are changed. At the door
of the church I observe a sort of fantastic idol,
venerated now as formerly—to pagans a god, to
Christians a saint. Those who do not think must
have their fetiches.

St. Jean-de-Luz is a village shaken down into the undulations of the mountain. A little Hôtel, with turrets after the manner of those of the Hôtel d'Angoulême in the Marais, was doubtless built for Mazarin in the time of Louis XV.

The Bidassoa, a pretty river with a Basque name, seems to form the frontier of two tongues as it does of two countries, and to preserve neutrality between French and Spanish.

We cross the bridge. At the southern end the coach stops. Passports are demanded. A soldier in torn cloth breeches and a green vest patched on the elbow and collar with blue, appears at the coach door. It is the sentinel. I am in Spain.

I am now in the land where they pronounce *b* for *v*, a circumstance which enraptured Scaliger's drunkard. "Felices populi," he cried, "quibus *vivere* est *bibere*."

I did not even look at the Île des Faisans, where the house of France was wedded to the house of Austria, where Mazarin, the athlete of cunning, fought hand to hand with Luis de Haro, the athlete of pride. But a cow was munching the grass. Is that sight less great? Is the meadow belittled? Macchiavelli would say, Yes ; Hesiod would say, No.

There are no pheasants on the island.   They are represented by the cow and three ducks,—figurants doubtless hired to play the part for the satisfaction of passers-by.

And this is the general rule.   In the Marais, in Paris, there are no marshes ; in the Rue des Trois-Pavillons, there are no pavilions ; in the Rue de la Perle, there are prostitutes ; on the Île des Cygnes, there is nothing but old shipwrecked shoes and dead dogs.   When a place is called the Île des Faisans, there you find ducks.   O curious, intrusive traveller, forget not this !

We are at Irun.

My eyes sought Irun hungrily.   It was there that Spain appeared to me for the first time, and astonished me so much with her black houses, her narrow streets, her wooden balconies, and her fortress-like doors—me, a French child brought up amid all the mahogany of the Empire.   My eyes, accustomed to spangled beds, swan-necked arm-chairs, sphinx-shaped andirons, gilded bronzes, and deep blue marbles, gazed with a sort of terror at the great carved chests, the tables with twisted legs, the beds with baldachins, the stumpy, contorted silver-work, the window-panes set in leaden lattice-work,

—at the whole of that old and new world which revealed itself to me.

Alas! Irun is Irun no longer. Irun is now more Empire and more mahoganied than Paris. It is nothing but white houses and green shutters. One feels that Spain, always in the rear, reads Jean-Jacques at this moment. O ye embellished villages, how hideous do ye become! Where is history? Where is the past? Where is romance? Where is memory? Irun now reminds one of the Batignolles.

There are scarcely more than two or three blackened houses with overhanging balconies still remaining. Nevertheless, I thought I recognized, and saluted from the depths of my soul, the house facing the one occupied by my mother, an old house which I contemplated with such wonder during long hours, and with which I, although a child, French, and brought up on mahogany, already felt some sort of sympathy. The house in which my mother lodged has disappeared in an improvement.

In the square there is still an old column of the time of Philip II., bearing the arms of Spain. The Emperor Napoleon, passing through Irun, leant his back against this column.

In leaving Irun, I recognized the lie of the road, one side of which rises while the other falls. I can remember it as if I saw it. It was morning. The soldiers of our escort, gay, as soldiers always are in time of war when they march with three days' rations, took the road which rises, while we followed that which descends.

Fuenterrabia had left a dazzling impression upon me. It had remained in my mind like the silhouette of a village of gold, with a pointed belfry, at the back of a blue bay, all immensely enlarged. I no longer saw it as I saw it before. Fuenterrabia is rather a pretty village situated on a plateau with a walk of trees at its base and the sea by its side. It is fairly near to Irun—half a league away.

The road buries itself among mountains magnificent in form and delicious in greenness. The hills wear coats of green velvet, worn here and there. A house appears, a great stone house with a balcony, and bearing an immense coat-of-arms which one takes at first for the escutcheon of Spain, so pompous is it and so imperially bedizened. An inscription declares : " Estas armas de la casa Solar. Año 1759."

A torrent skirts the highway. Every moment there is a bridge with an ivy-covered arch trembling

beneath some ox-waggon which is crossing it.   The
wheels shriek fearfully into the ravines.

For some minutes a man armed with a carbine
and dressed like a Paris faubourien has been running
alongside the diligence. He wears an all-round vest,
with wide breeches of tan-coloured cotton-backed
velvet, a cartridge-box over his stomach, and a
round glazed hat like that of our hackney-coachmen bearing this inscription: "CAZADORES DE
GUIPUZCOA."   In a word, he is a gendarme.

He escorts the diligence.   Are there robbers,
then ?   Impossible.   We have left France !   We
shrug our shoulders.   We enter a village, however.
What is the name of the place ?   Astigarraga.
And what is that long, green-painted coach at the
door of the inn ?   That is the mail-coach.   Why is
it standing still, unyoked and unloaded ?   It is
unloaded because it has no longer any load ; it is
unyoked because it has no longer any horses ; it is
standing still because it has been stopped.   Stopped !
By whom ?   By robbers, who have killed the
postillion, carried off the horses, stripped the coach,
and rifled the passengers.   And those poor devils
standing with that piteous air at the door of the inn ?
Those are the passengers.   Ah !   Indeed ?   One
wakes up.   So such things are possible.   Verily, it
is plain that we have left France.

The cazador goes off, and another presents him-self. The one who goes off comes to the door of the coach and asks you for alms. This is his pay.

One thinks of the golden pieces in one's pocket, and one gives him a piece of silver. The poor give a sou, the niggardly a liard. The cazador takes everything; he receives the peseta, takes the sou, and accepts the liard. The cazador scarcely does anything but run along the road, carry his gun, and demand alms—that is his whole business.

I set myself a problem : what would become of the cazador if there were no robbers? A nice question ! He would turn robber.

I fear so, at least. The cazador must, of course, live.

Two-thirds of the villages have been ruined by the Carlists, unless it be by the Cristinos. Scarcely six years ago the civil war was smouldering in Guipuzcoa and Navarre. In Spain, the highway belongs to the civil war from time to time, to the robbers always. The robbers are the nation's treasurers.

Just as it enters Hernani the road turns sharply to the right. A footpath for pedestrians runs along the side. There are crowds of peasants in bérets going to market to sell their cattle.

As the diligence was descending an incline at a

gallop, a poor terrified ox flung itself into the
hedge. A little boy of four or five who was driving
it took hold of its head and hid it in his breast,
patting it tenderly with his hand. He did to the ox
what his mother doubtless did to himself. The ox,
trembling in every limb, buried its big head, adorned
with enormous horns, confidingly beneath the small
arms of the child, casting a frightened side-glance at
the diligence as it was borne along by its six mules
with a fearful clatter of bells and chains. The child
smiled and spoke to it in low tones. Nothing could
be more beautiful and touching than the sight of
that blind brute force being reassured by intelligent
frailty.

The diligence reached the summit of a hill, and a
magnificent spectacle lay before us.

A promontory to the right, a promontory to the
left, and two bays; an isthmus in the midst, a
mountain in the sea; at the foot of the mountain, a
town. This is San Sebastian.

The first glance is magical; the second is amusing.
There is an old lighthouse on the promenade to the
left. In the bay, beneath the lighthouse, there is an
island. Then a ruined convent; a low, sandy beach.
Vessels laden with iron ore are being discharged on
the beach by ox-waggons. The port of San Sebastian is a curious tangle of complicated jetties.

On the right, the valley of Loyola, full of robin-redbreasts, in which the Urumea, a beautiful steel-toned river, describes a gigantic horseshoe. On the northern promontory there are some fragments of demolished walls, the remains of the fort from which Wellington bombarded the town in 1813. The sea breaks entrancingly.

Over the gate of the town there is a fine disfigured cartouche of the time of Philip II., which doubtless bore the arms of the town, but has been effaced by some miniature French revolution. Within the same gate, above the guard-room and the sentry, there is a large Christ of painted wood, shedding long drops of blood from beneath its crown of thorns ; by its side a holy water vessel. The soldiers of the guard play the guitar and the castanets.

The appearance of San Sebastian is that of a freshly rebuilt town, regular and square like a draughtboard.

As there are no buildings to describe, shall I give you some traits of local customs instead ?

While dining, I heard the sound of laughter and castanets in the street. I went out. A crowd of strange men surrounded me—ill-clad, clothed in rags, stately and elegant like the figures of Callot, with hats like Incroyables of the Directory, small moustaches, and handsome, intellectual, impudent faces. Round me there were shouts of "Los estudiantes! Los estudiantes!" They were students from Salamanca in vacation. One of them approached me, bowed low, and held out his hat to me. I threw in a peseta. He drew himself up again. All cried "Viva!" In this way they travel the country demanding alms. Some of them are rich. It amuses them. To ask alms is not at all a startling thing in Spain. It is done.

I entered a barber's shop. This artist inhabits a sort of cellar—three big walls without any window, and a door at the end. The dwelling is furnished with an exquisite Louis XV. mirror, two coloured prints of Austerlitz and Marengo, a small child, and four or five great wheels such as might have been found in the executioner's house long ago. This man speaks four languages, smells very badly, and shaves admirably. This is his history. He was born at Aix-la-Chapelle, and speaks German. The Emperor made a Frenchman of him, and the Empire a soldier, so he speaks French. In 1811 the Spaniards made him prisoner, and he speaks Spanish. He married in the district, taking to wife a "basquaise," as he calls her; so he speaks Basque. See what it is to have adventures in four different languages.

A tall, strapping Basque, who told me his name

was Oyarbide, offered to carry my belongings. He hefted them.—" They are heavy."—" How much do you want?" — " A peseta." — " Very well." — He loaded everything upon his head, and seemed to groan beneath the weight. We met a woman, a poor old creature, barefooted, and already laden. He went up to her, and said something in Basque which I did not understand ; the woman stopped. He transferred his whole burden into the great basket which she already carried half full upon her head, and then came back to me. The woman went on before us. Oyarbide, with his hands behind his back, walked along beside me and made conversation. He had a horse ; he offered it me for an excursion to Renteria and Fuenterrabia ; it would be eight pesetas for the day. We arrived. The old woman set down the luggage at the feet of Oyarbide, and made him an obeisance. I gave Oyarbide his peseta.—" Are you not going to give the poor woman anything ?" he asked.

VII.

SAN SEBASTIAN.

AM in Spain. I have one foot in it, at least. This is a land for poets and smugglers. The scenery is magnificent, wild as dreamers like it, rugged as robbers need it. A mountain in the midst of the sea ; the trace of bombs upon every house, the trace of the tempest upon every rock, the trace of fleas wherever one goes—this is San Sebastian.

But am I really in Spain here? San Sebastian hangs on to Spain as Spain hangs on to Europe, by a tongue of land. It is a peninsula in a peninsula. And here again, as in a host of other things, the physical aspect is a symbol of the moral state. The people at San Sebastian are scarcely Spanish ; they are Basque.

This is Guipuzcoa, the old land of the fueros,— the old free Basque provinces. A little Castilian is, indeed, spoken, but the general speech is *bascuence*.

The women wear the mantilla, but they have not the basquiña ; and this mantilla, moreover, which the Madrileñas wear with such grace and coquetry down to their eyes, is relegated by the Guipuzcoan women to the rear-summit of their heads, which however, does not prevent them being coquettish and graceful. In the evening they dance on the sward, clacking their fingers in the hollow of their hands. It is but the ghost of the castanets. The dancers sway with rhythmic suppleness, but without verve, without fire, without enthusiasm, without voluptuousness. It is but the ghost of the cachucha.

And then the French are everywhere. Out of twelve tradesmen keeping boticas in the town, three are Frenchmen. I make no complaint ; I merely state the faƈt. Besides, all these towns, on this side as on that, Bayonne like San Sebastian, Oloron like Tolosa—regarded, of course, only from the point of view of manners—are merely a mixture of nations. In them one feels the eddy of mingling peoples. They are the mouths of rivers. They are neither France nor Spain, neither river nor sea.

The situation, moreover, is a singular one, and worthy of study. And I would add that here a secret and profound tie, which nothing has been able to break, binds together, in spite of treaties, those diplomatic frontiers—in spite even of the

N

Pyrenees, that natural frontier—all the members of the mysterious Basque family. The old word Navarre is not merely a word. One is born Basque, one speaks Basque, one lives Basque, and one dies Basque. The Basque tongue is a fatherland, I had almost said a religion. Say a word in Basque to a mountaineer among the hills. Before pronouncing it you were to him scarcely a man ; afterwards you are his brother. Here the Spanish tongue is as foreign as the French.

This Basque unity is, no doubt, tending to decrease, and will ultimately disappear. The great States must absorb the small ; this is the law of history and nature. But it is strange that this unity, so slender in appearance, should have endured so long. France took one side of the Pyrenees, Spain the other. But neither France nor Spain has succeeded in disaggregating the Basque group. Beneath the fresh layers of history that have been piled upon it during four centuries, it is still perfectly visible, like a crater beneath a lake.

Never has the law of molecular adhesion, under which nations are formed, struggled more energetically against the thousand manifold influences which dissolve and recompose those great natural formations. I may here say that I wish the makers of history and the makers of treaties would study a little more than they are in the habit of doing, that mysterious chemistry in accordance with which humanity is made and unmade.

This Basque unity brings about curious results. Thus Guipuzcoa is an old land of communes. A century ago the ancient republican spirit of Andorra and Bagnères spread into the Jaizquivel Mountains, which are, in a fashion, the Jura of the Pyrenees. Here the people lived under a charter, while France was under a most Christian absolute monarchy, and Spain under a Catholic absolute monarchy. Here, from time immemorial, the people have elected their Alcaide, and the Alcaide governs the people. The Alcaide is mayor, the Alcaide is judge, and he belongs to the people. The Cura belongs to the Pope. What remains for the King? The soldier. But if he is a Castilian soldier the people will reject him. If he is a Basque soldier, the Cura and the Alcaide will have his heart, the King only his uniform.

At a first glance it would seem that such a people must be admirably prepared for the absorption of French innovations. It is not so. The old liberties are suspicious of the new. This the Basque people have proved.

At the beginning of the present century, the Cortes, which used to make revisions of the Constitution at every opportunity, and that quite opportunely at times, decreed the unity of Spain. Basque unity revolted. Basque unity, driven into its mountains, began the war of the North against the South. On the day when the throne broke with the Cortes, it was in Guipuzcoa that terrified, hunted royalty took refuge. The people of Rights, the land of the fueros shouted : " Viva el rey neto ! " The ancient Basque liberty made common cause with the ancient monarchy of Spain and the Indies against the revolutionary spirit.

And beneath this apparent contradiction there lay a profound logic and a true instinct. Revolutions— let us emphasize the fact—do not handle ancient liberties any the less rudely than they handle ancient power. They reconstitute everything, re-creating everything on a vaster scale ; for they labour for posterity, and take at the actual moment the measure of the Europe of the future. Hence those vast generalizations which are, as it were, the framework of future nations, which are so hardly absorbed by ancient peoples, and which take such small account of the old manners, the old laws, the old customs, the old liberties, the old frontiers, the old idioms, the old encroachments, the old ties which all things form, the old principles, the old systems, the old facts.

In the language of revolution the old principles are termed "prejudices," the old facts are termed "abuses." This is at once true and false. Whatever they be, republican or monarchical, ageing societies become covered with abuses like old men with wrinkles and old buildings with decay. But one must distinguish ; one must uproot the weeds and respect the building, uproot the abuse and respect the State. But this revolutions either do not know, do not wish to do, or cannot do. How, indeed, should they have time to distinguish, to select, to prune ? They do not come to weed the field, but to shake the earth.

A revolution is not a gardener ; it is the breath of God.

It passes once and everything crumbles ; it passes again and all is reborn.

Revolutions, then, maltreat the past. All that has a past fears them. In the eyes of revolutions, the ancient monarchy of Spain was an abuse ; so, too, was the ancient Basque Alcaidía. Both abuses felt their peril, and leagued themselves against the common enemy. The King leaned upon the Alcaide. And thus it came about that the old Guipuzcoan republic, to the great astonishment of those who see only the surface of things, fought for the old Castilian despotism against the Constitution of 1812.

This, moreover, is not without analogy with the events of La Vendée.   Brittany was a land of constitutions and liberties.   The day on which the Republic one and indivisible was decreed, Brittany felt confusedly that Breton unity was about to be lost in the greater unity of France.   She rose as one man to defend the past and fight for the King of France against the National Convention.

Ancient peoples who fight in this fashion are too feeble to descend into the plain, and engage in pitched battles with new races, new ideas, new armies.   They call nature to their aid ; they wage their wars on the moors, in the mountains, in the desert.   La Vendée made war on the moors ; Guipuzcoa made war in the mountains ; Africa makes war in the desert.

This war has left its mark everywhere here.   Amid the fairest scenes and the finest husbandry, among fields of tomatoes that reach up to one's hips, among fields of maize furrowed by the plough twice every season, you suddenly see a house without windows, without a door, without a roof, without inhabitants. What does it mean ?   You look.   The marks of fire are on the stones of the walls.   Who burnt this house ?   It was the Carlists.   The road turns. Here is another house.   Who burnt this one ?   The Cristinos.   Between Hernani and San Sebastian I resolved to count the ruins I saw from the road. In five minutes I counted seventeen. I gave it up.

On the other hand, the little anti-Esparteran revolution called "El Pronunciamiento" was accomplished at San Sebastian in the most peaceful manner imaginable. San Sebastian did not stir, letting the other towns of the province declare themselves as they pleased. Hereupon a message arrived from the people of Pampeluna. There must be a pronunciamiento at San Sebastian, otherwise they would march against it. San Sebastian was not frightened, but the poor town was wearied. The civil war of Espartero, coming after the civil war of Don Carlos, was too much for it. The chief personages of the town met in ayuntamiento ; the two officers of each company of the town militia were summoned ; a table with a green cover was placed in a room ; on this table something or other was drawn up, and this something was read from a window to the people who were in the square ; a few children who were playing hopscotch stopped for a moment and cried "Vivat!" The same evening these events were notified to the garrison in the castillo. The garrison gave its adhesion to what had been written on the table of the mayoralty and read from the window in the square. Next day the general took the mail-coach, the day after the

political chief took the diligence ; two days later
the colonel went off. The revolution was accomplished.

Such, at least, is the story as it was told me.

In crossing this lovely, devastated country, I
travelled with an old Carlist captain, perched like
myself on the top of "las diligencias peninsulares"
of Bayonne. He was a well-mannered man, distinguished-looking, grave and silent. I asked him
point-blank in Spanish : " Que pensa Usted de Don
Carlos ? " (What do you think of Don Carlos ?)
He answered me in French : " C'est un imbécile."
Take "imbécile" in the sense of *imbecillis*, feeble,
and you will have a just judgment, which will not
fall upon the man, but upon the particular times in
which he lived.

This war of 1833 to 1839 was both savage
and vehement. For five years the peasants lived
scattered among the woods and the mountains, without setting foot inside their own houses. Those
are sad times for a nation in which the home disappears. Some were enlisted, others were in flight.
One had to be either Carlist or Cristino. Parties
require one to be a partisan. The Cristinos burned
the Carlists, and the Carlists the Cristinos. This
is the same law, the same history, the same spirit
of human nature as of old.

Those who held aloof were hunted by the Carlists one day, and shot by the Cristinos on the morrow. There was always some fire smouldering on the horizon.

Nations at war observe the rights of men, but factions ignore them.

Here nature does all she can to make man's spirit serene, and man does all he can to cast a gloom over nature.

Don Carlos, in his own person, took no part in the war. He resided sometimes at Tolosa, sometimes at Hernani. Sometimes he went from one town to another, holding a little court, having levees, and living in accordance with the most rigorous Spanish etiquette. When he arrived in some village where he had not before lodged, the best house was chosen for him ; but he knew how to content himself with little. He usually went about in a dark-coloured frock-coat, without epaulettes or facings, with the Order of the Golden Fleece and the Star of Charles III. His son, the Prince of the Asturias, wore the Basque béret, and looked very well in it. Don Carlos, his wife the Princess of Beïra, and the Prince of the Asturias travelled on horseback ; and the Princess of Beïra was a pattern of courage under danger, and of gaiety under fatigue. The royal party was several times nearly surprised by Espar-

tero.   The Princess would then spring lightly into
the saddle and exclaim laughingly, " Vamos ! "

Ferdinand VII. had no love for Don Carlos, and
feared him.   He accused him of having plotted
during his reign, but this was not so.   Yet the last
person seen by King Ferdinand every evening
before falling asleep was his brother.   At midnight
Don Carlos would enter, kiss the King's hand, and
withdraw again, often without a word having been
exchanged between the two brothers.

The body-guard had orders to permit no one to
enter the royal chamber at that hour except Don
Carlos and the famous Father Cyrillo.   This Father
Cyrillo was a clever and an educated man.   His was
a figure well worthy of being drawn between two
such princes and two such brothers.   The factions
have disfigured him as it suited them, and that
with a strange fervour.

There were many Englishmen in the body-guard
of Ferdinand VII.   It was to them that the King
liked best to talk after mass when playing a game
of billiards, which was his most important business,
and lasted nearly the whole day.   When he was in
a good humour he used to give them cigars.

The truth is that Don Carlos was undone as
pretender on the day that Zumalacarregui died.
Zumalacarregui was a true Basque.   He was the

binder of the Carlist sheaf. After his death, the army of Charles V. was merely a loosened bundle of sticks, as the Marquis de Mirabeau said. There were two parties round Don Carlos, the court party, " el rey neto," and the party of Rights, " los fueros." Zumalacarregui was the man of " Rights." He counteracted the clerical influence with the Prince. He used often to say : " El demonio los frayles ! " He withstood Father Larranaga, the confessor of Don Carlos. Navarre worshipped Zumalacarregui. Thanks to him, the army of Don Carlos at one moment numbered thirty thousand regular com-batants, and two hundred and fifty thousand auxiliary insurgents, scattered over plain, forest, and mountain.

The Basque general, however, treated " his King " somewhat cavalierly. It was he who placed and transposed as he pleased that principal piece in the game of chess which was then being played in Spain. Zumalacarregui would write on a scrap of paper : " Hoy su Magestad irá á tal parte ! " And Don Carlos went.

The Navarre war closed suddenly in 1839. The treachery of Maroto, bought, it is said, with a million pesetas, broke up the Carlist army. Don Carlos, compelled to take refuge in France, was escorted to the frontier with musket-shots.

That day, some families in Bayonne had gone on
a pleasure party to the very point on the frontier
to which chance led Don Carlos. They witnessed
the Prince's entry and the last fight of the faithful
little band which surrounded him. As soon as he
had set foot on French territory the fusillade ceased.

There was there the poor hut of a goatherd. Don
Carlos entered it. As he entered he said to the
Princess of Beïra, by whom he was accompanied :
" Were you afraid ? "—" No, Señor," was her reply.

The Prince then asked for a seat, and had mass
said by his chaplain. Having heard mass he took
some chocolate and smoked a cigar.

The handful of men who had fought for him to
the last moment was composed entirely of Navarrese.
It was surrounded and made prisoner by a French
detachment. These poor soldiers went off in one
direction, and Don Carlos in another. He did not
address a word to them ; he did not even look at
them. The Prince and his army parted without a
farewell.

Elio, who had spent seventeen months in prison
by order of Don Carlos, was one of the band. When
he reached Bayonne, General Harispe said to him :
" General Elio, I have orders to make an exception
in your case. Ask anything you wish of me. What
would you like for yourself and your family ? "—

" Bread and shoes for my soldiers," answered Elio.
—" And for your family ? "—" I have just told you."
—" You spoke only of your soldiers," replied
General Harispe.—" My soldiers," said Elio, " are
my family."—Elio was a hero.

San Sebastian witnessed those events, and many
others besides. It was bombarded by the French
in 1719, and burnt by the English in 1813.

But I am told that the post is leaving. I am
hurriedly putting all this scrawl under cover without re-reading it. It seems to me that I may have
to finish this letter with a bombardment and a fire.

VIII.

WALKED out of San Sebastian the other day when the tide was high. At the end of the promenade, I held on towards the left by the wooden bridge over the Urumea, which one passes for a cuarto. A road made its appearance, and, following it at random, I went walking on into the mountains without quite knowing where I was going.

The external landscape, of which I was but vaguely conscious, had gradually developed within me that other inward landscape which we call reverie. My eyes were reversed and open within me, and it was no longer nature that I beheld, but my own spirit. I cannot tell what I did in this state, to which, as you know, I am subject. I only remember in a confused fashion that I remained standing for several minutes before some bindweed in which an ant was going to and fro, and that in my reverie this sight was transformed into this thought: An ant in

the bindweed. Labour and perfume. Two great
mysteries ; two great counsels.

I do not know how long I had been walking in
this way, when I was suddenly aroused by a shrill
hubbub made up of innumerable strange cries. I
looked, and found myself between two hills with a
horizon of tall mountains, and walking straight towards an arm of the sea in which the road I was
following sharply terminated some forty paces in
front of me. At the point where the road seemed
to plunge into the waves, I saw a strange sight.

Some fifty women, ranged in single file like a
company of infantry, appeared to be waiting for
someone, calling to him and claiming him with
hideously shrill cries. This astonished me greatly ;
but my surprise was redoubled when I realized in a
moment that the person thus awaited, called upon
and claimed, was myself. The road was deserted
and I was alone, and the whole storm of cries was
really directed at me.

I approached, and my astonishment was still
further increased. Speaking all at once, the women
showered upon me the most animated and alluring
expressions : " Señor francés, benga Usted con
migo ! "—" Con migo, caballero ! "—" Ven, hombre,
muy bonita soy ! "

They called to me with the most expressive and

most varied pantomime, but not one of them moved towards me. They seemed rooted to the earth like living statues to whom some magician had said : "Utter every cry, make every gesture ; but move not a step ! " They were, moreover, of all ages and appearances, young and old, ugly and pretty—the pretty, coquettish and adorned ; the old, in rags. In country districts, woman is less fortunate than the butterfly in her field. It begins as a grub ; here it is as a grub that woman ends.

As they all spoke at once, I could not hear what any one of them was saying, and it was some time before I understood. At length some boats moored to the shore explained the matter to me. I was among a lot of boatwomen who were offering to ferry me across the water.

But why boatwomen and not boatmen ? What was the meaning of this strangely ardent obsession, which seemed to possess a frontier which was never overstepped ? And then, where did they want to take me ? So many riddles—so many reasons for going on.

I asked the prettiest of them her name. She was called Pepa. I sprang into her boat.

Just then I noticed a passenger who was already in another boat. Separately, we ran the risk of being kept waiting a considerable time ; by uniting,

we might go off at once. As the last-comer, it was
for me to join the other. I therefore left Pepa's
boat. This made Pepa pout, and I gave her a
peseta. She took the money and continued pouting,
at which I felt curiously flattered ; for a peseta, as
my fellow-traveller explained to me, was double
the maximum fare for the passage. She had,
therefore, the money without the labour.

We left the shore, however, and rowed over a bay
where all was green, the waves and the hills, the
land and the water. Our little boat was managed
by two women, one old and one young, a mother
and daughter. The daughter, who was very pretty
and sprightly, was called Manuela, with the surname
of La Catalana. The two boatwomen had each
only one oar, and rowed standing, from the stern
forwards, with a slow, simple, graceful movement.
Both spoke French tolerably well. Manuela, with
her little oilcloth hat ornamented with a big rose,
her long plaited hair hanging down her back in the
fashion of the country, her bright yellow neckerchief,
her short petticoat, her well-cut skirt, showed the
most lovely teeth imaginable, laughed a great deal,
and was delightful. As for the mother, she, too,
alas! had been a butterfly.

My companion was a silent Spaniard, who, find-
ing me more silent than himself, elected, as it

O

invariably happens in such circumstances, to address himself to me. He began, of course, by finishing his cigar. Then he turned towards me. In Spain the end of a cigar is the beginning of a conversation. As I do not myself smoke, I do not converse. I never have had that great motive which constitutes the beginning of a conversation, the end of a cigar.

"Señor," observed my companion to me in Spanish, "have you seen it yet?"

To him I made answer in Spanish :

" No, Señor."

Observe the " No," and admire it. Had I said : " What ? " which would have been more natural, I should have had an explanation, and, probably, the key to my riddles then and there. But I wished to preserve my little mystery as long as possible, and did not at all care to learn where I was going.

" In that case, Señor," my companion resumed, "you are about to see something exceedingly fine."

" Indeed ? " said I.

" It is very long."

" Very long," thought I ; " what can it be ? "

" It is the longest in the province," added the Spaniard.

" Good ! " said I to myself [he had used the word *larga*], " so the thing is feminine."

"Señor," my companion went on, "have you seen any others before?"

"Sometimes," I replied—another answer after the manner of the first.

"I will wager that you have never seen any longer."

"Oh! oh! You might lose."

"Let us see; which are those that the Señor caballero has already seen?"

The interrogatory was becoming searching.

"That of Bayonne," I replied, without knowing what I was talking about.

"That of Bayonne!" exclaimed my companion; "that of Bayonne! Why, Monsieur, that of Bayonne is three hundred feet shorter than this one. Did you measure it?"

"Yes, Monsieur," I answered, with the same coolness.

"Well, measure this one."

"I intend to."

"You will see something! It could hold a squadron of cavalry in single file."

"Impossible!"

"It is as I say, caballero. I see that the Señor caballero is interested in them."

"Desperately."

"You are French," he resumed; then, with effusion, he added:

" Possibly you have come from France expressly
to see it?"

" Precisely; expressly to see it."

My Spaniard beamed.   He held out his hand to
me and said:

" Well, Monsieur" (he spoke this word in French,
a great courtesy), "you will be pleased with it.   It
is straight as an arrow, like a builder's line—magnificent!"

" The deuce!" thought I, "can it be that this
lovely bay extends into a Rue de Rivoli?   What
bitter mockery!   To flee the Rue de Rivoli even
into Guipuzcoa, and then find it jointed into an arm
of the sea—that would be melancholy!"

Our boat, however, still went on.   She doubled a
little headland dominated by a big ruined house
with its four walls pierced with doorways without
doors, and windows without frames.

Suddenly, as if by magic and without my having
heard the scene-shifter's whistle, the scene changed,
and I beheld a delightful spectacle.

A curtain of tall green mountains, their summits
standing out against a brilliant sky; at the foot of
the mountains a row of houses placed closely together; all the houses painted white, saffron, and
green, with two or three tiers of large balconies
shaded by the prolongation of their great, red,

hollow-tiled roofs ; on all the balconies a thousand
fluttering things, linen drying, nets, rags—red,
yellow, and blue ; beneath the houses, the sea ; half-
way up the hill on my right, a white church ; on my
left, in the foreground, at the foot of another
mountain, another group of balconied houses terminating in an old dismantled tower ; vessels of
every kind and boats of every size ranged before
the houses, moored beneath the tower, gliding over
the bay ; about the ships, the tower, the houses, the
church, the rags, on the mountains and in the sky, a
life, a movement, a warmth, a blueness, an atmosphere, a gaiety inexpressible,—this was what I had
before my eyes.

The spot, magnificent and charming like everything possessing the double character of joyousness
and grandeur, this unchronicled place which is one
of the loveliest I have ever seen and which no
tourist visits, this humble corner of land and water
which would be admired if it were in Switzerland
and celebrated if it were in Italy, but which is unknown because it is in Guipuzcoa, this little radiant
Eden into which I had been led by chance, not
knowing whither I was going, not knowing, even,
where I was, is called in Spanish Pasajes, and in
French Le Passage.

The low tide leaves half the bay dry and separates

it from San Sebastian, which is itself nearly separated from the world.   The high tide re-establishes
" the passage."   Hence the name.

The population of this village follows but one
industry, that of the sea.   The two sexes have
divided the labour between them in accordance with
their strength.   Man works the ships, woman the
boats ; man takes the open sea, woman the bay.
Man goes to the fishing and leaves the bay ; woman
remains in it and ferries over all those whom
business or curiosity brings from San Sebastian.
Hence the "bateleras."

These poor women have a passenger so rarely,
that they have had to come to an understanding.
They would have devoured each other over every
passenger ; perhaps they would have devoured the
passenger.   They have, therefore, laid down a line
which they never overstep, and a charter which they
never violate.   It is an extraordinary country.

When the tide rises they take their boats to the
point where the road is flooded, and there they
remain among the rocks, spinning their distaffs,
waiting.

Whenever a stranger appears they run to the
boundary which they have fixed, and everyone tries
to direct the passenger's choice upon herself.   The
stranger chooses.   His choice once made, all are

silent. The stranger who has chosen is sacred. He
is left to her who has secured him. The passage
is not dear. The poor give a sou, the bourgeois a
real, lords half a peseta, emperors, princes, and poets
a peseta.

But the boat had touched the landing-stage. I
was so dazzled with the place that I hastily threw a
peseta to Manuela and sprang ashore, forgetting all
that the Spaniard had told me, as well as the
Spaniard himself, who must—I have thought since—
have seen me depart with considerable amazement.

As soon as I had landed I took the first street
that appeared—an excellent method, which always
takes you where you want to go, particularly in
towns which, like Pasajes, have only one street.

I examined this single street from end to end.
It is composed of the mountain on the right, and, on
the left, of the backs of all the houses which have
their fronts on the bay.

Here there was a fresh surprise. Nothing could
be sweeter or more brilliant than Pasajes seen from
the water-side ; nothing could be more stern and
gloomy than Pasajes seen from the mountain-side.

Seen from this narrow street, tortuous and flagged
like a Roman road, these houses, which appear so
coquettish, pleasant, white, and brilliant from the
sea, present to the eye only high walls of blackish

granite, sparsely pierced with a few square windows
impregnated with the humid emanations of the
rocks, a dull row of strange buildings upon which,
carved in high relief, are profiled immense coats-of-
arms borne by lions or Hercules, and surmounted
by gigantic morions.   In front they are châlets ;
behind they are citadels.

I ask myself a thousand questions.   What is this
extraordinary place ?   What can be the meaning of
a street scutcheoned from one end to the other ?
One sees such streets only in the towns of the
Hospitallers, like Rhodes and Malta.   Usually coats-
of-arms do not elbow one another.   They love isola-
tion ; like everything that is great they require room.
A whole donjon is needed for one emblazonment, as
a whole mountain is needed for one eagle.   What
can a village covered with arms signify ?   Cottages
in front, palaces behind ; what can it mean ?   When
you arrive by sea, your breast dilates, and you think
you have a bucolic before you.   " Oh ! " you exclaim,
" the sweet, honest, simple fisherfolk ! "   You enter.
You are among hidalgos ; you breathe the atmosphere of the Inquisition ; you see rising at the other
end of the street the livid spectre of Philip II.

Among what people is one at Pasajes ?   Is one
among peasants ?   Is one among lords ?   Is one in
Switzerland or in Castile ?   Is not this a spot

unique in the world, this little corner of Spain where
history and nature meet and construct each one side
of the same town—nature with her most delightful
materials, history with her most sinister?

There are three churches in Pasajes, two black
and one white.

The chief one, which is black, is of a surprising
character. From the outside it is a heap of stones;
inside, it has the bareness of a sarcophagus. But
upon those sullen walls, unrelieved by any sculpture,
unenlivened by any fresco, unpierced by any window,
one suddenly perceives the shining and glittering of
an altar, which in itself is a whole cathedral.

It is an immense piece of woodwork placed
against the wall, carved, painted, joinered, wrought,
and gilded, with statues, statuettes, wreathed
columns, foliage, arabesques, volutes, relics, roses,
tapers, saints male and female, tinsel, and pasquils.
This begins on the ground and stops only at the
vaulted roof. There is no transition between the
nakedness of the wall and the ornamentation of
the altar. It is a magnificent piece of warm, florid
architecture, which vegetates, one knows not how, in
the gloom of that granite vault, and which, at
moments when one is least prepared, makes in the
dark corners clusters of gold and jewels.

There are four or five of these altars in the church

of Pasajes.   This custom, moreover, is common to
all the churches in the province, but it is at Pasajes
that it produces its most curious effect.

The first thing by which I was struck on entering
the church was a head carved in a wall facing the
portal.   This head is painted black, with white eyes
and teeth, and red lips, and it gazes at the church
with an expression of amazement.   As I was
examining this mysterious piece of carving, " el
Señor cura" passed.   He approached me, and I
asked him whether he knew the meaning of that
negro's head before the entrance of his church.   He
did not know, he informed me ; no one in the district had ever known.

At the end of two hours, having seen everything,
or, at least, glanced over everything, I re-embarked.
Manuela was waiting for me.   For it was all settled.
She had taken possession of me ; I belonged to her ;
I was her property.

As I was stepping over the side of the boat, some
one seized my arm, and I turned round.   It was the
worthy man with whom I had crossed the inlet in
the morning, and whose portrait I have forgotten
to give you.   I now repair my omission.   A shabby
tall hat with a narrow brim, a blue frock-coat worn
at the seams and buttoned at every other button, a
heavy watch-chain with a cornelian key, and the face

of a hard-up Jew who lends his name to doubtful
operations. I will now give you our dialogue on
board the boat.

Picture him talking in the most rapid Castilian
you can imagine.

"Well, Señor francés?"

"Well?"

"What do you think of it?"

"Of what?"

"Have you seen it?"

"What?"

"Have you measured it?"

"What?"

"Is it not the longest in the province?"

"Of what province, and what is it that is long?"

"Pardieu! The rope-walk!"

"What rope-walk?"

"The rope-walk you have just seen! Why, the
rope-walk here?"

"Is there a rope-walk here?"

"Ah! The Señor caballero francés is jesting and
wants to amuse himself; but he knows quite well
there is a rope-walk, since he has come two hundred
leagues expressly to see it."

"I? Not at all."

"Is it not fine?—like a builder's line?—long?
—magnificent?—straight as an arrow?"

" I know nothing about it."

"Well!" said the man, looking me straight between the eyes; "then, seriously, caballero, you have not seen it?"

"What?"

" The rope-walk?"

" Learn, Señor," I answered with dignity, " that I particularly dislike things that are long, magnificent, and like builders' lines, and that I would go a couple of hundred leagues not to see a rope-walk."

I pronounced these words in such a solemn fashion and with such an impressive accent that the man started back. He looked at me with a scared expression, and as the boat was leaving the shore I heard him say to the bateleras who remained on the steps, designating me with a shrug of his shoulders : " Un loco." (A madman.)

On returning to San Sebastian I announced in the inn that I was going next day to install myself at Pasajes.

This caused general consternation.

" What will you do there, Monsieur? Why, what a hole it is ! A desert !—a country of savages ! And you won't find any inn ! "

" I will lodge in the first house I come to. One can always find a house, a room, and a bed."

" But there are no roofs to the houses, no doors to the rooms, no mattresses to the beds ! "

" That ought to be interesting."

" But what will you eat ? "

" What there is."

" There will be only mouldy bread, sour cider, rancid oil, and goat-skin wine."

" I will try that ordinary."

" What, Monsieur, you have quite decided ? "

" Quite."

" You are doing what no one here would venture to do."

" Indeed ?   That tempts me."

" To go and sleep at Pasajes—such a thing has never been heard of ! "

And they almost crossed themselves.

But I would listen to nothing, and next day at high tide I left for Pasajes.

Would you now learn the result ?   See what my imprudence has led me into.

I shall begin by telling you what I have before my eyes at the moment of writing.

I am on a long balcony which overlooks the sea, leaning my elbows upon a square table covered with a green cloth.   On my right there is a window-

door opening into my room ; for I have a room, and
the room has a door.   On my left I have the bay.
Beneath my balcony are moored two ships, one of
which is old, and on that one a Bayonnese sailor
works and sings from morning until night.   Before
me, two cables' length off, there is another ship, quite
new and very lovely, which is about to leave for the
Indies.   Beyond this vessel, I see the old dismantled
tower, the group of houses called " el otro Pasaje,"
and the triple ridge of a mountain.   All round the
bay there is a great semicircle of hills, the undulations of which lose themselves on the horizon, and
which are dominated by the bare heights of Mount
Arun.

The bay is enlivened by the boats of the bateleras,
which are constantly coming and going, hailing
each other from one side of the water to the other
with cries like the crowing of a cock.   The weather
is magnificent, with the most lovely sunshine
imaginable.   I hear my sailor lilting, children
laughing, boatwomen calling each other, washer-
women slapping their linen against the stones in the
manner of the country, ox-waggons creaking in the
ravines, goats bleating among the hills, hammers
ringing in the dockyard, cables unwinding on
capstans, the wind blowing, the sea rising.   All
these sounds are music, for they are filled with joy.

When I lean over my balcony I see at my feet a narrow terrace with growing grass, a black flight of stairs descending to the sea, the steps of which are scaled by the rising tide, an old anchor buried in the mud, and a group of fisherfolk, men and women, standing in the water up to their knees, drawing their nets from the water and singing.

Finally, if I must tell you of everything, on the terrace and the stairs beneath my eyes there are some constellations of crabs, executing with slow solemnity all those mysterious dances dreamt of by Plato.

The sky has all the shades of blue from turquoise to sapphire, and the bay all the shades of green from emerald to chrysoprase.

Every grace has been bestowed upon this bay. When I look at the horizon which incloses it, it is a lake ; when I look at the rising tide, it is the sea.

What do you think of it ?   And, by the way—I have been thinking of it myself, and you remind me of it in your letter—for three weeks during which I have been travelling I have been unfaithful to my fancy of sending you the view from my window.   I shall repair this remissness at once.   At Bordeaux, my window overlooked a big wall ; at Bayonne, a street planted with trees ; at San Sebastian, an old woman killing fleas. Now, are you satisfied? I return with all haste to Pasajes.

The house in which I am living is one of the most dismal overlooking the street, and at the same time one of the brightest overlooking the bay. Above the roof, among the rocks, I see stairways clambering through patches of verdure up to the old white church, which looks like one heifer the more shaking the bell round its neck among the mountains. For, in the churches of Guipuzcoa, one sees the bell hanging uncovered at the edge of the roof beneath a sort of arcade resembling a collar.

The house has two floors and two entrances. It is strange and striking even among all the others, and carries to the highest pitch that two-fold character of the houses of Pasajes which is so original. It is the monumental patched with the rustic. It is a cottage mixed with and soldered into a palace.

The first entrance is a pillared doorway of the time of Philip II., sculptured by the divine artists of the Renaissance, mutilated by time and children playing, eaten away by the rain, the moon, and the sea wind. You know that fretted sandstone makes admirable ruins. This portal is of a beautiful chamois colour. The scutcheon remains, but the years have effaced the emblazonment.

You push open the little door on the right of the

portal, and find a staircase of beams and planks—
beams and planks black as coal, rudely cut, scarcely
shapen. At the top of the staircase, the timeworn
steps of which present wide gaps, the heavy door
of a fortress, in the middle of which a narrow grilled
wicket opens, grates upon its massive iron hinges
and introduces you into the house.

The antechamber is a whitewashed corridor,
tapestried with huge spiders' webs—for I do not
wish to conceal anything from you—and lighted
by a window looking into the street. Facing this
window, the escarpment of the mountain rears its
gigantic wall as far as the eye can reach.

The corridor, which extends to the staircase
of the second floor, has two doors opening off it.
That on the right leads to the kitchen, in entering
which one ascends two steps of massive wood; that
on the left opens into a large hall flanked at the
corners by four small rooms, which itself composes,
with its four cabinets and the kitchen, the first floor
of the house. Two of these cabinets are dark, and
have no other opening but the door into the hall.
They are slept in, however. The other two rooms,
like the hall, are on a level with the balcony, with
which they communicate by window-doors painted
green, and fitted with little panes which have
shutters. Each room has one of these windows.

P

The large hall has two of them, with a pretty case-
ment, almost square, opening between.

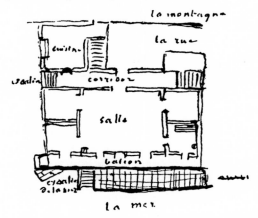

The interiors are whitewashed, like the frontage
on the lake.   The floors, blackened and decayed like
the staircase, resemble the wooden flooring of a
rustic bridge.   The doors are like the floors.   A
round table, some chests, and a few straw chairs—
this is the furniture of the large hall.   A coat-of-
arms, not very heraldic, however, is rudely painted
above the middle door.   There are no fire-places;
the climate dispenses with them.   The walls are of
stone and of the thickness of a donjon.

I occupy the room on the balcony at the left-
hand corner of the hall.   The other cabinets are

the cells of various inhabitants of the house, of whom I will tell you presently.

The second floor is like the first. A bedroom occupies the place of the kitchen. The balcony of the second floor shades that of the first, and is itself protected by the broad edge of the roof, which is embellished by the turning and carving of the rafters. The balconies are paved with squares of red brick, and are painted green.

But it would seem that all this must one day crumble away. There are crevices in the walls which let one see the landscape. Between the bricks of the upper balcony one can see the lower balcony, and the floors of the rooms bend beneath one's feet.

The staircase leading from the first to the second floor is most curious.

"Tout l'escalier branlait du haut jusques en bas,"

says Regnier of some house or other. This staircase trembles, and is at the same time massive. It is made of great beams, planks, and nails, rudely fashioned and fitted together three hundred years ago, which, although trembling with age, have still something robust and formidable about them. It is threatening in a double sense. There is no skylight, only an oblique ray of light from above. The steps, which have been rudely repaired by means of planks placed across and thrown as if at random, have the appearance of wolf-traps.   It is at once decrepit and imposing. Immense spiders come and go amid the gloomy medley. An oaken door four inches in thickness, garnished with massive, but rust-eaten, iron bars, closes the staircase and isolates the second floor from the first at will. Ever the fortress within the cottage.

What do you think of all this? It is gloomy, repulsive, terrible, you think? Why, no; it is charming.

First of all, nothing could be more full of surprises. This is a house such as could be seen nowhere else. Just as you are thinking yourself in a hovel, some piece of sculpture, some fresco, some useless but exquisite ornament, reminds you that you are in a palace. You go into raptures over some such luxurious and graceful detail, when the harsh cry of a bolt tells you that you are living in a prison. You go to the window ; there is the balcony, there is the lake, and you are in one of the châlets of Zug or Lucerne.

And then this mysterious house is penetrated and filled by a dazzling sunlight. Its distribution is pleasant, convenient, and original. The salt air from the sea purifies it, and the pure southern sun dries, warms, and vivifies it. Everything becomes joyous in this joyous light.

Everywhere else dust is filth; here it is mere age. The dust of yesterday is hateful; that of three centuries is venerable. And then, you must know, in this country of fishers and huntsmen the spider who hunts and spreads her net possesses rights of citizenship. She is in her own domain. In a word, I accept the house just as it is.

I have had my room swept, however, and have dismissed the spiders who occupied it before me.

What completes the strange appearance of the house is the circumstance that I have not seen any man in it. It is occupied by four women and a child: the mistress of the house, her two daughters, her servant Iñacia, a lovely barefooted Basque girl, and her grandson, a pretty little fellow of eighteen months.

Madame Basquetz, the landlady, is an excellent woman, with intelligent eyes, handsome, kindly, and cheerful, a little French in her origin, entirely French in heart, and speaking French exceedingly well. Her two daughters speak only Spanish and Basque.

The elder daughter is a sickly young woman, sweet and pensive. The younger, like all Spanish girls, is called Pepa. She is twenty, and has a slender form, a lithe figure, a well-shaped hand, a small foot—a rare thing in Guipuzcoa—big, black eyes, and magnificent hair.   In the evening she leans her elbows upon the balcony in an attitude of sadness, and if her mother calls her she turns round with cheerful vivacity.   She is at the age when the carelessness of the girl begins to disappear, insensibly veiled beneath the melancholy of the woman.

The child, which creeps about the staircase from one floor to the other, comes and goes all day, laughing, filling the house and warming it with its innocence, grace, and sweetness.   A child in a house is like the cheerful heat of a stove.

As he sleeps near my room, I can hear him cooing softly in the evening while he is being sung to sleep by the four women.

I have told you that the house has another entrance.   This is by a flight of steps without any balustrade, made of great blocks of freestone, which runs up to the kitchen from the street, and thence goes off to join other flights of stone steps which ascend the mountain through the foliage.

The house is built over the street, like the Château of Chenonceaux over the Cher, and the street runs beneath by means of an arch like that of a bridge, long, narrow, vaulted, and dark, lighted at night by a lantern.   In a niche, beside an air-hole covered by a grille of the fifteenth century, burns a holy candle dedicated by the following inscription to the welfare of poor mariners who pass :

VNA LIMOSNA PARA

ALVMBRAR AL S^{TO.} C^{TO.}

D. BVEN BIAJE.

AÑO 1756.

"An alms for the lighting of the Holy Christ of Safe Journeys.—1756."

You now know the house, and you know the inmates. I have told you where my room is, but I have not told you what it is.

Picture to yourself four white walls, two straw-bottomed chairs, a washhand-basin on a tripod stand, a child's hat ornamented with feathers and glass-trinkets hanging from a nail, a shelf with some pots of pomade and three odd volumes of Jean-Jacques Rousseau, a bed with an old-fashioned baldachin of very pretty chintz, with two mattresses as hard as marble, and the prettiest painted head imaginable, a slanting mirror, exquisitely framed, hanging on the wall, and a cellar-like door which does not shut. This is my room. Add to it the window-door of which I have already told you, and a table which is on the balcony. From my bed I can see the sea and the mountains.

In spite of the gloomy prophecies of the civilized people of San Sebastian, you see that I have succeeded in getting a lodging among the savages of Pasajes.

Have I managed to live? I will allow you to judge.

About ten o'clock, the graceful Pepa, who awakes with the dawn, comes and spreads a white napkin over my table with the green cover, which never leaves the balcony. She then brings me oysters taken that very morning from the rocks in the bay, two lamb cutlets, a fried loubine, which is a delicious fish, fried eggs sugared, a chocolate pudding, some pears and peaches, a cup of very good coffee, and a glass of Malaga. I drink cider besides, being unable to accustom myself to the goat-skin wine. This is my breakfast.

Here is my dinner, which is served about seven in the evening, when I have returned from my excursions on the bay or along the coast. An excellent soup, puchero with bacon and chickpeas, but without saffron and allspice, some fillets of haddock fried in oil, a roast chicken, a salad of watercress gathered in the brook which fills the wash-pool, petits pois with hard-boiled eggs, a cake of maize and milk flavoured with essence of orange, nectarines, strawberries, and a glass of Malaga.

While Pepita is serving me, as she comes and goes round about me, bringing those things which solicit my mountaineer's appetite, the sun goes down, the moon rises, a fishing-boat leaves the bay, all the sights of the ocean and the mountains deploy before me, wedded with all the sights of the sky. I talk Basque and Spanish to Pepita. I invent and tell her tales of sorcerers of the most incredible nature, in which I feign to believe, and she laughs and tries to dissuade me; I hear the boatwomen singing in the distance, and I do not observe that the porcelain is of delf and the silver of pewter.

All this costs me five francs a day.

At San Sebastian they probably think I have been starved to death or devoured by the savages.

Nothing, moreover, could have been easier than my settlement here. I asked Manuela if she knew any house in Pasajes where I could stay for a few days. At first the idea rather surprised Manuela, but I persisted in it and she conducted me where I now am. The worthy Madame Basquetz received me with a smile, and I gave her the price she asked. As you see, it was exceedingly simple.

The bay of Pasajes, sheltered on every side and from every wind, would make a magnificent port.

Napoleon thought so, and, as he was a good engineer, he had sketched out a plan of the necessary works.   The basin measures several leagues round, and the neck of water leading to the sea is so narrow that only one vessel can pass through at a time. This neck, which is compressed between two high ridges of rocks, is itself divided into three small basins separated by narrow straits easy to fortify and defend.

In the sixteenth century the Company of Caracas, afterwards amalgamated with that of the Philippines, had its entrepôt and stores at Pasajes.   For the protection of the bay it had the fine tower constructed which is to-day its ornament.   This tower was dismantled a few years ago by the Carlists.

The Carlists, it may here be said, have left melancholy traces at Pasajes.   They demolished and burned several houses.   That in which I am living was only pillaged.   " A great mercy ! " said my landlady to me, clasping her hands.

The English, too, have occupied Pasajes at various times, and that quite recently, moreover.

On the elevated points of the coast they had built several forts, now destroyed.   These have been burned by the inhabitants.   And, if all must be told, these conflagrations were bonfires.   The English are not loved in Guipuzcoa.   The landing of the

Duke of Wellington with the Portuguese in 1813 is a gloomy memory for the Basques. Like their own mountains, the hearts of these mountaineers have echoes long and deep, and the bombardment of San Sebastian resounds within them still.

The English have left no vestiges in the town of Pasajes other than the two syllables OLD.COLD.(?) which formed part of some shopkeeper's sign, and which are still visible beside a portrait of Philip II. upon the wall of the house I am lodging in.

The port of Pasajes is now almost deserted. It is frequented only by fishing-boats. Bayonnese ship-owners have built at Pasajes, under Spanish names lent them in Bilbao or Santander, vessels destined for the Spanish trade, which would not enjoy certain privileges if they were not built in Spain. Pasajes serves for the purpose. And hence the establish-ment, I believe in 1842, of the great rope-walk in the dockyard which I had so much disdained. This rope-walk is a long narrow stretch, and is really a fine rope-walk. I finished by visiting it. I am becoming civilized, you see.

The port is no longer militarily protected except by a little castillo situated on a rock half-way up the hill, at the entrance to the second articulation of the gorge. This fortress is held by innumerable fleas and a few soldiers.

Pasajes, moreover, could protect herself quite un-
aided.   She has been admirably fortified by nature.
The entrance of the port is dangerous.   Some
vessel is lost in it every year.   Last year, a ship
laden with planks worth some fifty thousand francs,
while seeking refuge in it during stormy weather,
was taken broadside on just as she was about to
enter the second basin of the channel, and thrown
by a wave upon the rock more than sixty feet above
the sea.   She did not fall again.   The sharp corners
of the rock seized her and buried themselves in her
at every point.   The spot where this big vessel lay
pinned down, is to-day marked by an iron cross
which trembles in the wind.

Would you now care to know the life that I am
leading here? As I do not close my window, and as
my door does not close, I am awakened as soon as
it is dawn by the brilliance of the sunshine and the
prattle of the child.   I do not hear the crow of the
cock, but I hear the song of the bateleras, and that
amounts to the same thing.   If the tide is rising, I
can see them from my balcony as I rise, hurrying
towards the other side of the bay.
There are always two in each boat, partly on
account of the heaviness of the boat. but much

more on account of the jealousy of husbands and
lovers. Thus couples are formed, each couple
having its name : La Catalana and her mother,
Maria Juana and Maria Andres, Pepa and Pepita,
the compañeras and the evaristas. The evaristas
are very pretty. The officers of the garrison of
San Sebastian like being rowed about by them ;
but they are sensible and really do row the officers
about. They always wear a bouquet on their glazed
hats, and when they bend over the oar, their short
skirt of black cloth with big pleats allows a well-
made leg and a well-shod foot to be seen. Those
who have stockings are few ; they are the aristocracy of boatwomen.

Pepa and Pepita, the two sisters, are even prettier
than the evaristas.

Nothing could be so vivid and pure as this bay
in the morning. I hear the bells of three churches
ringing behind me ; the sun shows up the furrows
of the old tower. Each vessel makes her track in
the bay, and seems to trail behind her a long silver
fir-tree with all its branches.

Before breakfast I take a walk in the village, or,
if you like, the town, for I do not know how to
describe this unique place. I am always discover-
ing something which I did not see the evening before. Now it is the sheds constructed in the rocks

which pierce the street and cut their way between
the houses ; the sheds contain the stock of wood,
stems of trees bristling like chestnuts, fragments of
boats, and the remains of ships. Now it is a woman
spinning before her door ; the thread leaves her
hand and ascends to the roof of the house, whence
it falls again, bearing at its extremity the spindle
which hangs before the spinster. Now it is the
oriental sun-blinds at the Gothic windows, and the
fresh faces behind the close lattice-work of black
wood. Now it is the pretty little girls with bare
legs, already bronzed by the climate, dancing and
singing :

> " Gentil muchacha,
> Toma la derecha.
> Hombre de nada,
> Toma la izquierda,"

which I should like to translate, according to the
spirit rather than the letter, in this fashion :

> " Fille adroite,
> Prends la droite.
> Homme gauche,
> Prends la gauche."

At Pasajes, one works, dances, and sings. Some
work, many dance, all sing.

In Pasajes, as in all primitive and rustic places,
there are only young girls and old women ; in other

words, only flowers and—but, in faith, you must
look for the other word in Ronsard. Strictly
speaking, woman, that magnificent rose which
blooms from twenty-five to forty, is a rare and
exquisite product of extreme, of refined civilization,
and exists only in the towns. Cultivation is re-
quisite to make woman; what is wanted is that
horticulture, if you will permit me the expression,
which we call the social spirit.

Where the social spirit does not exist, you will
not have woman. You will have Agnès, you will
have Gertrude, but you will not have Elmire.

At Pasajes one always sees girls washing clothes
and linen drying. The girls wash the clothes in
the streams; the linen dries on the balconies.

These balconies are the most interesting things
imaginable to look at and study. You cannot
think of all there is on a Pasajes balcony besides
the linen drying in the open air.

Even the balustrade, which is nearly always old
—in other words, twisted or carved—is worth the
trouble of examination. Then, from the ceiling of
the balcony—for every balcony has a ceiling formed
by the upper balcony or the eaves of the roof—
from this ceiling, I say, dangle fishing-lines, weels,
nets, coils of rope, sponges, a parrot in a wooden
cage, boxes full of red carnations with heads of

antlers interwoven beneath—little aerial gardens
that make you think of Semiramis. On the
wall, between the windows, hang bunches of immortelles bound into crosses, tattered garments, old
embroidered waistcoats, dish-clouts and dusters ;
then various fantastic things of which one cannot guess the use, and which are there by way of
ornament—four laths fixed together in a square,
an iron wire in a hoop, and a broken Basque
tambourine. Some sketches drawn in charcoal on
the white wall, some buckets with bright iron
hoops for drawing water, and a young girl laughing,
with her elbows leaning on the balustrade, complete
the furnishings of the balcony.

In old Pasajes, on the other side of the bay, I
saw a house of the fifteenth century, the balcony of
which, swarming and encumbered with more articles
than a Normandy farm-yard, is bounded by the
severe profiles of two knights carved upon two
great oak planks.

On the day of my arrival, as if to celebrate my
welcome, an old petticoat, composed of several rags
of every colour sewn together, was floating from
one of these balconies like a banner. This brilliant
piece of motley swelled itself out in the wind with
inexpressible pride and pomp. I have never seen a
harlequin's cloak more gorgeous.

At noonday the sun casts broad bands of horizontal shadow beneath all the roofs and balconies, setting off the whiteness of the façades, and making the town, when it is seen from a distance standing out against the dark, green background of the mountains, seem to live a life which is extraordinary in its effulgence.

The Plaza is especially brilliant. For Pasajes has a square, which, like all Spanish squares, is called the "Plaza de la Constitucion." In spite of this parliamentary and pluvious title, the Plaza of Pasajes shines and sparkles with admirable spirit. The Plaza is nothing but a prolongation of the street, widened and opening on the sea. Several of the tall houses surrounding it are perched upon colossal arcades. The central house bears upon its front the arms of the town in colours. The whole of the ground-floor is occupied by shops.

On certain Sundays the town treats itself to a bull-fight, and on these occasions the Plaza does duty as an amphitheatre, as is indicated by the structures of wooden beams fixed into the roadway along the parapet. Whether the Plaza be tauromachic or constitutional, however, nothing, I repeat, could be more gay, quaint, and pleasant to the eye.

The superabundant life which animates Pasajes is concentrated and reaches a paroxysm in the

Q

Plaza. The bateleras congregate at one side, the majos and sailors at the other. Children clamber and crawl, march and stagger, shout and play, all over the roadway. The painted frontages display all the colours of a parrot's plumage, the brightest of yellows, the freshest of greens, the ruddiest of reds. The shops and dwellings are caverns full of magical lights and shadows, in which, among all the glitterings and reflections, one dimly perceives all sorts of fantastic furniture, chests such as one sees only in Spain, mirrors such as one sees only at Pasajes.

Good, honest, genial faces beam in every doorway.

I told you just now of old Pasajes, which is also called "el otro Pasaje." There are, in fact, two Pasajes, one old and one new. The new Pasajes is three hundred years old. It is in it that I am staying.

The other morning I had a fancy to cross the water and see old Pasajes. It is a sort of southern Bacharach.

There, as at the Bacharach on the Rhine, "the stranger is strange," and pale-faced children and haggard old women stare at you in wonder as you pass.

One woman called out to me as I stopped before her house : " Hijo, dibuja eso. Viejas cosas, hermosas cosas." (" Draw this, my son. Old things, beautiful things.") The house was, indeed, a magnificent wreck of the thirteenth century, as dilapidated and crumbling as one could find.

The street of old Pasajes is a true Arab street, with whitened houses, massive and jolted, and pierced with but a few holes. Were it not for the roofs, one might think oneself in Tetuan. This street, which has ivy running from one end to the other, is paved with flagstones, great stony scales undulating like the back of a serpent.

The church spoils the composition. It is modern, and was rebuilt last century. I got them to open it to me for half a peseta. An inscription over the organ gives the date, which, however, is only too clearly written in the architecture :

MANVEL	MARTIN
CARRERA	ME HIZO
AÑO	1774.

This church is sullen, and old Pasajes is dull. Yet nothing could be less in keeping. The sullenness is the dulness of things that are paltry. And old Pasajes possesses grandeur.

You see, my friend, that my morning excursion is not without incident. Having made it, I return,

breakfast, and then go off by the roads among the
rocks.   I give my morning to the town, and my
day to the mountains.

I climb the mountain by perpendicular flights of
stairs with very high and narrow steps solidly built
into the slope, and mingling with the rude vegetation of the rock.   On reaching the top of one flight,
one finds another.   In this way they are joined together end to end, and tower towards the heavens
like those terrible ladders which one sees tottering
in the impossible and mysterious architecture of
Piranesi.   The ladders of Piranesi, however, thrust
themselves into the infinite, while the stairways of
Pasajes have an end.

On reaching the top of these stairways I usually
find a cornice, a goat-path or sort of gutter formed
by the rain and the torrents which makes a border
along the mountain.   I make my way along this at
the risk of falling on the roofs of the village, of falling down a chimney into some flesh-pot and adding
myself as yet another ingredient to some olla
podrida.

The tops of mountains are to us a sort of unknown world.   There refugees of nature living

apart, grow, and palpitate, and blossom. There the fierce and the charming, the wild and the peaceful, are joined together in a kind of mysterious hymen. Man is far away, and nature is tranquil. A sort of confidence, unknown on the plains where the sound of human footsteps is heard, modifies and calms the instinct of the animals. It is no longer the fearful, uneasy life of the fields. The butterfly does not flee ; the grasshopper lets itself be taken ; the lizard, which is to the stones what the birds are to the leaves, comes from its hole and looks at you as you pass. There is no other sound but the wind, no other movement but that of the grass beneath and the clouds overhead. Upon the mountain the soul is lifted up and the heart is purified. Thought has its share in the profound peace. One feels close to one the open eye of Jehovah.

The mountains of Pasajes have for me two special attractions. The first is that they reach down to the sea, which every moment turns their valleys into gulfs and their ridges into promontories. The second is that they are of sandstone.

Sandstone is somewhat despised by geologists, who, I believe, classify it among the parasites of the mineral kingdom. For myself, I set great store by sandstone.

You know, my friend, that, to thoughtful minds,

all the parts of nature—even those which, at first sight, are the most incongruous—are united to each other by innumerable secret sympathies, the invisible threads of creation which the contemplator perceives, which make of the great whole an inextricable network, living only one life, nourished by but one sap, one in the midst of diversity, and which are, so to speak, the very roots of being.   To me, therefore, there is a harmony between the oak and the granite, which awaken, the one in the vegetable kingdom, the other in the mineral sphere, the same ideas as the lion and the eagle among the animals—of power, grandeur, strength, and excellence.

There is a harmony, too, still more subtle, but to me visible enough, between the elm and the sandstone.

Sandstone is the most interesting and the most strangely formed of stones.   It is among the rocks what the elm is among the trees.   There is no appearance which it does not take, no caprice which it does not have, no dream which it does not realize. It has every shape ; it makes every grimace.   It seems to be animated by a multiple soul.   Forgive me the expression with regard to such a thing.

In the great drama of the landscape, sandstone plays a fantastic part.   Sometimes it is grand and severe. sometimes buffoonlike : it bends like a wrestler, it rolls itself up like a clown ; it may be a sponge, a pudding, a tent, a cottage, the stump of a tree ; it appears on the ground in little yellow, flaky lumps among the grass in some field, and mimics a flock of sheep lying asleep ; it has faces that laugh, eyes that look, jaws that seem to bite and munch the ferns ; it seizes the brambles like a giant's fist suddenly issuing from the earth. Antiquity, which loved perfeƈt allegories, ought to have made the statue of Proteus of sandstone.

A field strewn with elms is never wearisome, a mountain of sandstone is always full of surprises and of interest. Whenever inanimate nature seems to live, she moves us with a strange emotion.

It is in the evening especially, at the disquieting hour of twilight, that this portion of creation begins to take shape as it turns phantom. It is a gloomy, mysterious transfiguration.

Have you observed at nightfall on our highways round about Paris the monstrous, supernatural profiles of all the elms which the career of the coach brings successively before you ? Some gape ; others twist themselves towards the sky, and open mouths that utter fearful roars. Some there are that laugh a fierce and hideous laugh, such as becomes the darkness ; the wind sways them ; they bend backwards with the contortions of the damned. or lean

over towards each other to whisper in their great
leafy ears words of which you hear I know not
what fantastic syllables as you pass.   Some there
are with huge eyebrows, ridiculous noses, dishevelled
hair, enormous wigs.   This takes nothing from the
mournfulness and dread of their fantastic reality.
They are caricatures, but spectres.   Some are
grotesque ; all are terrible.   The dreamer imagines
that he sees, marshalled in menacing, shapeless files
along the roadside, and bending over him as he
passes, the unknown but possible phantoms of the
night.

One is tempted to ask whether these are not the
mysterious beings who have darkness for their
element, and who are composed of shadow as the
crocodile is composed of stone, and the humming-
bird of air and sunshine.

All thinkers are dreamers ; reverie is thought in
its fluid, undetermined state.   There is no great
mind that has not been possessed, charmed,
frightened, or, at least, astonished, by the visions
evoked by nature.   Some have spoken of them,
and, as it were, preserved within their works, to live
for ever the immortal life of their style and thought,
those wonderful, fugitive shapes, those nameless
things of which they had caught a glimpse " in the
obscurity of the night."   *Visa sub obscurum noctis.*

Cicero calls them "imagines," Cassius "spectra,"
Quintilian "figuræ," Lucretius "effigies," Virgil
"simulacra," Charlemagne "masca." [1] In Shake-
speare, Hamlet speaks of them to Horatio. They
preoccupied Gassendi, and Lagrange dreamt of
them after translating Lucretius and meditating
upon Gassendi.

I am thinking aloud to you, my friend. One
thought leads me on to another. I let myself go.
You are good, and sympathetic, and indulgent. You
are accustomed to my pace, and you let me think
with a loose rein. But here I am rather far from
the sandstone, at least in appearance. I must return
to it.

The aspects presented by sandstone, those curious
copies of a thousand things which it makes, possess
this peculiarity : the light of day does not dissipate
them and cause them to vanish. Here at Pasajes,
the mountain, cut and ground away by the rain, the
sea, and the wind, is peopled by the sandstone with
a host of stony inhabitants, mute, motionless,
eternal, almost terrifying. Seated with outstretched
arms on the summit of an inaccessible rock at the
entrance of the bay, is a hooded hermit, who,
according as the sky is clear or stormy, seems to be

[1] " Stryga vel masca."

blessing the sea or warning the mariners. On a desert plateau, close to heaven, among the clouds, are dwarfs with beaks like birds, monsters with human shapes, but with two heads, of which one laughs and the other weeps—there, where there is nothing to make one laugh and nothing to make one weep. There are the members of a giant, *disjecti membra gigantis;* here the knee, there the trunk and omoplate, and there, further off, the head. There is a big-paunched idol with the muzzle of an ox, necklets about its neck, and two pairs of short, fat arms, behind which some great bramble-bushes wave like fly-flaps. Crouching on the top of a high hill is a gigantic toad, marbled over by the lichens with yellow and livid spots, which opens a horrible mouth and seems to breathe tempest over the ocean.

IX.

ROUND ABOUT PASAJES.

WALKS IN THE MOUNTAINS—WRITTEN WHILE WALKING.

I.

3rd August, three in the afternoon.

HILE cruising in the roadstead I observed a kind of ruin at the top of a mountain. Its profile is not at all that of an old ruin. The demolition is modern, probably recent. The English during their stay in Pasajes, and the Carlists and Cristinos during the last war, constructed forts on the heights. It is no doubt one of these forts which has since been thrown down. I am going off to inspect it.

I am climbing the mountain. There is, apparently, a path, but I do not know it. I am going through the furze at random. The ascent is long, almost perpendicular, and very trying. I am sitting down among the sandstone half-way up.

The horizon rises and the sea appears down below. The sound of the bells on the goats grazing down in the precipice reaches my ear. Near my feet I see a beautiful green buprestid covered with golden spots.

I have resumed my climb. The summit is curved and rounded, and it is becoming easier.

I have reached the ruin. A stone chimney, black with smoke, rises above the walls.

An immense pile of demolished cut stones. A ditch full of rubbish. I have climbed over the stones.—They are mixed with tiles and broken bricks.—I am on the plateau.

A road for wheeling gun-carriages, laid with flagstones, quite new—it might have been made yesterday.

The grass, however, grows in the spaces between the flags.

I enter the first ruin.—A square room built of stone.—A great thick wall.—Three loopholes covering the channel house. In the middle, an enormous fire-place of stone and brick—that of which I have seen the stalk—all demolished, very strange in appearance.—Several brick compartments, cubical and circular ; probably an oven for heating the cannon-balls. The interior is nothing but a pile of rubbish. No human sound reaches here. One

hears but the wind and the sea.   It is beginning to
rain.   The stones slip beneath my feet.   I have
come out with difficulty.

A second square room about ten feet in every
direction ; it is like the first.   Three loopholes
covering the village.   A window looking on the
sea.   A beam in an embrasure ; it is rotten ; I have
taken a piece of it.   Two other small rooms without windows ; one all blackened with smoke.   I
have made a plan of it, with my elbows leaning on
the top of the wall.   There is burnt wood mixed
with the débris.   The three rooms have no longer
any roof ; not even a vestige of one remains.

I have entered the second ruin.   It is a large
room, less encumbered with rubbish, with a small
fire-place at the end.   On one side, a smaller room ;
both are square.   Everything is torn down, destroyed,
broken in pieces.   Hideous insects flee beneath the
stones which I raise with the end of my stick.   The
rain is increasing.   A mist covers the sea and the
plain.   I am about to redescend.

I resolve to climb the remainder of the ruin.
There is a heap of stones which must have been
a third part of the house.   Behind this heap there
is a little tilled field twelve feet square, covered
with fragments of burnt wood.   The ditch borders
the field and surrounds the three ruined buildings.

—It is raining hard. A sort of night is spreading. The mist is thickening more and more. Everything round me has disappeared. I no longer see anything but the ruins, the flagged road, and the plateau.—I shall not be able to recognize my way, and shall lose myself on the slopes.—With the help of God!

A magnificent butterfly hunted by the rain has just taken refuge on a stone before me. It is less afraid of me than of the storm. I redescend at random. It has become clearer. The rain has slackened, the day has returned.—I perceive the little roadstead.—It is swarming with four-oared fishing-boats gliding over the water. From the height at which I am, the roadstead full of boats resembles a puddle covered with water-spiders.

II.

4th August, half-past two, on the mountain.

A desolate scene.—Violent wind.—A little bay closely crushed between the capes of the channel. —The waves break angrily upon a rocky bank which half closes the bay and which the ebb-tide leaves uncovered. Beyond, the open sea is dark and troubled. The sky is leaden. The sunshine and the shadow wander over the water.

In the distance, a trincador from Fuenterrabia, her two sails in the wind, is struggling to enter the bay. She is heading for the channel. The surge tosses her violently from stem to stern ; every wave lifts her up and then hurls her perpendicularly into the liquid ravine, which swells and heaves her up anew. Just now a goatherd on the mountain said to me, " Iguraldia gaiztoa." [1]—There is the vessel ; she almost touches the breakers, which the sea covers with foam. The masts heel over, the sails flap. She is passing. She has passed.—A grasshopper is singing in the grass beside me.

Three o'clock, on the brow of the precipice.

Bare rocks like death's-heads. Heath. I have stuck my stick into the heath and am writing standing. Flowers everywhere, grasshoppers of a thousand colours, and the loveliest butterflies imaginable. Far away beneath me I hear the laughter of young girls whom I cannot see.

One of the rocks before me has a human profile. I have sketched it. The cheek seems to have been devoured ; so, too, do the eye and the ear, and one imagines one sees bared the interior of the mouth

[1] Basque for " bad weather."

of the Fallopian aqueduct.   In front of this rock
and above it, another block has the shape of a
bulldog.   It seems to be barking at the open sea.

Five o'clock.
I am upon a rocky point at the extremity of
a cape.   In climbing the slope I have gone round
the rock.   In order to clamber up, I placed my
hands and feet into those curious holes with which
the rocks of this coast are honeycombed, and which
resemble the prints of enormous soles.   In this way
I reached a sort of console with a back, which
projects over the abyss.   I am sitting upon it ; my
feet are dangling in space.

The sea, nothing but the sea !—Magnificent,
eternal spectacle ! It pales against some black
rocks below.   The horizon is misty, although the
sun is scorching me.   The wind is still high.—A
sea-gull sweeps majestically through the depths a
hundred fathoms beneath me.

The noise is continuous and heavy.   From time
to time one hears a sudden crash, a sort of abrupt
thud in the distance, as if of something falling.
Then there are sounds resembling a multitude of
human voices ; one might think one was listening
to the murmur of a crowd.

A silvery fringe, slender and brilliant, winds beneath the coast as far as the eye can reach.— Behind me, a great upright rock describes the form of an immense eagle stooping towards its nest, its two talons resting on the mountain.— Gloomy, superb sculpture of the ocean.

Six o'clock.

Here I am upon the very point of a high mountain, upon the loftiest summit I have reached during the day.   Here again I have had to scramble up on my hands and knees.

I discover an immense horizon. All the mountains as far as Roncevaux. The whole sea of Bilbao on the left, the whole sea of Bayonne on the right. I am writing this with my elbows upon a block shaped like a cock's crest, which forms the extreme edge of the mountain. On the left, someone has cut deep in the rock with a pick the three letters :

L. R. H.

and, on the right, the two letters :

V. H.

Round this rock there is a little triangular

plateau covered with dry heath, and surrounded by a sort of ditch which is very rugged. In a crevice, however, I perceive a pretty little piece of pink heather in flower. I have plucked it.

Seven o'clock.

Another castillo, much larger than that of yesterday. A thousand insects torment me. I am in the enceinte after having scaled the trench. A great square of stone walls surmounted by an earthen wall, still intact in places, and covered with grass. Four Basque herdsmen in bérets and red vests are sleeping in the shade of the trench. A big white dog is sleeping on the top of the wall.

The remains of rooms. In one of them the fragments of a dismantled fire-place are still visible. In the middle of the large enceinte, a smaller one, of which one corner has been burnt and blackened with smoke. Behind this small enceinte, a terrace reached by a staircase with four steps.

One of the herdsmen awoke and approached me. I said to him with a grave air, "Jaincoa berorrecrequin." [1] He went off astonished.—He has been rousing the others. I see them through the embrasures examining me with a singular air.

[1] "God be with you."

—Is it an uneasy air? Is it a menacing air? I do not know; perhaps it is both. I have no other weapon but my stick. The dog, too, has awakened and is growling.

A wonderful carpet of green turf, thick as fur, and strewn with myriads of Easter daisies and camomiles in flower, covers the whole ruin into the farthest recesses.

I am going to mount the terrace.

Here I am. I am sitting on the top of the dry brick wall. Behind me is the sea, before me a circus of mountains. On my left, on a distant summit which touches the clouds, I distinguish the demolished fort which I visited yesterday; on my right, more distant still, the Wellington fort and the old tower of the lighthouse beyond San Sebastian. In a hollow, the valley of Loyola; in another hollow, the valley of Hernani.

One of the herdsmen approached me once more. I gazed at him fixedly, and he fled crying : " Ahuatlacouata! Ahuatlacouata!"

I am about to redescend.

While descending.

A spectacle which reminds me of that which I saw yesterday. A little triangle of water set in an immense ring of mountains; in the water a few plant-lice. The water is the bay; the plant-lice are the vessels.

III.

5th August, noon.

While following the road which runs half-way up the hill, after having passed the castillo, its sentry-box and its sentry, I encountered a wash-pool.

This wash-pool is the most charming of caverns. An enormous rock, which forms one of the sharp corners of the mountain, and is prolonged to a considerable height above my head, here makes a sort of natural grotto. This grotto distils a spring the water of which falls abundantly, although drop by drop, from all the crevices of the vault. It is like a shower of pearls. The entrance of the grotto is carpeted with a vegetation so rich and thick that it is like an immense porch of verdure. All this vegetation is full of flowers. Amid the branches and the leaves a long blade of grass forms a sort of microscopic aqueduct, and serves as conduit to a tiny stream of water which travels along its whole length and falls from its extremity, rounding itself against the dark background of the grotto like a silver thread. A sheet of limpid water confined by a parapet fills the whole grotto. The uncemented stones allow the water to escape and run away among the pebbles.

The path passes at a little distance from the parapet, which is separated from it by a broad, fresh plot of water-cress. One sees the water through the leaves and hears the murmur of the spring beneath the grass. On turning round one perceives the bay of Pasajes, and, on the horizon, the open sea.

Three young girls, with their legs in the water up to the knee, were washing their linen in the wash-pool. They could not be said to be beating it, but striking it. Their method consisted in violently slapping the stone of the parapet with the linen, which they held in their hand. One was an old woman. The two others were young girls. They stopped for a few moments, looked at me, and then resumed their work.

After a silence of a few moments the old woman said to me in bad French: "You come from the mountain, Monsieur?" I answered her in indifferent Basque: "Baï, bidea nequesa."[1] The girls gave each other a sly look and began to laugh.

One was fair, the other dark. The fair one was

[1] "Yes, a difficult road."

the younger and prettier.   Her hair, which was
twisted into a single plait behind, in accordance
with the fashion of the country, assumed on the top
of her head a pale yellow tint like tresses of silk
which have been exposed to the air and of which
the colour has faded.   The young washerwoman,
moreover, was most graceful with her red petticoat
and blue corset, the two favourite colours of the
Basques.

I approached her, and began the conversation in
Spanish :

"What is your name?"

"Maria-Juana, at your service, caballero."

"How old are you?"

"Seventeen."

"You belong to this country?"

"Yes, Señor."

"Are you of the townsfolk?"

"No, Señor ; I am a batelera."

"A batelera!   And you are not at sea?"

"It is low tide; and then, you know, one has to
wash one's clothes."

Here the girl grew bolder and continued by herself :

"I was on the shore the other day, caballero,
when you arrived.   I saw you.   You first of all
engaged Pepa to take you over ; but you were with

Señor Leon and the Señor had already embarked, so, as Manuela La Catalana was his boatwoman, you went over with Manuela. Poor Pepa! But you gave her a peseta.—You remember, Maria Andres," said she, turning to her companion, "you remember, the Señor caballero chose Pepa first?"

"And why did I choose her?"

The girl looked at me with her big innocent eyes, and answered without hesitation:

"Because she was the prettiest."

She then began striking her linen again. The old woman, who had finished her work and was now going away, said as she passed near me:

"The muchacha is right, Señor."

As she said this she placed her basket on the ground and sat down at the edge of the path, fixing upon the two girls and myself her small gray eyes, pierced as with a gimlet amid her wrinkles.

"Would you like me," said I, "to help you put the basket on your head?"

"A thousand thanks, caballero! No one helped me yesterday, and no one will help me to-morrow. It is better that no one should help me to-day."

"What is the name of this herb in Spanish?" said I, pointing with the end of my stick to the water-cress.

"Verros, Señor."

" And in Basque ? "

She replied with a very long word which I do not remember sufficiently well to write.

I turned to the girls.

" Maria Juana," said I, " what is the name of your querido ? "

" I have none."

" And Maria Andres ? "

" Maria Andres has one."

The young girl said this with deliberation, without appearing surprised at the question or embarrassed by her answer.

" What is the name of the querido of Maria Andres ? "

" Oh ! He is a fisherman, a poor mozo. He is very jealous. See ! There he is on the bay ; you can see him from here in his boat."

Here the old woman interrupted :

" And a lucky thing that he doesn't see you ! He would be pleased to see Maria Andres talking and laughing with the Señor ! To speak to a Frenchman ! Sweet Jesus ! Better tattle with the four demons of east, west, north, and south ! "

A soldier passed. I saluted the young girls with my hand. They returned my salute with a smile, and I pursued my way.

IV.

6th August, three o'clock.

I heard a young cock crowing in the distance, and continued my walk. I reached this spot by an exceedingly rough road cut in the rock for the ox-waggons as far as a ravine here, which is strangely wild. The rocks which jut out of the heath on the steep slope of the mountain all resemble gigantic heads. There are death's-heads, Egyptian profiles, bearded satyrs laughing among the grass, melancholy knights with stern features. Every kind of face is here—even that of Odry, who sneers at one from beneath a wig of brambles.

To the right, through the break of two mountains, I perceive an arm of the sea, three villages, two ruins, one of which is a convent, a charming valley, and a chain of tall peaks covered with clouds.

The village of Leso, the nearest of the three villages, has a fine Gothic church of simple, heavy proportions. One might take it for a fortress. God himself dwells in the citadels of this country, where war is never extinguished at one side of the horizon without breaking out at another.

Half-past five.

Here the view is impressive in its magnificence.
The horizon is composed of two parts, sea and
mountain.   The coast extends away before me as
far as the eye can reach.   It has the angle and the
form of the immense scarp of an immense intrench-
ment covered over with heath.   A precipice, which
has the same angle, forms the counterscarp.

From the land side, the angry sea storms and
shatters this entrenchment, on the crest of which
nature has placed a parapet that might have been
built with a square.   Here and there the intrench-
ment crumbles away in great strips, which fall in
a single mass into the ocean.   Picture to yourself
slates eighty feet in length.   Where I am, the
assault is furious, the ravage terrible.   An enormous
breach has been formed.

I am sitting at the extreme point of a projecting
rock which overlooks this breach.   A forest of ferns
fills the top of the cavity.   A multitude of pigmy
oaks, which the sea wind mows down to the level
of the grass, are growing round about me.   I have
plucked a pretty red leaf.

Minute fishing-boats float on the floor of the gulf
beneath my feet.   Mackerel, loubines, and sardines
glisten in the sun at the bottom of the boats like

masses of stars.   The clouds cast brassy tints over
the sea.

Seven o'clock.

The sun is setting. I am coming down. A child
is singing on the mountain. I can see him passing
at the end of a hollow road, driving six cows before
him   The mountain's pinnacles cast their great
shadows upon a russet field, over which some sheep
are passing.

The sea is a faint bluish green.   It is becoming
darker.   The sky is overcast.

X.

LESO.

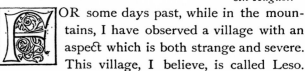OR some days past, while in the moun-
tains, I have observed a village with an
aspect which is both strange and severe.
This village, I believe, is called Leso.
It is situated at the extremity of the arm of the sea
by Pasajes, at a spot where it is left dry by the receding tide. Yesterday, as the sun was declining, I
took an ox-path which leads to it half-way up the hill.

This road is often very rough, being paved in
places with sandstone and marble flags, and broken
here and there by species of abrupt stairways
formed by the flags as they fall in pieces. For the
rest, it runs over the brow of two mountains, at
present covered with an immense cope of flowers
by the purple heather and the yellow broom.

I left behind me on my right a large farm-house
built of stone, with a lancet door; then, on my left,
an exceedingly wild gorge in which a torrent forces

its way in the strangest and fiercest fashion through a ruin which has once been a house. I crossed this torrent by a small one-arched bridge, and climbed the slope of the opposite mountain.

There were women singing. Children were bathing in puddles of water. Some French workmen from Bayonne, who are at present building a vessel on the bay, were passing in a ravine carrying, between the seven of them, a long piece of timber. I heard the bells of the oxen and the rustle of the trees. The landscape was magnificent in its brightness. The wind breathed life into everything, and everything was gilded over by the sunlight.

I then encountered a ruin on the right, a ruin on the left ; yet another ; then a group of three or four behind a clump of apple-trees, and I suddenly found myself a few steps from the village.

Here I am making a wrong use of the word ruin ; I ought to employ only the word wreck. These " ruins " are ordinarily composed of four walls without a roof and pierced with a few windows, most of them stopped up with a platform of bricks and transformed into loopholes, with marks of fire everywhere, and in the interior a cow or a couple of goats browsing peacefully upon the grass on the pavement or upon the ivy on the wall. These wrecks are the work of the last war.

As I entered the village a solemn-looking beggar, a centenarian at the very least, rose up in the angle of a wall and demanded alms of me with an impressive gesture of protection.   I gave this century a sou.

I entered a dismal street lined with big black houses, all of stone, some with balconies of massive iron of old workmanship, some others with enormous coats-of-arms carved in high relief in the middle of the façade.

Livid faces, which seemed to have been startled out of their sleep, made their appearance in the doorways as I passed.   In place of curtains, nearly all the windows were hung with great spiders' webs. I looked into the houses through these long narrow windows, and saw interiors like sepulchres.

In a moment there was a head at every window —a head even older than the window itself.   These gloomy, cadaverous heads, as if dazzled by a light too strong for them, were all nodding, bending over each other, and talking in whispers.   My coming had caused a commotion among this swarm of spectres.   I seemed to be in a village of phantoms and lamias, and all these shades seemed to be gazing with anger and affright upon a living being.

The street I had entered was tortuous, and was cut, as it were, into two floors.   The right side leaned its back against the mountain, while the left buried itself in the valley.

Many of the houses were of the fifteenth century, and had two great doors.   On the master keystone of the first door was carved, in the most delicate and elegant manner, the number of the house interwoven with some religious symbol, a cross, a dove, a branch of lily.   On the master keystone of the second door were cut the attributes of the owner's occupation, a wheel for a wheelwright, an axe for a woodcutter.   Everything in the village had a strange and dismal grandeur.   A sign was a bas-relief.

Here there was profound wretchedness, but it was not a vulgar wretchedness.   It was a wretchedness that dwelt in houses of freestone, a wretchedness that had balconies of figured iron like the Louvre, and arms on slabs of marble like the Escurial.   A colony of ragged noblemen in cottages of granite.

I did not see any young faces except those of some ragged children who followed me at a distance, and who, as soon as I turned round, hung back without running away, like young frightened wolves.

Every other house was a ruin, generally covered with ivy and encumbered with brambles, sometimes old, but more frequently recent.

By stepping over the fragments of a wall I reached a house which appeared to be uninhabited. The whole façade fronting what had been the street had the gloomy look of a dwelling without an inmate, with doors carefully shut, and windows with green shutters of Louis XIII. woodwork, which were everywhere closed. I climbed over a small fence in order to go round the house, and on the other side I found it open, but open in a fearful fashion, open from top to bottom by the complete destruction of one side, the wall of which lay in a single piece on the ground in a field of crushed maize. I walked over this wall as if it had been a pavement, and entered the house.

What desolation ! At a single glance I saw the four disembowelled stories. The staircase had been burnt. The well of the staircase was now merely a great hole into which all the rooms opened. The walls, red and horrible, bore the marks of flames everywhere.

As the staircase was wanting I was only able to go over the ground floor.

The house had been very large and very lofty. It was now upheld only by a few pillars and beams made slender by the fire. I could see it tremble as it hung above my head. From time to time a stone, a brick, or a strip of plaster, detached itself and fell at my feet, making an ominous sound of life in that dead house. On the third floor, a half-burnt plank remained hanging by a nail; the wind made it sway to and fro and creak dismally. In the rooms I again saw the solidly bolted shutters. There were some shreds of paper upon the walls. One room was painted rose colour. In the kitchen, at a point now inaccessible, I observed above the mantel-piece of the high fire-place a little ship drawn in charcoal by a child's hand.

One comes forth from a secular ruin with one's soul exalted and expanded. From a ruin of yesterday one comes forth with an oppressed heart. In the ancient ruin I think of the phantoms; in the recent ruin I think of the possessor. The phantoms are the less dismal.

This forbidding village is overlooked by a huge, tall, lugubrious church of granite.

Seen from a distance, it is not a church, but a block of stone. On approaching, one distinguishes some holes in the wall, and in the apsis three or four ogive windows of the fifteenth century. As it was doubtless found that these let too much light into this stone box, the ogives are walled up, only a narrow œil-de-bœuf having been left in the centre of each of them. The walls are of a reddish-brown, rough, and gnawed away by lichens.

S

The façade is a large square-cut wall, without window or bay, presenting to the eye no opening other than the doorway, which is mean and depressing, with two worn columns and a bare fronton. The façade is gashed from top to bottom by two long toothings of black stones. It is flanked on the right by a long, narrow tower which scarcely overtops the ridge of the roof.

Seven or eight hideous old women sat huddled solitarily at intervals round the church. I do not know whether the arrangement was the result of chance, but each of the old women appeared to be mated with a gargoyle which stretched out its neck at the edge of the roof above her head. From time to time the women raised their eyes to heaven and seemed to be exchanging tender glances with the gargoyles.

One of these savage-looking beggars turned upon me a look more fixed and more wild than the others. I went straight up to her, which seemed to astonish her. I then pointed to the church and said, " Guiltza," which signifies in Basque " the key." The living gargoyle, tamed by this magic word and by a half-peseta which I threw into her apron, rose up and said, " Baï," that is to say, " Yes." And she disappeared behind the church.

I remained alone before the porch. The other

old women had all risen and formed themselves into a group at one corner, from which they scrutinized me.

A few moments later the one who had gone reappeared with a key in her hand. She opened the church-door and I entered.

Was it the hour, the approaching night, the disposition of my mind, or even the emanations of the building? Never have I experienced a more icy sensation than that which I felt as I entered this church.

It had a lofty nave, as bare within as it was without, immense, cold, wretched, and gloomy, scarcely lighted by the dim, earthy glimmer of the dying day.

At the back, behind the tabernacle, on a stone estrade, an immense altar-piece stretched from the floor up to the vaulted roof, laden with statues and bas-reliefs, formerly gilded, now tarnished, marshalling upon a surface sixty feet in height the formidable saints of the Inquisition intermingled with the tragic and forbidding architecture of Philip II. This altar, seen dimly through the gloom, had about it something strangely pitiless and terrible.

The old woman had lit a candle-end, which flickered in a large lamp of embossed tin, fashioned in good taste, which hung before the altar. This

candle-end took nothing from the gloom and added
something to the horror.

The priest approaches the altar by a wide staircase inclosed by a balustrade of massive stone
admirably wrought in the sombre, elaborate manner
of the period of Charles V., which corresponds with
what in France we call the Francis I. style, and
with what is called in England Tudor architecture.

I ascended this staircase, and thence I examined
the church, which is truly majestic and funereal.

The old woman had gone into some dark corner,
I know not where.

The door had been left half-open, and in the
distance I could see the plain already covered with
gloom, the darkening sky, and the inlet, now a great
stretch of dry sand; in the foreground, a ruin which
was a cottage; in the middle distance, a ruin which
was the house of an Alcaide; in the background a
ruin which was a convent. Were not this ruined
cottage, this ruined house, this ruined convent, this
sky from which the light was fading, this shore
from which the sea was receding—were not all these
a perfect symbol ?   It seemed to me that, from the
recesses of this mysterious church, I beheld, not
a fortuitous piece of country, but the figure of
Spain.

Just then a strange sound reached my ear.   I

listened, and, being unable to believe my ears, listened again. For I heard something which astonished me, and showed how profound the revolution which is being accomplished in this country already is. The band of children who had followed me at a distance had seen the church-door opened, and had taken up their position in the porch, where they were now singing mass and vespers at the top of their voices, derisively and with long bursts of laughter, mimicking the priest at the altar and the chanters in the choir.

Shall I tell you, my friend, that at that moment I felt my soul filled with infinite pity for these poor children, who will be bereft of religion before they have been given civilization?

And then, from the children my pity went out to that poor, old nave of the Holy Office obliged to submit to that affront in silence. What a retribution, and what a reaction! Children now make sport of that which so long made men tremble! Oh! if stones have feelings, if the soul of institutions is communicated to the edifices which they build, with what sullen, unutterable anger must these austere and formidable walls have been moved at that moment to their very foundations! And to think that this took place beside the very cradle of St. Ignatius, a couple of leagues from the valley of

Loyola!—As the children sang the nave grew
darker, and the night which was filling the church
seemed to be a symbol of the night which had
overshadowed their faith.

Unfortunate church of St. Dominic! Thou
hadst thought to vanquish Satan and thou art van-
quished by Voltaire!

So everything in Spain is in ruins! The houses,
the dwelling of man, are devastated in the fields.
Religion, the dwelling of the soul, is devastated in
men's hearts.

It was night when I left the church. Every
window and door in the village was shut. Not a
light, not an inhabitant was to be seen. It was as
if these sepulchres had been closed again, and the
spectres had once more fallen asleep.

In one place, however, I distinguished a light. I
made my way towards it. The shutter of a window
on the ground floor was partly open, and in a low
room I saw an old woman crouching on the ground,
motionless, with her back against a freshly whitewashed wall. A lamp, which hung from a nail,
was burning above her head—the old Spanish lamp
the shape of which is such as may be seen in tombs.
I thought I was a witness of the ravings of Lady
Macbeth.

The reflection of this lamp enabled me to read

this inscription over the door of the opposite
house :

POSADA

LHABIT

I should have expected to find anything there
except an inn.

The moon was rising behind the Jaizquivel
Mountains as I left the village.   I easily found my
way again.   But in the state of mind in which my
visit to that strange place had left me, it was with
difficulty that I recognized the country which had
delighted me but a few hours before.   This landscape, so bright in the sunlight, was made mournful
by the light of the moon.   The horizon was dis-
tended by the solitude of night.

I neared Pasajes.   A few wayfarers began to
show themselves on the road.

I had my eyes fixed upon the ruin of a distant
castillo which stood out in the moonlight on the
crest of a rather lofty mountain at the further
extremity of a narrow, wild, and desert valley.

What had attracted my attention was a light
which had just made its appearance in this ruin at the
extremity of the gable.   About this light there was
something strange and inexplicable—first, the place
where it was shining, and then the manner in which

it was shining. It behaved like a lighthouse, flaring up and then going out, then flaring up again and suddenly throwing out a flash like a large star. What was this fire, and what did it mean?

As I reached the gorge where the bridge is, a begging woman, who usually stands at the entrance to the rope-walk, and to whom I give alms nearly every morning, was crossing the roadway to climb to her cabin half-way up the hill. As she perceived me she turned round, crossed herself, and, pointing the light out to me, said, "Los demonios." I passed on.

A little further on, at the beginning of the steep flagging which runs down to Pasajes, a man—a fisherman—was standing on a block of red marble, and, like the old woman, he was looking at the light. "Que es eso?" said I, approaching him. Without taking his eyes off the light, the man answered, "Contrabandistas."

As I was ascending my staircase, I met my landlady, the excellent Madame Basquetz.

"Ah! Monsieur," said she, "how late you are! And you have not supped? Why, where can you have been?"

"At Leso."

"What! You have been to Leso?"

'Yes. Madame."

A moment afterwards she repeated, with a thoughtful air :

" To Leso ? "

" Why, yes," I rejoined.   " And you—have not you ever been to Leso ? "

" No, Monsieur."

" And why ? "

" Because no one in the country ever goes to Leso."

" But why does no one go ? "

" I don't know."

XI.

PAMPELUNA.

 AM in Pampeluna, and I cannot describe all that I feel. I had never seen this town, and yet I seemed to recognize every street, every house, every door. The whole of the Spain which I saw in my childhood appears before me here as on the day when I heard the first ox-cart pass. Thirty years of my life are effaced ; I become a child again—the little Frenchman, " el niño," " el chiquito francés," as I was called. A whole world that had been slumbering within me awoke, palpitated, and thronged through my memory. I had thought it almost obliterated, but now it is more vivid than ever.

This is indeed the true Spain. I see arcaded squares, pavements of flint mosaic, tilt-boats, houses with painted furbelows, which make my heart beat. It seems as if it were but yesterday. Yes, it was only yesterday that I passed beneath that covered gateway which leads to the little staircase ; it was only the other Sunday, on my way to the promenade with my young schoolfellows of the Seminario de los Nobles, that I bought some sort of pepper gimblettes (*rosquillas*) in that shop, from the pediment of which hang goat-skins for holding wine ; I played at ball along that high wall behind the old church. To me all this is unquestionable, real, distinct, palpable.

There are some skirtings of walls, coloured in extravagant marble, which delight my soul. I spent two delicious hours in commune with an old green shutter with small panels which opens in two pieces, in such a way as to form a window when half opened and a balcony when opened altogether. This shutter had been in a corner of my mind for thirty years without my having suspected it. " Why," said I to myself, " there is my old shutter ! "

How mysterious is the past ! And how true it is that we deposit ourselves in the objects which surround us ! We think them inanimate, but they live. They live the mysterious life which we have given them. At every phase of our life we strip off our entire being and leave it forgotten in some corner of the world. That whole combination of inexpressible things which has been ourselves remains there in the shadow, making but a single unity with

the objects upon which we have impressed ourselves
unawares. Some day, at length, we chance to see
those objects once more. They suddenly rise up
before us, and immediately, with the all-powerful-
ness of reality, our past is restored. It is like a
sudden flash of light. They recognize us, they are
recognized by us. They bring back to us, radiant
and intact, the store-house of our memories, and
render up to us an entrancing phantom of ourselves—of the child that played, the young man that
loved.

I left San Sebastian, then, yesterday.

Two kinds of roads are produced by mountains :
those that wind flat along the ground like vipers,
and those that snake along with sudden vertical
undulations like boas. You will allow me these
two comparisons, which serve to illustrate my
thought. The road from San Sebastian to Tolosa
is of the latter kind ; that from Tolosa to Pampeluna is of the former. In other words, the road
from San Sebastian to Tolosa rises and falls over
the crests of the hills, while the road from Tolosa
to Pampeluna follows the sinuosities of the valleys.
The one is charming, the other wild.

As I left San Sebastian I gave a last look at the
peninsula, at the sea whitening superbly over the
sand, at Mount Orgullo, at the three convents which

have been burnt at the gates of the town, one by the Cristinos and two by the Carlists.

Hernani has no public buildings—a church of a sort with a Pompadour portal, which, however, is tolerably ornate, and a paltry ayuntamiento. But Hernani has delightful surroundings, and a street which is worth a whole cathedral. The chief street of Hernani, which is lined throughout with projecting emblazonments, miniature balconies, and seigneurial doorways, and is closed by an old ruined postern at present surmounted, not by battlements, but by clumps of flowering nasturtium, is a magnificent book in which may be read, page by page, house by house, the architecture of four centuries.

In passing through the town I was sorry that there was nothing to indicate to the passer-by the house in which Juan de Urbieta was born, the Spanish captain to whom fell the honour of taking Francis I. prisoner on the day of Pavia. Urbieta did the deed like a gentleman, and Francis I. suffered it like a king. Spain owes Urbieta a marble slab in the chief street of Hernani.

These mountains, moreover, are full of illustrious names. Motrico is the birthplace of Charruca, who died at Trafalgar. Sebastian de Elcano, who went round the world in 1519 (observe the date), and Alonzo de Ercilla, who wrote an epic poem, were

born, the one at Guetaria, the other at Bermeo.
The valley of Loyola, in 1491, saw the birth of
Ignatius, who from being page turned saint, and
the bridge of Lozedo saw the landing of Charles V.,
on his way from Germany to St. Just,[1] who from
being Emperor turned monk.

Tolosa, which is the Iturissa of antiquity, has
more charm than Hernani, more life and more
ornateness, but less grandeur and solemnity.

In spite of the fine rain which had been falling
since morning, I saw the whole town.   A few old
houses, one built in the reign of Alfonso the Wise,
the astronomer-king ; a tolerably fine church, which
they have turned into a granary for forage ; the two
pretty rivers, the Oria and the Araja—this is all I
had for my pains.

On the front of a first floor in the principal street
there is an inscription on black marble which begins
with " SIC VISUM SUPERIS," and ends with " EL
EMPERADOR LE . . . CABALLERO."   I had begun to
copy it, but this unexampled act caused such a
crowd round about me in a few minutes that I gave
the inscription up.   At a time like this, when the

---

[1] In common with other French writers, the author falls
into the error of supposing " St. Just " to be the equivalent of
Yuste, the name of the monastery in Spain where Charles V.
ended his days.— *Translator.*

ayuntamientos are trembling like leaves, I am afraid of causing a revolution at Tolosa through inadvertence.

Hernani, through which I passed as a child, and which had remained in my memory, possesses the Spanish physiognomy much more than Tolosa. The fourteen diligences which leave Tolosa daily carry away every morning something of the old manners, the old ideas, the old customs—something, in short, of what goes to make old Spain.

And then, the people work at Tolosa. There is the Urbieta hat factory, a paper manufactory, a host of curriers' shops, of factories for making nails, horseshoes, wrought-iron pots, balcony railings of polished iron, sabres, and muskets. The whole mountain is full of forges. Now, if anything can change the face of Spain it is work.

Spain is essentially the nation of gentlemen, which for three centuries has lived by doing nothing at the expense of the Indies and America. Hence the emblazoned streets. In Spain they used to await the galleon as, in France, they vote the budget. Tolosa, with her activity, her industry, her mills, her torrents, her shadows, her anvils, and her din, resembles a pretty French town. It would seem that she must trouble her neighbour, Old Castile, with her rumbling, and that that province must often be tempted to turn round, half-asleep as she is, to beg her to be silent.

As soon as I had alighted at Tolosa I was surrounded at the door of the fonda by a swarm of women-servants with short petticoats and bare legs, active, bright, and some of them pretty, who took possession of my baggage. All of them endeavoured to say some words in French to me.

At three o'clock this morning, well before daybreak as you see, I installed myself in the coupé of the diligence "Coronilla de Aragon," and left Tolosa.

We traversed the street and the bridge, and entered upon the highway at a furious gallop in the blackness of the night, drawn by eight mules, urged, excited, lashed, spurred, goaded, and exasperated by three men.

One of these three men was a child, but he alone was the equal of the two others.

He seemed to be no more than eight or nine years old. This savage urchin, of whom I had caught a glimpse by the stable lantern before starting, with his Henri II. hat, his clown's blouse, and his leather gaiters, had an Arab profile, almond-

shaped eyes, and the most graceful bearing imaginable. As soon as he had mounted he became
transformed. I seemed to see a gnome who had
turned postillion. He was almost imperceptible on
his immense mule, and seemed to be screwed into
his saddle, brandishing with his tiny arm a monster
whip, every cut from which made the team bound
forward, and precipitated pell-mell, headlong into
the darkness, that whole enormous equipage, ringing, jolting, leaping, rolling over the roads and
bridges with the noise of an earthquake. He was
the fly on the coach, but how terrible a fly !

Picture to yourself a demon dragging a thunder-
bolt.

The mayoral, sitting on the right of the box,
grave as a bishop, wielded like a sceptre a gigantic
whip, the end of which reached the eighth mule at
the head of the team, and the sting of which seemed
to burn like fire. From time to time he shouted :
" Anda, niño ! " (" Get on, child ! ") And the little
postillion would bend furiously over his mule, and
the whole thing would bound as if the coach had
taken wings.

On the left of the mayoral was a great ragamuffin
of about twenty, almost as fantastic as the postillion.
This was the zagal. This strange fellow, girdled
with a rope, shod in tatters, dressed in rags and

T

bonneted with a béret, risked his life a score of
times in the hour.   Every minute he would fling
himself to the ground, leap with one bound to the
head of the team, swear at the mules, calling them
by their names with fearful shrieks—" La Capitana !
La Gallarda ! La Generale ! Leona ! La Carabinera !
La Colegiana ! La Carcaña ! "—he would lash, goad,
pinch, sting, strike, and kick, urging to a triple
gallop the diligence which he no longer seemed
able to follow, and which passed him with the speed
of lightning.   Then, at a moment when one thought
him a quarter of a league behind, at the swiftest
instant of our flight, a man, who seemed to have
been hurled from a bomb, would suddenly fall on
to the box beside the mayoral.   This was the zagal
resuming his seat.

And he resumed it in the calmest possible fashion,
without any flurry or shortness of breath, without a
drop of perspiration upon his forehead.   A miser
who has just given a liard to a beggar is assuredly
more perturbed.   Whoever has not seen a Navarrese
zagal running along the road from Tolosa to Pampeluna, does not know the full significance of the
famous proverb, " to run like a Basque."

My head was heavy with that sort of slumber
into which the traveller is plunged by the fatigue
of a bad night, the fresh morning air, and the

lurching of the coach. You know the somnolence, at once vague and lucid, in which the spirit floats half-quenched, in which the realities confusedly perceived tremble, grow, flicker, disappear, and become dreams even while they remain realities. A diligence becomes a whirlwind and remains a diligence. The mouths of people speaking sound like trumpets. At the relays, the postillion's lantern flashes like Sirius, and the shadow which it projects upon the roadway seems an enormous spider seizing the coach and shaking it between its antennæ. It was through this exaggerating reverie that my eight mules and my three postillions appeared to me.

But is there not sometimes reason in hallucinations and truth in dreams? And are not those mysterious states of soul full of revelations?

Well, shall I say it? While in that condition in which so many philosophers have vainly endeavoured to examine themselves, my mind was assailed by singular doubts—questions fantastic and new. What, I asked myself, can be passing, and what does pass, within these poor mules, which, in the sort of somnambulism in which they live, vaguely illumined by the flickering gleams of instinct, deafened by a hundred bells about their ears, almost blinded by the guardaojos, imprisoned by the harness, terrified by the clatter of chains, wheels, and stones which follows them unceasingly, feel themselves furiously beset amid this darkness and tumult by three devils whom they do not know, but whom they feel, whom they cannot see, but whom they hear? What does the dream, the vision, the reality mean to them? Is it a punishment? But they have done no crime. What do they think of man?

My friend, the dawn was beginning to break; one corner of the firmament was whitened over with that forbidding pallor which always accompanies the first gleams of morning; everything living a separate and distinct life was still asleep in the nests lost beneath the leaves, and in the cottages buried among the woods; but to me it seemed that nature was not asleep. The trees, seen dimly in the darkness like phantoms, emerged little by little from the mists in the deep gorges of Tolosa, and appeared at the edge of the sky above us as if stretching their heads over the tops of the hills; the grass trembled on the banks of the road; upon the rocks the black, tangled brambles writhed as if with despair; I heard no sound, no voice, no sigh; but to me, I say, it seemed that nature was not asleep, and that, in the trees, in the grass, and in the brambles, it was she, the common Mother, who was bending, in anguish ineffable and unutterable pity, from the edge of the road and the tops of the mountains, to see those poor, terrified mules pass and suffer in their flight through the night, those wretched, abandoned animals who are her children even as we are, and who live closer to her than we.

Oh, my friend, if nature really watches us at certain times, if she sees the brutal acts we commit without any need and as if for pleasure, if she suffers by the wicked things men do, how melancholy is her attitude and how terrible her silence!

No one has probed these questions. Human philosophy has concerned itself little with man outside of man, and has examined only superficially, and almost with a smile of disdain, the relations of man with things, and with animals which, in his eyes, are merely things. Are there not here unsounded depths for the thinker?

Is one to think oneself mad because one has the sentiment of universal pity in one's heart? Do there not exist certain laws of mysterious equity which are set free by the great scheme of things, and which are outraged by the unthinking and needless cruelty wrought by men upon animals? No doubt the sovereignty of man over things is not to be denied; but the sovereignty of God is higher than that of man. Do you think, now, that man, without violating some secret and paternal purpose of the Creator, could have made the ox, the ass, and the horse the galley-slaves of creation? Let him make them serve, if he will, but let him not make them suffer. Let him kill them even, if he must— that is his need and his right; but at least—and I insist upon this—let him make them suffer nothing needlessly.

For myself, I believe that pity is a law like justice, and that kindness is a duty like uprightness. That which is weak has a right to the kindness and pity of that which is strong. Animals are weak, for they are without intellect. Let us then treat them with kindness and compassion.

In the relations of man with the animals, with the flowers, with all the objects of creation, there is a whole great ethic, scarcely perceived as yet, which will at length break through into the light, and which will be the corollary and the comple- ment to human ethics. I admit the exceptions and restrictions, which are innumerable; but to me it is certain that, on the day when Jesus said, "Do not unto others that which you would not have them do unto you," in His mind "others" was bound- less—"others" went beyond man and embraced the universe.

The principal purpose for which man has been created, his great end, his great function, is to love.

God would have man love. The man who does not
love is beneath the man who does not think. In
other words, the egoist is inferior to the imbecile,
the evildoer is lower in the human scale than the
idiot.

Everything in nature gives man the fruit that it
bears, the benefits which it produces. All things
serve man according to their own laws. The sun
gives its light, fire its heat, the animal its instinct, the
flower its perfume. It is their way of loving man.
They follow their law, never failing it, never fleeing
from it. Man should obey his. He should give to
humanity and render to nature that which is his
light, his heat, his instinct, and his perfume—love.

No doubt it was a first duty—men had to begin
with it, and the various legislators of the human
mind were right to neglect every other care for it—
no doubt it was necessary to civilize man in relation
to man. That work is already advanced and is
making progress every day. But man must be
civilized also in relation to nature. Here everything is yet to be done.

This, then, is my reverie. Take it for what it is;
but whatever you may say to it, I assure you that
it arises from a profound feeling within me. Let
us now think of it, but speak no more of it. We
must cast the seed and let the furrow do the rest.

What am I to tell you ?   I am fascinated ; for
this is a charming country, most quaint and interesting.   While you have rain in Paris, here I have the
sun and the blue sky, and just sufficient clouds to
make magnificent vapours upon the mountains.

Everything here is capricious, contradictory, and
strange.   It is a mixture of primitive and degenerate
manners, of simplicity and corruption, of nobility
and bastardy, of pastoral life and civil war, of
beggars with the bearing of heroes and heroes with
the looks of beggars ; it is an ancient civilization
which has rotted away in the midst of a young soil
and a new nation ; it is old, yet it is being born ;
it is rancid and yet fresh.   It is indescribable.
Especially is it amusing.

Unique country, in which incongruities are every
moment mated, at the end of every field, at the
corner of every street !   The women-servants at the
tables d'hôte bow like duchesses on receiving a
couple of sous.   Look at that village girl passing.
She is marvellously pretty, delightfully bonneted,
decked and adorned like a Madonna.   Cast your
eyes down, and you see a horrible, ragged skirt from
which project fearfully large feet, bare and dirty.
The Madonna terminates in a muleteer.   The wine

is execrable ; it tastes of the goat-skin. The oil is abominable ; it tastes of I know not what. The signs of all the shops offer you wine and oil : " Vino y aceyte." The highways have foot-pavements, the beggars have jewels, the cottages have coats-of-arms, their inmates have no shoes. All the soldiers play the guitar in all the guard-rooms. The priests climb to the tops of the coaches, smoke cigars, eye women's legs, eat like tigers, and are as thin as nails. The roads are scattered over with picturesque vagabonds.

O decrepit Spain ! O newest of countries ! A great history, a great past, a great future ; a hideous, pitiful present. O worthlessness ! O wonder ! One is repelled ; one is attracted. Once more, I say, it is indescribable.

In the evening one again sees these vagabonds on the tops of the hills, with a carabine across their backs, casting their silhouettes against the sky.

The gorge which leads from Tolosa to Pampeluna would be celebrated were it but known. It is, however, one of those roads which no one ever takes. A zigzag journey through Spain would be a voyage of discovery. There are seven or eight high-roads, and these everybody follows. No one knows the places between.

Europe, moreover, is threatened with something similar. The desertion of the intermediate districts is one of the probable results to be apprehended from railways. Civilization will certainly find a remedy, but she will have to seek it.

There is a class of people—of minds, if you like —whom enthusiasm fatigues or leaves untouched, and who, before all the beauties of art or of creation, get over everything with the ready-made phrase : " It is always the same thing." To these profound scorners, what is the sea ? A cliff or a dune, and a big blue or green line which looks dismal. What is the Rhine ? Some water, a rock, and a ruin ; then water, a rock, and a ruin again ; and so on in rotation from Mayence to Cologne. What is a cathedral ? A spire, some ogives, some stained glass, and some buttresses. What is a forest ? Trees, and then more trees. What is a gorge ? A torrent between two mountains. " It is always the same thing ! "

O honest imbeciles, who never suspect the immense part played in this world by detail and shade ! In nature it is life, in art it is style. O proud, disdainful simpletons, who know not that the atmosphere, the sun, a gray or clear sky, a gust

of wind, an accident of light, a reflection, the
season, the fancy of God, the fancy of the poet, the
fancy of the landscape, are so many worlds ! The
same motive gives us the bay of Constantinople, the
bay of Naples, and the bay of Rio de Janeiro. The
same skeleton gives us Venus and the Virgin. The
whole of creation, this manifold, diversified, dazzling
and melancholy spectacle, studied by every thinker
since Plato, contemplated by every poet since
Homer, may, indeed, be reduced to two things—
—some green and some blue. Yes, but God is the
painter. With the green He has made the earth ;
with the blue He has made the sky.

The gorge of Tolosa, then, is a gorge like other
gorges—" always the same thing "—a torrent between two mountains. But this torrent utters a cry
so horrible, and the bearing of the mountains is so
imposing, that, in entering it, man feels himself puny
and small. A forest is intermingled with the rocks,
and from the highest summits descend great sheets
of living rock, strewn with tall oaks which are almost
inexplicable. One sees the tree, one sees the rock,
and one asks oneself where the root is and on what
it can live.

As in all the grander works of nature, there are
here delightful nooks, banks of turf, rivulets that
have parted from the torrent and murmur along

beside it with a sweet gurgle such as young eaglets
must make in the nest, grass full of flowers and
scents, a thousand charming resting-places for the
eye and the mind. Man alone remains gloomy.
The passing peasants wear a meditative look.
There are no villages. Here and there are tall
stone houses pierced with three or four small
windows, which, however, have still been found too
large, for they are half walled up.

In this country, I am obliged to repeat, the
window is no longer a window ; it is a loop-hole.
The house is no longer a house ; it is a fortress.
There is a ruin at every step. For all the civil
wars of Navarre for four centuries have rushed
headlong into the ravine along with this torrent.
This water, now white with foam, has many a time
been red with blood. This, perhaps, is why the
torrent wails so dismally. This, assuredly, is why
man meditates.

This gorge is cut in two by a high mountain—a
fine rise, from the point of view of the traveller, a
nasty hill, in the language of the postillion. The
road, which is exceedingly fine, moreover, wriggles
and twists along the side of the precipice with
alarming turns. Two oxen had been added to
our eight mules, and the diligence, towed by this
enormous team, mounted at a walk. At the middle

of the ascent, a big stone post informs you that you are six leagues from Pampeluna : " Seis leguas á Pamplona." The mountains form wonderful groups round the precipice. Reapers the size of ants are cutting their corn far below.

I had alighted from the coach, and, as I walked along to the noise of the chains, the oxen, and the mules, I gathered a bunch of wild flowers. I met a beggar and gave him a real. Then, at the top of the mountain, I encountered a waterfall, and into it I threw my bouquet. One must give alms to the naiads also.

There I climbed to the top of the coach again, and the oxen were unyoked. Just then the six front mules, feeling themselves free, went off at a gallop. The mayoral, the postillion, and the zagal ran off after the mules swearing, and leaving the coach where it stood. The diligence was still upon a very steep slope. The two wheel-mules, left to keep it back alone, had not the strength ; their feet slipped, and the coach began to roll back slowly towards the precipice. The terrified passengers cried for the drivers, who did not hear them. The hind wheel was now only a few inches from the brink when the beggar, a poor old man, completely bent and almost paralytic, approached and pushed a stone in front with his foot. This sufficed.

The stone formed an obstacle to the wheel, and the coach stopped.

There was a priest beside me on the seat. He crossed himself and said : " God has saved twenty people." I answered : " With a flint-stone and an old man."

The drivers led back the mules, which had already got far away.

An hour later we came out between two immense promontories which are the mountain's last towers on this side on the plain of Pampeluna.

Pampeluna is a town which fulfils more than it promises. At a distance one shakes one's head, for no monumental profile makes its appearance. When in the town the impression changes. In the streets one is interested at every step ; on the ramparts one is charmed.

The situation is admirable. Nature has made a plain round as a circus, and has surrounded it with mountains ; in the centre of this plain man has made a town. This is Pampeluna.

According to some, it is a Vascon town with the ancient name of Pompelon ; according to others, a Roman town founded by Pompey. To-day Pam-

peluna is the Navarrese city of which the House of
Évreux has made a Gothic town, of which the
House of Austria has made a Castilian town, and
of which the sun almost makes an Eastern city.

The mountains all round about are bare; the
plain is dried up. A pretty river, the Arga, yields
nourishment to a few poplars. The gentle undulations which run from the plain to the mountains
are covered with Poussin structures. It is not only
a fine plain, but a fine landscape.

Seen at close quarters the town has the same
appearance. The streets, with their black houses
enlivened with colours, balconies, and streaming
banners, are at once gay and severe.

A magnificent square tower of dry brick, with
the simplest and most dignified outline, dominates
the promenade planted with trees. It is the
thirteenth century modified by Arab taste, as it is
in Germany and Lombardy by Byzantine taste. A
portal in the style of Philip IV. ornaments richly
the lower portion of this tower, which, without it,
would perhaps be a little bare. This portal, which
is in no way obtrusive or exaggerated, is here a
happy addition. It is almost rococo, and yet it is
Renaissance.

Spanish rococo, moreover, is, like everything produced by Spain, belated. It borrows from the six-

teenth century, and preserves into the seventeenth,
and even the eighteenth, the smallness of the
columns and the complicated folds of the frontons,
so graceful in the Henri II. period.   These forms
of the Renaissance, intermingled with the chicory-
work and rock-work, give the Castilian rococo a
strange originality made up of nobility and caprice.

This magnificent tower is a belfry.   The old
church to which it was attached has disappeared.
Who destroyed it?   Most likely it has been burnt
down in one of the numerous sieges which Pampeluna has sustained.

As I said this to myself, a corner of the belfry,
in which a deep breach seemed to have been made
by shells, confirmed this conjecture in my mind.
However, I pushed open a door at the foot of the
tower and entered a frightful church built in
approved taste, in the vilest and poorest style, after
the manner of the Madeleine and the guard-house
in the Boulevard du Temple.   This perplexed me.
Can it have been to build this platitude decorated
with triglyphs and archivaults that they demolished
the old church of the thirteenth century, half
Romanesque, half Moorish?

Alas!   The "elegant school" has penetrated to
Spain, and this feat is worthy of it.   It has disfigured old cities more than all the sieges and fires.

I would rather give a building a shower of shells
than an architect of the elegant school. Bombard
the old edifices, for pity's sake, but do not restore
them! Shells are merely brutal; the classical
masons are stupid. Our venerable cathedrals boldly
brave bombs, grenades, bar-shot, and Congreve
rockets; they tremble to their foundations before
M. Fontaine. At least rockets, balls, grenades, and
bombs do not carve Corinthian capitals, scoop out
flutings, and cause eruptions of freshly-cut ovoli
round a full Romanesque cintre. St. Denis has
just been restored, and is St. Denis no longer; the
Parthenon has been bombarded, and is still the
Parthenon.

The houses, nearly all built of yellow brick, the
obtuse roofs with their hollow tiles, the dust which
fills the air, the russet plains, and the scorched
mountains on the horizon, give Pampeluna a
strange, earthy look which at first sight is depressing; but, as I have said, everything in the town
itself delights the eye. The fantastic taste for
ornament, inherent in the peoples of the south,
takes its revenge upon the fronts of the houses.
The medley of colouring, the brilliance of the
frescoes, the groups of pretty women leaning half
over the street and talking with signs from one
balcony to the other, the varied and fantastic dis-

U

play of the shops, the lively hubbub and the per-
petual jostle of the crossings, have about them
something animated and dazzling.

The taste at once savage and elegant found in all
semi-civilized nations is revealed at every turn.
Now it is a common-place well, with its brim of
almost undressed stone supporting six small columns
of white marble, surmounted by a cupola which
serves as a pedestal to the statue of a saint ; now
it is a doll Madonna surrounded by paintings, laden
with gewgaws, tinsel, and spangles, installed beneath
a daıs of red damask at the corner of an arcaded
walk covered with whitewash.

This taste, which is impressed upon the decora-
tion and furnishing of the churches, sheds some
grace and light within.   At Pampeluna, the external
architecture of the buildings being very severe, the
internal architecture at least escapes being tiresome.
For myself, I am grateful ; and to my thinking the
chief merit of the rock-work and chicory art—and
one that ought to secure it forgiveness for all its
vices—is the constant effort which it makes to
please and interest.

With the exception of the Cathedral, about which
I will tell you presently, the churches of Pampeluna,
although having nearly all old naves, have preserved
few traces of their Gothic origin.   In one of them,

however, I observed, over a door in the middle of a
high wall, a bas-relief of the fourteenth century representing a knight starting on the Crusade.   Man
and horse disappear beneath their caparisons of
war.   The knight, proudly morioned, with the
Cross on his shield, urges his steed, which presses
quickly onwards.   On a hill behind the baron one
perceives his castle with its crenelated towers, with
the portcullis still raised, and the gate, from which
he has just issued, and which, perhaps, he may
never re-enter, still open.   Over the keep is a thick
cloud, which opens a little and permits the passage
of a hand, an omnipotent, fatal hand, the outstretched finger of which points out to the knight
his way and purpose.   The knight's back is turned
upon the hand; he does not see it, but one divines
that he feels it.   It urges him forward, it holds him
back.   It is full of mystery and grandeur.   I fancied
I saw revivified, rudely but superbly cut in the
granite, the beautiful Castilian romance which
begins thus : " Bernard, with lance in hand, rides
swiftly by Arlanza's shores.   He is gone, the gallant
Spaniard, valiant and undaunted ! "

All the churches have an altar to San Saturnino,
who was the first apostle of Pampeluna, and another
to San Fermin, who was its first bishop. Pampeluna
is the most ancient Christian town in Spain, and

she is vain of the fact, if, indeed, there can ever be any vanity in regard to the matter. These two names, Fermin and Saturnino, are not merely in all the churches ; they are on all the shops as well. At every street corner one reads: SATURNINO, ROPERO. —FERMIN, SASTRE.

I was struck with the portal of a mansion in a street which I no longer remember. Picture to yourself a broad archivault, round which creep, climb, and twist, like a vegetation of stone, all the fantastic tulips and all the extravagant lotus-work which rococo intermingles with its coquilles and volutes. Then, instead of scaly sirens and naked naiads, summon forth from the lotus-work and tulips kettle-drummers in three-cornered hats and moustached halberdiers dressed like the foot-soldiers of the Chevalier de Folard. To this add rock-work and garlands, in the midst of which gunners are loading their pieces, and arabesques which daintily hold at the end of their tendrils drums, bayonets, and bursting grenades. Over the whole throw the full and heavy, but tolerably pliant, style of the time of Charles II., and you will have some conception of the little military and pastoral poem chiselled over this doorway. It is an eclogue garnished with cannon-balls.

The first object sought by the eye when one perceives a town on the horizon is the Cathedral. In approaching Pampeluna I had observed in the distance, towards the eastern end of the town, two abominable steeples of the time of Charles III., a period which corresponds to our worst Louis XV. These two steeples, which are intended for spires, are alike. If you care to picture one of them, imagine four big corkscrews supporting a sort of big, swollen vasculum, surmounted by one of those classical pots, vulgarly called urns, which look as if they had been born of the union of an amphora and a pitcher. And all this in stone. I was perfectly enraged.

"What!" said I. "So this is what they have made of that almost Romanesque Cathedral which saw the building of the citadel of Philip II., which saw Ignatius of Loyola wounded by a French arquebus, and which Charles d'Évreux, King of Navarre, thought so beautiful that he desired to have his tomb made within it!"

I was tempted not to visit it. On reaching Pampeluna, however, and observing the piteous look of the two steeples at the end of a street, I was seized with a scruple and made my way towards the portal.

Seen close at hand, it is still worse. The two excrescences I have just described, cut like cabbage-stalks and adorned with the name of spires, are supported by a colonnade which I can compare with nothing unless it be the colonnade of St. Denis du Saint-Sacrement in our Rue St. Louis in Paris. And these abominations are given out in the schools for Greek and Roman art. Oh, my friend, how ugly is ugliness when it aspires to be beautiful!

I shrank back from this architecture and was about to give the church up, when, on turning to the left, I observed behind the façade the tall black walls, the pointed flamboyant fenestration, the exquisite bell-turrets, the massive counterforts of the venerable Cathedral of Pampeluna. I recognized the church of my dreams.

It stands there, gloomy, sad, and humiliated, as if undergoing I know not what punishment, hidden behind the odious portal by whose "good taste" it is eclipsed. What a mask is this façade! What fool's-caps are these two steeples!

Reconciled and satisfied, I entered the edifice by a lateral portal of the fifteenth century, which is simple, little adorned, but elegant. The doors are studded with nails and fleurs de lys, and the iron knocker, composed of dragons tearing each other, is of a fine Byzantine character.

I was delighted with the interior of the church. It is Gothic with magnificent windows.

I told you just now of the entrance of a mansion which is quite a pretty little poem. The Cathedral of Pampeluna is a poem also, but a great and beautiful poem ; and, since I have been led into this assimilation, which arises so naturally between the things of architecture and the things of poetry, let me add that the poem is in four cantos—the high altar, the choir, the cloister, and the sacristy.

It was a little past five in the morning when I entered the Cathedral. It had just been opened, and was still dark and empty. The first beams of the rising sun pierced the windows of the lofty nave horizontally, and stretched from one ogive to another great beams of gold, which stood out sharply against the gloom of the background, shining resplendently through the tenebrous church. An old and much bent priest was saying early mass before the high altar.

The high altar, barely lit by a few lighted candles, half surrounded by a waving wall of tapestry and hangings fastened to the pillars of the apsis and intercepting the light, seemed, amid the haze by which it was enveloped, to be a heap of precious stones. Round about stood all sorts of glittering furnishings such as one sees only in Spanish churches,

credences, cabinets, chests, and inclosed cupboards
with small drawers. At the back, behind some
clusters of lilies, over the high altar, in the midst of a
sort of glory, which, perhaps, was merely gilded
wood, but which the hour and the place invested with
a strange majesty, between the two glistening sides
of an open cupboard with folding-doors, shone a
Madonna in a robe of silver, the Imperial crown on
her head and the Child Jesus in her arms.   I caught
sight of all this through a wonderful iron grille of
the time of Joanna the Mad, wrought by the magical
craftsmen of the fifteenth century, all laden with
flowers, arabesques, and figures.   This grille, which
is over twenty feet in height, and is approached
by a staircase of a few steps, closes the chancel
on the only side from which the eye can penetrate it.

Nothing could have been more impressive, at that
sacred and sublime hour of morning, than that white-
haired man, alone in the midst of that great church,
robed in splendid garments, speaking in low tones
and turning over the leaves of a book, performing a
mysterious act in that magnificent, dark, silent
hidden place.   The mass was said for God and for
immensity, and for an old woman who was listening
huddled behind a pillar a few steps away from me.

All this was sublime.   The old church, the old

priest, and the old woman seemed to be a sort of trinity and to form but one. The two sexes and the building composed a symbol from which nothing was wanting. The priest had been strong and was now broken, the woman had been beautiful and was now faded, the building had been perfect and was now mutilated. The man, grown old in his body and in his work, worshipping God in the presence of that dazzling sun which nothing cools, nothing extinguishes, nothing ruffles, nothing changes—tell me, do not you think this sublime?

I was moved to the depths of my heart. No discordant thought arose from this melancholy contrast. On the contrary, I felt that it inspired an inexpressible sense of unity. Assuredly, nothing but a deep, unfathomable mystery can thus unite in one intimate and religious harmony the incurable decrepitude of the creature and the eternal youth of creation.

When the mass was finished I turned round and looked at the choir, which in the churches in the north of Spain faces the altar.

The choir of the Cathedral of Pampeluna, a lofty and gloomy piece of sixteenth century joinery, consists of two rows of stalls occupying the three sides of an oblong, the fourth side of which is filled and shut off by a grille, a magnificent piece of iron-

work of the same period.   One of the saints of the
liturgy is carved full-size in the oak behind each
stall.   The woodwork is cut throughout with the
pliant, graceful chisel of the Renaissance.   In the
centre of the short side of the oblong facing the
grille, and, consequently, the altar, stands the
Bishop's throne surmounted by a charming pierced
bell-turret.   The present Bishop of Pampeluna,
who did not live very harmoniously with Espartero,
is at the present moment in France—at Pau, I
believe, where he took shelter two years ago.

I was fatigued with having walked all the morning, and I sat down upon the vacant throne.   A
throne!   Do you not think the place of repose
curiously chosen?   I did so, nevertheless.   The
Bishop's choir-book was on his desk before me.   I
opened it.   It was torn at nearly every page.

The grille of the choir, in which angels hover and
serpents writhe as in a magic foliage, faces the
grille of the high altar.   The art of the fifteenth
century and the art of the sixteenth confront each
other, each with its most prominent and most
opposite characteristics; the one is the more delicate, the other the more diffuse.   One cannot tell
which is the more charming.

In the centre of the choir another iron grille,
resembling a huge cage, incloses and protects—

while at the same time permitting it to be seen—
the cenotaph of Charles III. of Évreux, King of
Navarre.

This is an exquisite tomb of the fifteenth century,
worthy of a place at Bruges with the tombs of
Mary of Flanders[1] and Charles the Bold, at Dijon
with the tombs of the Dukes of Burgundy, or at
Brou with the tombs of the Dukes of Savoy.   The
motive is not varied, but it is so simple and so
lovely !   The king with his lion and the queen with
her greyhound are lying side by side, crowned,
upon their bed of marble—a pathetic conjugal
tomb, round which winds a procession of small
weeping figures marshalled beneath little mouldings
of the most exquisite workmanship.   A portion of
the tomb is horribly mutilated.   Nearly all the
statues are broken in two.

Seven or eight enormous missals of those in-
fortiatic[2] proportions which furnished Boileau with

---

[1] Commonly known as Mary of Burgundy.—*Translator.*

[2] An allusion to these lines in " Le Lutrin : "

> " À ces mots, il saisit un vieil infortiat
>   Grossi des visions d'Accurse et d'Alciat,"

the " Infortiatum " being one of the divisions of the Corpus
of Roman law.   Francesco Accorso and Andrea Alciati
were eminent Italian jurists, the former in the thirteenth,
the latter in the sixteenth century.—*Translator.*

so wonderful a rhyme and so delightful a line, bound
in parchment and ornamented with copper corners,
are ranged round the cenotaph and placed upon
the ground like the shields of resting soldiers.
They are set against the grille of the tomb.   It
would seem that chance, in making the books of
the church lean against the tomb, was not without
a meaning.

A great organ-case in the manner of last century,
much gilded and decorated, dominates the entire
choir, but without marring it.   Over it one reads
this verse, which, moreover, is inscribed over nearly
all the organs in Spain: "LAUDATE DEUM IN
CHORDIS ET ORGANO."   Beneath this is the date:
"AÑO 1742."

The chapels surrounding the high altar and the
choir are ornamented, one might almost say encumbered, with those enormous carved and gilded
altar-pieces which this old Catholic country has
always loved.   Their vogue is excessive.   In one
chapel I saw one of these altar-pieces which was of
the fifteenth century, and in one of the aisles
another of the thirteenth.   In the middle of this
altar-piece a large Byzantine Christ was hanging
by three nails.   It was entirely black, with a frizzled
beard and prominent ribs, and was muffled in an
immense petticoat of white lace.

What in the world should the lace be doing there?

Some banners fixed to the walls, some Madonnas in niches of red damask, and some tombs sculptured in the wall at various heights, completed the furnishings of the church.

As I left the choir some strange effect of chiaroscuro drew me away to the right towards the lateral door facing that by which I had entered, and I suddenly found myself in one of the finest cloisters I have ever seen in my life.

It is a vast quadrilateral surrounded by large ogives, the outlines of which form a rich and vigorous fenestration of the fourteenth century. Some of the pointed windows bear the traces of recent, and, I make haste to add, of intelligent restoration. Above the ogival gallery, a second lower gallery with carved joists supports the hollow-tiled roof, which is over-topped here and there by bell-turrets of black stone exquisite in form. The court of the cloister is an exceedingly well-kept garden, in which clipped box-trees describe all those fascinating arabesques which are seen in gardens of the seventeenth century.

Everything in the cloister is fine, the dimensions and the proportions, the form and the colour, the composition and the details, the light and the

shadow.   Now it is an old fresco which animates
and enlivens the wall, now a marble tomb gnawed
away by the years, now an oak door mended and
patched in such a fashion as to mingle strangely
the joiner-work of all the different periods.

Some Navarrese fleurs de lys, old and half torn
away, waved in the wind above the iron fencing of
the garden as I passed, while beside them bloomed
in all their perfume and splendour the eternal fleurs
de lys of the good God.

The pavement upon which one walks is composed of long black flags.   Every flag bears a
number and covers a tomb.   There is something
cold and precise in this method of labelling the
departed.   I am quite ready to become dust, or
ashes, or a shade, but to become a cipher is re-
pugnant to me.   It is nothingness without its
poetry ; it is too great a nothingness.

At one of the corners of the cloister, some
lancet windows, partly walled up, stretch round a
mysterious kind of room.   It is a chapel.   But
why, one asks, has it been separated from the
church ?

I saw in it merely somewhat dilapidated furnishings, a crucifix, a wooden altar, and a lamp of
embossed tin.   I admired, however, the iron grille
which incloses the two aisles of the chapel opening

on the cloister, and which is a precious example of the complex and vigorous iron-work of the fourteenth century. This grille is the most interesting object in the chapel, both as regards workmanship and material. Yet it is merely of iron; but that iron is illustrious.

At the battle of Tolosa, the Miramolin[1] had his camp surrounded by an iron chain, which the King of Navarre severed with one blow of a hatchet. Like the hair of Berenice, which took its place among the stars, this chain has remained one of the constellations of the coat-of-arms. It has composed the arms of the kingdom of Navarre, and even recently it possessed half of the shield of France. Well, it is with the iron of that chain that this grille has been made. This, at least, is what is revealed to the passer-by, and affirmed, in a notice placed above the grille, by this quatrain of somewhat barbarous and enigmatic Latin :

CINGERE QVÆ CERNIS CRVCIFIXVM FERREA VINCLA
  BARBARICÆ GENTIS FVNERE RUPTA MANENT.
SANCTIVS EXUVIAS DISCERPTAS VINDICE FERRO
  HVC ILLVC SPARSIT STEMATA FRVSTA PIVS. AÑO 1212.

[1] The name given by writers in the Middle Ages to the Sultans of Morocco and other Mohammedan sovereigns. It is a corruption of the Arabic "amir al-muminin," the Commander of the Faithful.—*Translator*.

I have nothing to say to this quatrain unless it be that the workmanship of the grille denotes the fourteenth century and not the thirteenth at all.

The inner portal by which I entered the cloister from the church is of the fourteenth century also. It has tympana, arches, capitals, colonnettes, medallions, and statuettes, all in the finest style of that fine period. Add to this that the portal, protected by the cloister against the action of the atmosphere, and by chance against the plasterers, has preserved the gilding and painting of the time in all their lustre and nearly all their freshness. I was filled with wonder.—" Pardieu," thought I, " one might well kneel before this !"

I turned round and saw someone kneeling before it in reality, kneeling on the flags. And who? A woman of about forty, still beautiful, with distinguished-looking features, and enveloped in a rich mantilla of black lace. As I was looking at her with surprise, another woman—this one old and ragged—entered the cloister and knelt beside the first. Then came a third. Observe that we were outside the church.—" This," said I, " is indeed a devout worship of architecture !"—A little observation explained everything. On the framework of the portal there was a doll Madonna, and on the wall beside it this inscription :

EL EMINEN^{MO} S^R CARDE
NAL PEREIRA CONCEDIO
80 DIAS DE YNDVLGEN^A
Y EL S^{R.} OBISPO MURILLO
40 AL QVE REZARE VNA
SALVE DE RRODILLAS DE
LANE ESTA S^{MA} YMAGEN
DE N^{RA} S^{RA} DE EL AMPARO [1]

It is probable that this inscription is the chance, of which I spoke just now, that has prevented the plastering. The portal has been saved by the doll.

As I was finishing my copy of the inscription, the beautiful kneeling devotee rose up, and as she passed close to me, almost without going out of her way, said to me over her shoulder : "The French caballero who is looking at everything ought to go and see the sacristy." She then walked quickly away.

I re-entered the church and searched everywhere. At length, by dint of pushing open all the doors, I discovered the sacristy.

Oh ! That was indeed a sacristy after the heart

---

[1] The most eminent Señor Cardinal Pereira has granted eighty days' indulgences, and the Señor Bishop Murillo forty, to whosoever will recite a salve kneeling before this most sacred image of Our Lady of Succour.

of a fair Spanish devotee! Picture to yourself an
immense rock-work boudoir, gilded and turned,
florid and showy, ambered and captivating. The
wall-paper imitates the damask which it has replaced; the pavement of brick and stone imitates
mosaic.   Everywhere there are beautiful ivory
Christs, swooning Magdalens, leaning mirrors, sofas
with great cushions, dressing-tables with goats' feet,
corners with small tables of Aleppo breccia.   A
brilliant light, mysterious recesses, extraordinary
and diversified furnishings, priests coming and going,
chasubles sparkling in the half-open drawers, I know
not what perfume of a marquis, I know not what
odour of an abbé—this is the sacristy of Pampeluna.

It was a worthy bishop, Cardinal Antonio
Zapata, who offered this gallantry to the Cathedral.
The transition is sudden; it is almost a shock.
Dante pervades the cloister, Madame de Pompadour
the sacristy.

After all, even there, one thing completes the
other, and there is harmony at bottom.   The sacristy
invites to sin and the cloister to penitence.

Already masses were being said in all the chapels,
and the church was filled with the faithful, chiefly
women.   I made a round of it for the last time.

On the side of the great portal the choir is protected by a massive wall, against which leans a

tomb of white marble. The epitaph, in letters of gold now almost effaced, indicates that there lie the remains of the brave Don Bonaventure Dumont, Comte de Gages, who defeated the Imperialists and M. de Savoie in person in many an encounter.

One of these encounters makes a very fine battle-piece, which is to be seen carved in bas-relief above the epitaph. In it there are cannons levelled, horses prancing, officers commanding, solid battalions with lances crossed resembling bramble-bushes entangled by a furious wind. Nothing could be stranger than this petrified, silent mêlée, motionless for ever in that gloomy church, through which one hears from time to time the feeble, inter-mittent rattle of the choir-boy.

The great tumult of the battle and the great silence of the tomb leave a solemn lesson in one's heart. This, then, is the glory of the soldier in death ! It is silent. The glory of the poet and the thinker speaks and sings eternally.

While I was given up to I know not what reverie before this tomb, the sound of the organ and a loud, wild, lugubrious chant broke out suddenly on my left in the neighbouring chapel, and caused me to turn my head.

A bier, which had doubtless only just been carried in, was lying on one of the flag-stones of

the pavement. One could see the wood, scarcely
hidden by a black sheet which was worn and full
of holes. Four tapers burned round about ; three
round loaves were ranged upon a plank on the
ground by the head of the coffin. Four large pine
torches flared a few paces to the right, and by their
reverberations I dimly saw, in a gloomy chapel, the
priest in a black chasuble with a white cross saying
the mass for the dead. The chant of the organ
descended from above like a supernatural sound.
One could not perceive whence it came. Round
me, a crowd of women of every age, grouped in a
sort of semicircle at some distance from the bier,
all gracefully bonneted and enveloped in the mantilla of black silk, squatting on the pavement of the
church after the Spanish fashion, in the indolent
and charming attitude of women of the seraglio,
their eyes more often raised than lowered, were
playing with their fans, listening to the mass and
watching the passers-by.

I looked alternately at the tomb of the Comte
de Gages and the wretched burial of the unknown.
Both alike are nothingness ; the one honoured, the
other despised. My friend, if the things which we
call inanimate could suddenly speak, what a conversation there would be between that marble tomb
and that bier of deal.

In the evening I walked upon the ramparts, alone and pensive.

There are days in our lives which stir up the whole of the past within us. I was full of thoughts which could not find expression. The grass upon the counterscarps waved in the wind and sighed gently at my feet. The guns thrust their heads over the battlements as if to look out over the plain. The hills on the horizon, blurred by the twilight, had assumed magnificent shapes. The plain was covered with darkness. The Arga, furrowed with a thousand glittering reflections, glided through the trees like a silvery adder.

As I passed the entrance of the town I heard the creaking of the chains of the drawbridge and the dull shock of the falling portcullis. They had just closed the gate. At this very moment the moon rose. Then—forgive me the absurdity of quoting myself—these lines which I wrote fifteen years ago came back to my mind:

"Toujours prête au combat, la sombre Pampelune,
  Avant de s'endormir aux rayons de la lune,
    Ferme sa ceinture de tours."

In Spanish towns there are many " ventas," or taverns—some " posadas," or inns—and very few " fondas," or hotels.   At San Sebastian there is only the " Fonda Ysabel," so named to distinguish it from the French hostelry kept by an honest and worthy man called Lafitte.   At Tolosa and Pampeluna the fonda has neither name nor sign.   It is called simply " la fonda," which clearly signifies that it is the only one.

The room which I occupy in the fonda of Pampeluna " al segundo piso " (on the second floor) has two large windows overlooking the Gran Plaza.

This plaza is in no way remarkable.   At the present moment they are building at one end, the eastern, some hideous thing resembling a theatre, which is to be of freestone.   I recommend this thing to the first man of understanding who may be bombarding Pampeluna.

Forgive me, my friend, this dismal pleasantry.   I do not erase it, because it really arises from the very nature of things.   Is it not the destiny of every Spanish town to be periodically bombarded?   Last year Espartero bombarded Barcelona.   This year Van Halen is bombarding Seville.   What will be bombarded next year, and who will bombard it,

I know not. But be sure that there will be a bombardment. This being so, I pray for the inhabitants, for the houses, and for the cathedrals; but, as one must give the bombs their due, I joyfully accord them every copy of the Paris Bourse with which I meet.

Having said this, let us return to Pampeluna and go up again to my room.

It is a sort of whitewashed hall, with two beds, one of which is large and is called by the women-servants "el matrimonio." On the walls are some coloured pictures representing lovers smiling at others representing spouses sulking. Further, a small table, two straw-bottomed chairs, and an enormous door, with panels counter-buttressed with an oak framework, with the bolts of a prison and the lock of a citadel.

It appears that in Spain the possibility of being taken by assault is provided for on every floor of every house. To arm his window and balconies with close shutter-blinds in order to defend his wife from the gallants, and his door with heavy iron-work to defend his house from pillage—this is the two-fold solicitude of the Spanish citizen. Jealousy makes the window, and fear makes the door.

Half of the Gran Plaza of Pampeluna is at present occupied, or, rather, invaded, by a colossal scaffolding which has been erected for some bull-fights which are to take place in about ten days, and which are putting the town in a bustle. This "corrida" is to last four days, from the 18th to the 22nd of August. On the first day the fighting will be with "novillos," and on the last day, Muchares, an "espada" famed throughout the district, will kill the bull.

The amphitheatre is square. It obstructs the ground floors of two sides of the Plaza, the balconies and windows of which, on the day of the corrida, will serve as so many first or second tier boxes. The garrets will contain the gods. This theatre, for it is really one, is simply built of skeleton carpentry, with innumerable benches in tiers, and of the rudest construction. I can distinguish the numbering of the planks from my windows.

To all this add three unyoked diligences and a guard-room with its sentry walking in front of the fonda, and you will have the "landscape" seen from my window.

The Town Hall of Pampeluna is an elegant little building of the time of Philip III. The façade presents a curious example of a kind of ornamenta-

tion peculiar to the seventeenth century in Spain.
It consists of flat arabesques and volutes which look
as if they had been pinked into the stone with a
punch. I had already seen one house in this manner
in the strange and dismal village of Leso. The
fronton of the Town Hall is surmounted by lions,
bells, and statues, which make an amusing riot to
the eye.

What has amused me no less is the Fair which is
being held at present in a little square exactly
opposite the Town Hall. The open-air shops full
of gewgaws and pasquils, the shopkeepers full of
merry words, the jostling passers-by, the busy
buyers—that whole whirlpool of shouts and laughter,
abuse and song, called a fair, makes a greater
tumult and has a greater gaiety beneath the sun of
Spain than elsewhere.

Amid this crowd, leaning his back against one of
the pillars of the Town Hall, stood a formidable-
looking fellow of great stature. His big bare feet
projected from his leggings of red net-work. A
white woollen muleta with madder stripes covered
his head, entirely enveloping it in its sculptural folds,
and showing only his tawny face with its prominent
cheek-bones, its square nose, its angular jaws, its
projecting chin, and its black bristling beard—a face
of Florentine bronze with the eyes of a wild cat

In the midst of the noise and movement this man stood motionless, grave and silent.   Assuredly he was no Spaniard ; he was an Arab.

A couple of paces from this statue, an Italian mountebank with a pair of big spectacles on his nose, was exhibiting his marionettes, beating a drum, and singing on his trestles the ancient refrain of Punchinello, " Fantoccini, buraccini, puppi," of which we have made in France the villanelle :

> " Le Pantalon
> De Toinon
> N'a pas de fond."

The pantaloon and the savage gazed at each other like two inhabitants of different planets, and without understanding each other.

One cannot go through a fair, and especially this one, without purchasing.   I made no resistance, opened my purse, and sent all that was sold me to the fonda.

On my return, I found on my table a perfect pedlar's pack.   It contained amulets from Saragossa in gold, silver-gilt, and filigrane, garters with mottoes from Segovia, holy-water vessels of glass from Bilbao, tin night-lamps from Cauterets, a box of lucifer matches from Hernani, a box of pine-sticks which serve as candles at Elizondo, paper from

Tolosa, a mountaineer's sash from the Pass of Panticosa, an alpenstock, hempen shoes, and two Pampeluna muletas, which are of excellent wool, coarse workmanship, and exquisite taste.

Apart from this fair and some of the crossings, Pampeluna remains dull and silent all day long. But as soon as the sun has set, as soon as the windows and the lamps are lighted, the town awakens, life bursts forth everywhere, everything is suffused with brightness, and the town hums with activity like a beehive. A flourish of trumpets and cymbals sounds from the Gran Plaza ; it is the band of the garrison giving the town a serenade. The town responds. On every floor, at every window, upon every balcony, one hears voices and singing, and the sound of guitars and castanets. Every house vibrates with sound like an enormous bell. Add to this the angelus ringing from all the belfries in the town.

You might think, perhaps, that this combination is discordant, and that the result of all these mingled concerts is merely an immense and consummately conducted charivari. You would be mistaken. When a whole town transforms itself

into an orchestra the result is always a symphony.
The shrill tones are softened by the wind, the false
notes are stifled by the distance, everything plays
its due part in the ensemble, and the effect is harmonious. On a small scale it would be a din; on a
large scale it is music.

This music enlivens the population. The children
play in front of the shops; the inhabitants issue
from the houses; the Gran Plaza is covered with
pedestrians; priests and officers salute women in
mantillas; conversations are hidden behind fans;
the muleteers banter wenches beneath the arcades;
a soft glare falls from a hundred wide open and
brightly illuminated windows and dimly lights the
Plaza.   The people come and go and pass each
other in the shadow, and nothing could be more
charming than this discreet medley of pretty faces
and suppressed but merry laughter.

In this lovely climate the freedom of the priests
is in no way scandalous.   It is a familiarity which
the manners permit.   Still, from the window whence
I was observing everything, I heard three priests,
covered with their prodigious sombreros and enveloped in their great black cloaks, talking in front
of the fonda, and I must confess that one of them
pronounced the word "muchachas" in a fashion
which would have made Voltaire smile.

About ten in the evening the Plaza empties and Pampeluna falls asleep. But the sound does not die away all at once ; it is prolonged, and does not end when sleep begins. The first hours of the town's slumber seem still to vibrate with all the joys of the evening.

At midnight there is silence. One hears only the voice of the serenos calling the hour, which suddenly sounds from the neighbouring tower just as you are falling asleep, and is then repeated less loudly a little further off by another tower at the end of the Plaza, until, growing fainter and fainter from steeple to steeple, it dies away in the darkness.

XII.

THE CABIN IN THE MOUNTAINS.

HE sun was setting, and the mists were beginning to rise from the torrents which one heard roaring deep down in the lost ravines. There was no vestige of a habitation. The gorge grew more and more wild.

I was overcome with fatigue. Half-way up the hill, a few paces to the right of the pathway, I observed, at the foot of a high perpendicular rock, a block of white marble half buried in the earth. A tall fir-tree which had fallen from the escarpment, dead with age, had been stopped by the block in rolling down the slope, covering it with its withered and unlovely branches. In my wearied condition, I hung our mattresses and wraps in imagination to this block and this dead tree, which seemed to me to constitute a comfortable bed-room.

I called my companions, who were some twenty paces in front of me, and explained to them my scheme of nocturnal architecture, declaring that it

was my intention to bivouac there. Azcoaga began
to laugh. Irumberri's sole answer was to gaze at
the smoke from his cigar as it soared towards the
sun. Escamuturra el Puño (the Fist) seized my
hand.

"Have you thought of it, Señor francés?" said
he; "are you determined?"

"I am not determined," said I, "I am knocked
up."

"You want to sleep there?"

"I resign myself to sleep there."

"Pshaw! Why, just look at what your lodging
would be made of. It is only the dead who sleep
in chambers of marble and fir."

Mountaineers, like sailors, are superstitious.
Now I confess that in the mountains I am a
mountaineer, and that at sea I am a sailor. In
other words, I am superstitious in both cases—un-
reasoningly, frankly superstitious, just as those about
me are. This sepulchral reflection of Escamuturra
made me think.

"Come," he went on, "a few steps farther, amigo.
I swear to you, Señor, that a half-quarter league
from here we shall find a good stopping-place."

"A half-quarter Spanish league!" I exclaimed.
"It is now six o'clock. We shall arrive at midnight."

Escamuturra answered gravely :

" We shall arrive at midnight if the devil stretches the road, and in twenty minutes if the Frenchman stretches his legs."

" Andamos," said I.

The caravan resumed its march.

The sun went down and twilight came on. I must say, however, that the devil did not stretch the road. For about half an hour we had been climbing a steep pathway which wound like a serpent among blocks of granite that seemed to have been scattered over the mountain's flank by some giant. All at once a grass-plat made its appearance, than which nothing could have been sweeter, fresher, more grateful to the foot, or more unexpected.

" Here we are ! " said Escamuturra, turning round towards me.

I looked on before me to see where we were, but I saw nothing but the dark, bare line of the mountain. The grass-plat was confined like an avenue between two low walls of dry stones which I had not at first observed.

Meanwhile my companions had mended their pace, and I did likewise.

Presently I saw a sort of sharp, black hump re-sembling a roof surmounted by a chimney gradually rise up, like a thing issuing from the earth, and stand out against the clear sky of twilight.

It was, in fact, a house hidden in one of the folds of the mountain.

I examined it as we approached. The day was not yet completely extinguished. I made what is called in the language of strategy a reconnaissance.

The house was tolerably large, and was built, like the inclosure of the grass-plat, of dry stones mixed with blocks of marble. The roof of clipped stubble imitated a stairway. I have since found the same fashion in some poor hamlets in the Pyrenees.

At the foot of the wall facing the slope of the mountain there was a square hole from which flowed a little sheet of fresh, limpid water, which fell upon the rock, and then went off with a merry, happy noise to lose itself in the ravine.

The low, heavy door was shut. There was only one window, pierced on the same side as the door. It was very narrow, and three-fourths of it was stopped up with rudely-built bricks.

Like all lonely habitations in Guipuzcoa and Navarre, this wretched dwelling had the look of a fortress. But here there was danger rather than safety, for the thatched roof was only breast-high, and one might have forced the place to surrender with no other artillery than a lucifer match.

Y

For the rest, there was no light within ; there was neither voice, nor step, nor sound. It was not a house, but a black mass, gloomy and silent like a tomb.

Escamuturra alighted, approacned the door, and began to whistle softly the first part of a fantastic and fascinating melody. Then he stopped short and waited.

Nothing stirred within the cabin. Not a breath answered. The night, which had now quite fallen, added something strangely sullen and funereal to the profound, mysterious silence.

Escamuturra began his melody again ; then, on reaching the same note as before, he stopped. The cottage still preserved its silence. Escamuturra recommenced for the third time, more softly still, whistling, so to speak, below his breath.

We were all four bending down at the door listening. I confess that I held my breath and that my heart beat a little.

Suddenly, as Escamuturra was finishing, the following part of the melody made itself heard in the house behind the door, but it was whistled so feebly and so low that it was, perhaps, stranger and even more dreadful than the silence. It was lugubrious by reason of its very sweetness. It was like the song of a spirit in the tomb.

El Puño clapped his hands three times.

A man's voice was then heard in the cabin, and the following rapid and laconic dialogue in the Basque tongue was exchanged through the darkness between the questioning voice and the answering Escamuturra :

"Zuc ? " (You ?)

"Gûc." (We.)

"Nun ? " (Where ?)

"Hemen." (Here.)

"Cembât ? " (How many ?)

"Laû." (Four.)

A light gleamed in the interior of the house, a candle was lit, and the door opened—slowly and noisily, for it was barricaded.

A man appeared upon the threshold.

In his hand, raised above his head, he held a great iron candlestick in which a pine-torch was flaring.

His was one of those burnt and tanned faces which have no age. He might have been thirty years old, or he might have been fifty. For the rest, he had fine teeth, a keen eye, and a pleasant smile—for he did smile. A red handkerchief encircled his forehead, after the manner of the Aragonese muleteers, binding his thick black hair about his temples. The top of his head was shaven, and he wore a broad white muleta, which covered him from his chin down to his knees, short breeches of olive velvet, white linen leggings with black button-holes, and hempen shoes upon stockingless feet.

The lights and shadows alternated over the man's face by the light of the pine-torch flaring in the wind. Nothing could have been stranger than its genial smile shining through that gloomy flacker.

Suddenly the man perceived me, and his smile vanished like the light of a lamp when one blows it out. He frowned and fixed his eyes upon me. But he did not utter a word.

Escamuturra touched him on the shoulder with his hand, and, indicating me with his thumb, said in an undertone:

"Adichquidia." (A friend.)

The man made way for me to enter, but his smile did not reappear.

Meanwhile Azcoaga and Irumberri had driven the mules into the cabin. Escamuturra and our host talked in low tones in a corner. The door had been shut again, and Irumberri had carefully readjusted the barricade as if he were quite familiar with the task.

While Azcoaga was unloading the mule, I seated myself on a pack, whence I examined the interior of the dwelling.

The house contained only one room—that in which we were—but this room contained a whole world.

It was a large, low apartment, with a ceiling composed of laths and thin white planks, and supported here and there by beams which were utilized as pillars. The ceiling allowed the hay with which the upper part of the house beneath the angle of the roof was filled, to come through and hang down in long wisps. Open partitions, resembling trellis-work rather than partitions, formed capricious divisions throughout the apartment.

One of these compartments, on the left of the door, inclosed one corner of the cabin, the window, the fire-place—an enormous cavern of stones blackened by the fire—and the bed, or rather a sort of coffin in which a bistre palliasse and a russet blanket grimaced in a thousand folds. This was the bedroom.

Facing the bedroom was another compartment containing a calf lying on a dung-heap, and some fowls roosting in a sort of box. This was the stable.

In a third compartment at the opposite corner was heaped a shapeless pyramid of bristling tree-stumps and thorny branches—the stock of wood for the winter. Some goat-skins of wine and some mule-harness were arranged with a certain degree of care beside the firewood.   This was the cellar.

There was a carabine in the corner of the wall next the window, between the cellar and the stable, while, in another compartment packed with lumber of every description—old muletas, old panniers, broken tambourines, and guitars without strings—I saw glistening beneath a basket of rags the handle of a navaja, fine, black, and gallooned with copper like the sleeve of an Andalusian.   In the shadow close by, I distinguished two or three carabine barrels buried under some rags, and a sort of metal trumpet, wide and bell-shaped, which I at first took to be the mouth of a mountain clarion, but which was a blunderbuss.   This heap of rags was the arsenal.

A big block of rock which filled the corner on the right of the door, and over which the wall was built, formed a declivity of granite in the interior of the cabin, and served as a bolster for some trusses of straw which had been thrown on the ground. This was doubtless the hostelry.

A perfectly naked child, which probably slept on the straw and had been awakened by our arrival, sat crouching on the slope of the granite block, its knees pressed against its breast and its arms folded across its knees, and gazed upon us with terror in

its eyes. At first sight I took it for a gnome; I
then recognized it as a monkey; at last I discovered
that it was a child.

Two tall fire-dogs of wrought iron, rust-eaten by
the fire and the rain, were visible in the fire-place

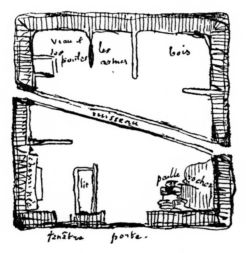

standing erect upon their four massive feet, and
stretching out their long necks terminating in two
gaping jaws. They seemed to be the two dragons
of the dwelling, ready either to bark or to bite.

For the rest, the cabin contained no other culi-
nary utensil but the frying-pan hanging in the
fire-place, which, with the iron candlestick, the fire-

dogs, and the bed, constituted the whole of the
furniture.

Near the bed there was a jar of oil, and beside
the door another jar full of milk.   A wooden bowl
of the purest and most elegant form was hooked
on to the rim of the milk-jar.   It was almost an
Etruscan vessel.

Two lean yellow cats, which we had aroused as
well as the child, prowled about us with an expression of menace.   By the fashion in which they eyed
us, it was clear that they would have asked nothing
better than to be tigers.

I fancied that I heard a pig grunting in some
obscure corner.

The house had that sugary and sickly odour
which is exhaled by every Spanish cottage.

There was, moreover, neither table nor chair.
Whoever entered either remained standing, or else
sat down on the ground.   Anyone who had a
pack sat upon that.   In this house the expression
" to sit down to table " was meaningless.   For
some moments I remained immersed in this
melancholy reflection.   For I was dying of hunger.

In such circumstances one's sadder thoughts
come from the stomach.

I was taken out of my reverie by a faint and
pleasant sound, a sort of gentle, continuous murmur

which I had heard since entering the cabin. When one has nothing for dinner, what can one do in one's lodging but look about? So I did look, but could not discover whence the sound came.

At length, as I cast my eyes upon the ground, I distinguished in the darkness a sort of metallic vibration, a band of luminous watered silk, and I observed that the cabin had a brook flowing right through it.

This brook, which flowed rapidly in a slanting inclined plane, over a hollow beam sunk to a level with the ground, entered the cabin by a hole made in one of the walls and left it through the opposite wall. There it formed in the ravine the tiny water-fall which I had observed when we arrived.

It was a curious chamber, where the mountain seemed to feel at home and to enter without cere-mony. The rock made it its lodging; the brook made it its house of call.

While I was making these observations in the elegiac attitude of a visionary who has not supped, the mules, unloaded and unmuzzled, were peace-fully pulling down the long wisps of hay which hung from the ceiling.

Seeing this, Escamuturra made a sign to the host, who drove them towards the end of the cabin and threw each of them a bundle of fodder.

Meanwhile my companions had installed themselves, one on a pack like myself, another on a saddle laid upon the ground. Azcoaga had lain down at full length, wrapped in his muleta.

Our host had piled in the fire-place some bundles of furze on the top of a heap of dry ferns. He then applied his pine-torch to the pile. In a twinkling a great crackling fire with clouds of sparks and a beautiful ruddy roaring flame rose in the hearth, filling the cabin, throwing into relief against their dark backgrounds the cruppers of the mules, the fowl-coop, the sleeping calf, the hidden blunder-busses, the rock, the brook, the wisps of straw hanging from the ceiling like threads of gold, the rugged faces of my companions, and the wild eyes of the frightened child.

The black fire-dogs with their monster mouths stood out against a background of red-hot embers, and seemed to be a couple of hell-hounds panting in the furnace.

But it was nothing of all this, I confess, that engaged my attention ; it was entirely elsewhere.

A great event had just taken place in the cabin.

The host had taken down the frying-pan from its nail.

XIII.

CAUTERETS.

TO LOUIS B.

CAUTERETS.

WRITE to you, dear Louis, with the worst of eyes. Writing to you, however, is an old and sweet habit which I would not lose. I would not have a single stone of our friendship dislodged. We have been brothers now for nearly twenty-five years— brothers in heart, brothers in thought. We see creation with the same eyes, we look at art with the same respect. You love Dante, as I love Raphael. We have passed together through many days of struggle and trial without ever weakening in our sympathy, without ever receding a step in our devotion. Let us, then, remain to the last what we have been from the first. Let us change nothing in what has been so good and so sweet. In Paris, we can clasp each other's hands ; when separated, we must write.

When I am away from you I need to send you a
letter to tell you something of what I am seeing,
and thinking, and feeling. This time it will be
shorter, or, rather, less long than usual. My own
eyes compel me to spare yours. Do not complain ;
you will have less scribble and more friendship.

I have come from the sea, and am now among
the mountains. This is, so to speak, but a change
of emotion. The mountains and the sea speak to
the same side of one's spirit.

If you were here (I cannot prevent myself from
constantly indulging in this dream) what a delightful life we should have together ! What pictures
you would carry back in your thoughts, to give
them afterwards to art even more beautiful than
you received them from nature !

Picture it to yourself, Louis. I rise every morning at four, and at that hour, at once dim and
clear, I go off into the mountains. I walk along by
a torrent, I plunge into the wildest gorge imaginable, and, under the pretext of dipping myself in
hot water and drinking sulphur, every day I have a
new spectacle, unexpected and marvellous.

Yesterday, the night was rainy. The air was
cold, and the drenched fir-trees were blacker than
usual. The mists rose from every part of the ravines
like vapours through the crevices of a solfatara. A

hideous, terrible noise came from the darkness
away down in the precipice at my feet; it was the
angry cry of the torrent hidden beneath the mist.
Something strangely vague, supernatural, and impossible, mingled with the landscape. Everything
about me seemed gloomy and pensive. The gigantic
spećtres of the mountains appeared to me through
the rents in the clouds as if through torn winding-
sheets. The dawn illuminated nothing; but, through
a crevice above my head, I perceived far away in
the distance a corner of the sky, at once blue, pale,
icy, dismal, and dazzling. All that I could distinguish of the earth, the rocks, the forest, the
meadows, and the glaciers, flitted about confusedly
in the mists, and, carried through space by the
wind, seemed to be flying away into a gigantic
network of clouds.

This morning, the night was clear. The sky was
strewn with stars ; but what a sky, and what stars !
The sky had the freshness, the grace, the melancholy,
the inexpressible transparence of morning ; the
glittering stars standing in the pale sky formed a
vault of crystal scattered over with diamonds.
Against this luminous vault the enormous mountains, black, shaggy, and deformed, leaned on every
side. Those to the east cast against the brightest
spot in the lightening sky the fir-trees on their

summits, which there looked like leaves that have
been transformed into lace-work by the vine-fretters
consuming everything but the fibres.   Those to
the west were black at their base and throughout
nearly all their height, but had a ruddy haze about
their crests.   There was neither cloud nor mist.
The dark flank of the mountain was animated by
a vague, delightful movement.   One could distinguish the grass, the flowers, the stones, and the
furze quivering together in a sort of sweet and
joyous vibration.   The sound of the gave [1] was no
longer horrible ; it was but a great murmur mingling
with the great silence.   Not a sad thought, not
a vestige of unrest, was evoked by this harmonious
whole.   The entire valley was like an immense
urn, into which the sky was pouring the peace of
the spheres and the brilliance of the constellations
during the sacred hours of dawn.

It seems to me, my friend, that these things are
more than mere scenery.   They are a glimpse of
nature at certain mysterious moments when everything seems to dream—I had almost said to think ;
when the dawn and the rocks, the cloud and the
thicket, live more visibly than at other hours, and

[1] " Gave " is the local name for a brawling river, the word
being derived from the same Celtic root as the English word
Avon.—*Translator.*

seem to thrill with the low beat of the universal life.

I have a strange fancy—but one which, to me, is very nearly a reality—that at those moments when the eyes of man are closed some unknown thing makes its appearance in nature. Do you not think as I do? Might not one say that, in the moments of sleep, when thought ceases in man, it begins in nature? Is it that the calm is more profound, the silence more absolute, the solitude more complete, and that then the waking thinker is better able to seize in its marvellous and subtle details the extraordinary scheme of creation? Or can there be in this some revelation, some manifestation of the great Intelligence entering into communication with the great whole—some new attitude of nature? Does nature feel herself more at ease when we are not by? Does she then reveal herself more freely?

It is certain that, in appearance at least, those objects which we call inanimate live a crepuscular and a nocturnal life. This life exists, perhaps, only in our minds. The realities of sense come before us at certain hours under an unaccustomed aspect; we are moved by them; they form a mirage within us, and we take the new ideas which they suggest to be a new life which they possess.

These are the problems.   You may resolve them.
As for me, I confine myself to dreaming.   I devote
my mind to the contemplation of the world and the
study of its mysteries.   I spend my life between a
note of admiration and a note of interrogation.

XIV.

GAVARNIE.

HEN you have crossed the Pont Des-
douroucat and are only a quarter of
an hour's journey from Gèdre, two
mountains are suddenly parted and an
unexpected sight is disclosed.

You may have seen the Alps, the Andes, and
the Cordilleras; you may have had the Pyrenees
before your eyes for weeks; but, whatever you may
have seen, that which you now behold resembles
nothing that you may have met with elsewhere.
Hitherto, you have seen mountains; you have contemplated excrescences of every form and of every
height; you have explored grassy ridges, slopes of
gneiss, of marble, of schist, precipices, summits
rounded and jagged, glaciers, forests of fir-trees
mingling with the clouds, peaks of granite and
peaks of ice; but nowhere, I repeat, have you seen
what you now see on the horizon.

In the midst of the capricious curves of the

mountains, bristling with angles both obtuse and acute, suddenly appear innumerable straight lines, simple and subdued, horizontal and vertical, parallel and cutting each other at right angles, and combined in such a fashion that their union produces the form of some extraordinary—some impossible object, at once resplendent and real, and impregnated with azure and sunlight.

Is it a mountain? But what mountain ever presented those rectilinear surfaces, those regular planes, those rigorous parallelisms, those strange proportions, that geometrical aspect?

Is it a wall? There are, indeed, towers by which it is counter-buttressed and supported; there are battlements, cornices, architraves, strata, and stones, which the eye can distinguish and almost number; there are two clean-cut breaches which awaken in one's mind thoughts of sieges, trenches, and assaults. But there is snow also—broad bands of snow spread over the strata, the battlements, the architraves, and the towers. We are in the heart of summer and the south. This, then, is eternal snow. But what wall, what human architecture, ever reared itself to the line of the eternal snow? Babel, that effort of the whole of human kind, sank beneath its own weight before having attained to it.

What, then, is this inexplicable object which

cannot be a mountain, but which has the loftiness of one; which cannot be a wall, but which has the form of one?

It is at once a mountain and a wall. It is the most mysterious edifice of the most mysterious of architects. It is the Colosseum of nature—Gavarnie.

Picture to yourself this magnificent silhouette as it makes its first appearance at a distance of three leagues. It is a long, dark wall, every projection and indentation of which is marked by lines of snow, every platform of which is covered with a glacier. Near the middle are two great towers. One of these, which is towards the east, is square, and turns one of its corners towards France. The other, which is nearer the west, seems to be less a tower than a sheaf of turrets. Both are covered with snow. Towards the right are the breaches, deep notches cut into the wall like two vases filled with clouds. Finally, at the western extremity, and still towards the right, is a kind of enormous border, puckered with a thousand tiers, and presenting to the eye, in monster proportions, what would be called in architecture the section of an amphitheatre.

Picture this to yourself as I saw it—the black wall, the black towers, the dazzling snow, the blue sky; in a word, a thing of perfection—great beyond expression, serene even to sublimity.

The impression which one receives is like no other. It is at once so strange and powerful that it effaces everything else, and one is rendered for some moments indifferent to all that has no part in this magic vision, even after it has disappeared round a turn in the road.

Meanwhile the landscape about you is exquisite. You enter a valley in which you are surrounded by every magnificence and every grace.

Gèdre-Dessus and Gèdre-Dessous, villages, like Tracy-le-Haut and Tracy-le-Bas, in two stories, with their stairway-like gables and their old church of the Templars, are clustered and strewn over the flanks of two mountains, by the side of a gave white with foam, beneath the delightful vegetation of brilliant, fantastic thickets. All this is vivid, entrancing, joyous, and exquisite. It is Switzerland and the Black Forest suddenly mingled with the Pyrenees. A thousand pleasant sounds float towards you, like the voices and the words of this sweet landscape—the singing of the birds, the laughter of children, the murmuring of the gave, the susurrus of the leaves, the softened breathing of the wind.

You see nothing, you hear nothing. Of this graceful whole you scarcely receive even a vague, indefinite impression. The apparition of Gavarnie is ever before your eyes, and radiates through your thoughts like those supernatural horizons which one sometimes sees on the confines of one's dreams.

In the evening, on returning from Gavarnie, I experienced one delightful moment. This is what I beheld from my window :

A huge mountain filled the earth ; a huge cloud filled the sky. Between the cloud and the mountain there was a narrow band of the twilight sky, vivid, pale, and limpid, with Jupiter glittering like a golden nugget in a stream of azure. Nothing could have been more melancholy, more soothing, and more lovely than that little streak of light between those two masses of darkness.

XV.

LUZ.

UZ is a charming old town—a rare thing in the Pyrenees—deliciously situated in a deep triangular valley. Three great floods of daylight stream into it through the three embrasures of the three mountains.

When the Spanish bandits and smugglers came from Aragon by the Brèche de Roland and the dark and dreadful Pass of Gavarnie, they suddenly perceived a great light at the end of the gloomy gorge, like that seen through the door of a cellar by those within. They hastened on and found a big village all lit by the sun and full of life. This village they appropriately named Luz (Light).

It has a rare and curious church built by the Templars. With its crenelated enceinte and its donjon doorway it is a fortress rather than a church.

I walked round, between the church and the crenelated wall. The churchyard is there, strewn with great slates, upon which crosses and names of mountaineers hollowed out with a nail have been effaced by the rain, the snow, and the feet of passers-by.

A door, now walled up, was the Porte des Cagots. The Cagots, or cretins, were pariahs. Their door was low, as far as can be judged by the indistinct line described by the stones with which it is walled up.

The exterior holy-water vessel is a charming little piece of Byzantine workmanship, to which two almost Romanesque capitals still adhere.

I stopped at an inscription on a tombstone. It had been effaced by time, scraped by a knife, and was covered with dust. One can distinguish several Spanish words—" aquí," " abris." The words " filla de . . . ," however, seem to indicate the patois. I almost succeeded in deciphering the last line, which however, conveys no meaning :

SUB DESERA LO FE

The corbels of the exterior wall of the apsis bear curious designs. The principal portal, which represents Jesus among the four symbolical animals, is in the finest Romanesque style, solid, robust, powerful, and severe. There are the remains of colouring on the walls, representing mosaics and buildings. The interior of the church is like that of any barn.

Under the arch of the portal of the entrance tower are some Byzantine paintings, restored and half whitewashed over, which have lost much of their character.   Above the arch there is a Christ wearing the Imperial crown.   Beneath, there are angels of the Judgment day blowing their trumpets, with the inscription: SVRGITE . MORTVY . VENYTE . AD . JUDICIUM.   At the four corners are some vestiges of the four Evangelists—the ox, with the inscription :   SANC . LVC . , the eagle, with SANC . . . The mould has formed a cloak, beneath which the rest is lost.   There is also a winged lion, very fine in style, bearing the inscription : SANT MARC . , and, in the shadow, an angel's head with this remnant of a legend : . . . CTE MYCHAEL.

XVI.

OLÉRON.

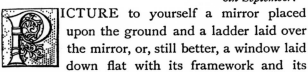ICTURE to yourself a mirror placed upon the ground and a ladder laid over the mirror, or, still better, a window laid down flat with its framework and its panes. Make the window a quarter of a league round about, and you will have a salt-marsh. When the glass becomes dimmed it is the salt forming.

Imagine a long, narrow, flat tongue of land, which, seen as a bird flies, would appear to the eye covered with these immense windows, leaving between them scarcely room for some narrow strips of land strewn with thorn-broom and tamarinds; here and there some meadows, and some vineyards manured with sea-weed which yield an oily, bitter wine; some clumps of trees, and some pathways; some white villages at long intervals along the low shore: on the French side, a band of fortifications:

on the side next the ocean, an escarpment called
the Côte Sauvage ; at the southern point, dunes
strewn with pines, indicating the vicinity of the
great landes.   Cover this country with the dirty
gray mists which rise from every part of the marshes,
and you will have the island of Oléron.

If, after having contemplated the whole, you con-
sider the detail, the dreariness grows with every
step you take, and you are oppressed with a gloomy
heaviness of heart.

A flat, muddy shore, a bleak horizon, two or
three windmills turning heavily ; some lean cattle
grazing in a wretched pasturage ; at the edge of
the marshes, great piles of salt—gray or white
cones according as they are covered with stubble to
keep through the winter, or exposed to the sun to
dry ; at the doors of the houses, beautiful but
pale girls, livid children, bent and trembling men
—but few of them old ; fever everywhere,—this
is the lugubrious little world into which you have
penetrated.

It is not easy to reach Oléron.   One must
really want to get there.   The traveller is taken
here only step by step.   It would seem that they
wish to give him time to reflect and to alter his
mind.

From Rochefort he is taken to Marennes in a

kind of omnibus which leaves Rochefort twice a day. This is the first initiation.

There is a journey of three leagues through the salt-marshes. There are vast plains above which the fine English steeples of Moise and Marennes with their sharp points of stone rise like two obelisks in a churchyard; all along the road, sheets of stagnating water; in all the fields, which are marshes, enormous padlocked inclosures; not a single wayfarer; from time to time a customs official standing, musket in hand, and with a pale, terrified face, before his cabin of mud and gorse; not a single tree; no shelter from the wind and rain in the winter, or from the sun in the dog-days; an icy chill or the heat of a furnace; in the middle of the marshes, the pestilent village of Brouage buried within its square of walls, with its ruins of the time of the religious wars, its low houses, whitened like the sepulchres of which the Bible speaks, and its spectres shivering before the doors amid all the warmth of the south. This is the first stage.

Should you persist, a coucou-driver takes possession of you at Marennes, and introduces you, the fifteenth passenger, into a receptacle made to contain six persons at most. Then, with these fifteen patients inside and a mountain of packages on the top, the vehicle starts off for the Pointe through

the landes and the heath, to the lame and stagger-
ing trot of a single horse.

Should you still persist, you are there loaded or
embarked—choose whichever word you like—upon
one of those precarious ferry-boats to which the
inhabitants have given the name of "risk-alls."
The vessel has three boatmen, four oars, two masts,
and two sails, one of which is called the storm-sail.
You have two leagues of sea to traverse on this
piece of timber.   The sailors who load the boat
begin by safely stowing the oxen, horses, and carts
in the best compartment.   The luggage is next
arranged ; and then, in the spaces that remain,
between the horns of an ox or the wheels of a cart,
the passengers are inserted.

There you meditate, at the mercy of the wind, the
sun, or the rain.   During the passage you listen to
the groans of the sea-sick passengers or the roar of
the Strait of Maumusson, which is at the point of
the island, and is heard by mariners fifteen leagues
away.   By way of diversion, this noise is explained
to you.

The Strait of Maumusson is one of the ocean's
navels.   The waters of the Seudre, the waters of
the Gironde, the great ocean currents, and the little
currents at the southern extremity of the island,
there press from four different points at once against

the quicksands which the sea has heaped up upon
the coast, and transform this mass into a vortex.
It is not a whirlpool, for the sea appears level and
smooth upon the surface.   One can scarcely distinguish the slightest flexure; but beneath the
tranquil water one hears an awful sound.

Any large vessel which touches the vortex is
lost.   She suddenly stops and slowly sinks—sinks
uninterruptedly, and diminishes in height little by
little.   Soon her port-holes are no longer seen, then
the deck plunges beneath the waves, then the yards
and the top-sails.   One can no longer distinguish
anything but the point of the mast. Then there is a
little ripple on the sea, and all has disappeared.
Nothing can arrest the terrible spiral which has
seized hold of the vessel in its slow and awful movement.

Boats which draw little water, however, may
boldly cross the vortex. "Without danger," say
the sailors.   A moment afterwards they add : " But
old Monier, the pilot at the Château, had one day
just time to jump into the sea, leaving his vessel to
sink, and swam for four hours before getting out of
the vortex."

With gossip of this sort we at length reach our
destination, the storm-sail is lowered, the cable is
thrown ashore, and the gangway is put out.

On the right there is a fortress which is the prison; on the left there is a hideous low shore which is the fever.   One lands between the two.

Pretty women-servants, looking charming in their great white caps, which they wear most gracefully, wait for you on the jetty, take your portmanteau and bag, and walk off in front of you.

You pass along a rampart beneath which some hundreds of men, dressed in gray, haggard and silent, and guarded by gendarmes, are crowded together in every attitude of labour, digging out trenches in the pestiferous slime.   They are poor soldiers condemned to the chain-and-ball, for the most part deserters through home-sickness, nostalgics whom the law does not disgrace, who are severely punished by special regulation, and who come here to die although not condemned to death.

While engaged in such reflections you reach the Cheval Blanc, which is the inn of the place.   A good inn, when all is said.   You are conducted to a vast whitewashed room, in the middle of which a great baldachined bed sticks out, making a sort of promontory after the manner of the seventeenth century. The walls are white, the sheets are white, the landlord is genial, the landlady charming.   Everything in the house is becoming and pleasant.   Only do not

look at the water with which they have filled your
ewer, and which in these parts is called fresh.

On the evening of my arrival at Oléron I was
overcome with sadness.

To me the island seemed desolate and sinister,
and yet I did not dislike it. I walked along the
shore, stepping among the seaweed to avoid the
mud. I skirted the trenches of the Castle. The
prisoners had just re-entered, the roll was being
called, and I could hear their voices answering one
after another to the voice of the inspecting officer,
who seemed to be flinging their names at them.
On my right the marshes stretched away as far as
the eye could reach ; on my left the leaden sea
was lost in the mists that masked the coast.

On the whole island I saw no other human
creature but a soldier on sentry duty, motionless at
the horn of an entrenchment, and standing out
against the mist. Away on the horizon I could
scarcely distinguish the fortress which is called
the Pavé, isolated in the sea between the island
and the mainland. On the open sea there was not a
sound, not a sail, not a bird. In the west, low in
the sky, appeared an enormous round disc, which

seemed in the livid mist but the reddened, ungilded impression of the moon.

I had death within my soul.   Perhaps I saw everything through my own dejection.   Some other day, perhaps, at some other hour, I shall receive a different impression.   But that evening everything seemed to me funereal and melancholy.   It seemed to me that the island was an immense coffin lying on the surface of the sea, and that the moon was but a torch illuminating it.

NOTE.

N the 8th of September Victor Hugo wrote :

"I had death within my soul."— "That evening everything seemed to me funereal and melancholy."—"It seemed to me that the island was an immense coffin lying on the surface of the sea."

Next day, Victor Hugo, having fled from the pestilent island upon which he had experienced this feeling of depression, was at Rochefort. As he was awaiting the departure of the diligence, he entered a café where he asked for some ale. While there, his eye chanced to fall upon a newspaper.

A by-stander saw him suddenly turn pale, place his hand against his heart as if to prevent it breaking, rise up, leave the town, and walk along the ramparts like a madman.

The newspaper which he had read reported the catastrophe of Villequier.

Five days before, on the 4th of September, 1843, his daughter Léopoldine had perished in an excursion on the Seine.

She had been married scarcely six months previously to Charles Vacquerie, who, being unable to save her, had chosen to die along with her.

They are buried at Villequier in the same coffin.

It was in this manner that the Pyrenean journey was interrupted. The unhappy father returned with all haste to Paris.

Those beautiful and sad poems in the "Contemplations" entitled "Pauca meæ" have since been read by all, and will be read for ever.